DESIRED BY THE WOLF

SHADOW SHIFTERS SERIES

MILA YOUNG

CONTENTS

Shadow Shifters Series   v
Desired By The Wolf   vii

Chapter 1   1
Chapter 2   12
Chapter 3   23
Chapter 4   33
Chapter 5   41
Chapter 6   54
Chapter 7   63
Chapter 8   70
Chapter 9   83
Chapter 10   94
Chapter 11   102
Chapter 12   110
Chapter 13   122
Chapter 14   134
Chapter 15   145
Chapter 16   152
Chapter 17   163
Chapter 18   176
Chapter 19   182
Chapter 20   194
Chapter 21   202
Chapter 22   210
Chapter 23   216
Chapter 24   223
Chapter 25   228
Chapter 26   236
Chapter 27   249
Chapter 28   254

About Mila Young   261

He's her enemy, her fated mate, her darkest desire, and her only savior from the encroaching danger.

Death has followed Alena Novac's circus family for years. When the police arrest her brother for a murder he didn't commit, she has only a week to rescue him before he transforms into his wolf form in prison and exposes their wulfkin existence to the world.

Enre Ulf, a former member of the Varlac, the fearsome ruling wulfkin clan, plans to infiltrate Alena's circus clan and take out their treacherous alpha to save his home in Transylvania. Except he never expected his wolf to claim Alena as his mate, or feel compelled to save her brother to help protect the secrets of the wulfkin. Now he must overcome his pasts and convince Alena to do the same to save their packs' futures

CHAPTER 1

ALENA

I sprinted after my brother, Nicolai, wanting to wring his neck each time the brushwood tore at my pants. If this continued, I'd end up in my underwear, frozen and drenched, if the storm clouds were any indication. But we had to track down our fellow wulfkin, Ash, before a human found her.

Dodging a low branch covered with ivy, I trailed after Ash's pungent, sweaty smell through the strip of woodland that ran alongside a freeway.

"I hate Ash being locked away." Nicolai slowed his run. "Alena." His voice climbed as if I hadn't heard him the first time. He glanced over his shoulder.

"I don't like it either, but you'd rather allow her to roam free and eat our circus customers? Yeah, real smart. She has no control while she's stuck in her wolf form. And we wouldn't be out here, freezing, if *you* didn't keep letting her out." I hadn't intended for my response to sound so bitter, but Nicolai drove me insane with his antics.

He tripped over a root but caught himself and raced ahead, speaking with his back to me. "Put me in charge of her. I'll stay with her every second." Looking back, he flaunted his smile, the one that made girls either hate or love him.

I definitely wasn't in the latter group this morning. Dark hair framed his pale face, and with his strong chin, he reminded me of our father, though I'd never seen Father wiggle his eyebrows that way.

"And have her run off like this every day?" My hair snagged on a tree limb. Groaning, I stopped and rubbed my head, glaring at the auburn strands twisted around bottle-green leaves. I'd knock some sense into Nicolai. This was all his fault. Didn't he realize Ash was unpredictable in her wolf form?

He halted several paces away. "She responds to my music. It calms her. She'll behave, I promise." And then he broke into beatboxing, his shoulders bopping and his fists pumping to the tune he made with his mouth.

I refused to waste time on Nicolai's deranged ideas—we had to catch the escapee wulfkin before any humans frightened her and she attacked. If I were stuck in my wolf form twenty-four seven, it would mess with my mind, so I had no plans of giving up on finding Ash a cure. Two weeks ago, we'd been blessed with a red moon—the Lunar Eutine—a time when moonwulf were transformed into wulfkin and the moon no longer controlled our wolf side. I'd changed, as did Ash, but because of her young age, something went terribly wrong and she ended up stuck in her wolf shape, unable to shift back into human form. No one knew why, but I would find a way to break her free.

Especially since Interpol was on our doorstep asking about Ash going missing a couple of weeks ago from her mom's place. It didn't help that she'd last been seen at our circus. The poor girl wasn't even part of our pack, but her wolf side drew her to us, and now it was our responsibility to help her.

A truck zoomed down the nearby freeway, coughing puffs of gray smoke between the enormous oaks of the forest, and I snapped to attention. *Focus.*

We broke back into our run, my boots launching a couple of stones ahead of me. At least I'd had the sense to wear hiking boots after being dragged out of bed at an ungodly hour. As we approached the end of the narrow woodland, Ash's scent strengthened.

"Father's going to be pissed," I called out.

Nicolai huffed and leapt over a dead log. "Don't care. I plan on leaving the pack. I'm not taking over from Father as alpha. No one wants a moonwulf like me, still controlled by the moon, to rule over a pack. They consider anyone who didn't change into a wulfkin to be weak. You go be the strong alpha."

Every part of me yearned to smack him in the head. "Stop being selfish. Your future isn't just about you. Don't forget about me. We need to stay close." With Nicolai being reckless, my days might be shorter than I'd like. As twins, we'd been born with a curse that linked our souls, and if one of us died, so did the other.

Nicolai halted. "Sis, relax. You ain't gonna catch no guy with your face all scrunched up."

I whacked him in the arm—twice, for good measure. "This is the *last* time I'm helping you when you let Ash out of her cage. Don't ever ask me again."

One boy screwing up my life was terrible enough, but with tradition expecting me to find a mate now that I was a wulfkin, I couldn't handle two.

I sniffed the wind. Ash. Her pungent smell skimmed the back of my throat. "Hurry, she's close." We broke into a dash through the ribbon of trees. Nicolai retrieved a leather cord from his pocket, and while I hated the idea of any animal being leashed, it was a necessity with Ash so she wouldn't run away again.

Another semitruck gunned down the road, motor grunting, horn blaring. The rush of air slapped my side, sending hair into my eyes and causing a flurry of cascading leaves around us.

Nicolai remained caught up in a tune in his mind by the look of his hands scratching an invisible record. I loved my brother, I did, but at twenty-three, he still had foolish dreams of becoming the world's best DJ.

Inhaling deep pockets of arctic air, I froze. Ash's scent had shifted to our left— toward the homes. *Shit.* The truck must have terrified her.

"She's on the move." I changed gears, crossing the woodland away from the freeway as adrenaline tightened my muscles. Foliage cracked under our steps.

"Ash," Nicolai called out.

Thunder boomed across the heavens. The first trickle of rain licked my brow as we emerged from the cluster of trees into a lane behind a row of homes. Tall, wooden fences concealed the cottages. I counted on those barriers and the morning darkness to cloak Ash from prying eyes.

The car fumes, chimney smoke, and damp soil smells carried on the wind diluted her scent, but she was close, though I couldn't pinpoint her exact location. And another odor drifted on the breeze too: a wulfkin I didn't recognize.

I stopped near a fence and tried to collect my thoughts. "What's wrong?" Nicolai halted several steps ahead.

My hackles raised. Rival packs often sent scouts to spy on us before they attacked.

The threat came with being Europe's largest pack. But this would be the first scout we'd found since arriving in

Bulgaria. Better find Ash fast and inform Father about the trespasser.

I scanned the residential area—two alleyways faced us, weaving in opposite directions. Licking my dry lips, I turned to Nicolai. "There's an unknown wulfkin here. Be careful. Go left, I'll take the other path, and if you find Ash, take her straight home. Don't wait for me."

"I got this." Worry streaked his tone despite his words. "Her paw prints head left, so I'll track her down."

Those rare moments when I could get Nicolai to concentrate, he was an incredible tracker, even as a moonwulf. Outside the full moon, moonwulf generally retained no strength or wolf qualities, yet Nicolai had a natural hunting talent. At the next Lunar Eutine, he'd finally transform into a wulfkin. He would be able to choose when he transformed into his wolf form, instead of turning into a savage and uncontrollable wolf once a month under the full moon. As a wulfkin, our transformations were magical, giving us full control over our furry side. Except the next destined eutine wasn't for another ten to twenty years.

"Go," I said and bolted into a deserted alley flanked by lofty fences that cast long shadows. Eeriness folded in around me, and the prickling instinct at the base of my belly was on full alert. The whole scene seemed off, but I couldn't identify the problem. Were we being stalked by this intruding wulfkin? My first instinct told me to grab Nicolai and get home, but we couldn't leave Ash behind.

Rain pitter-pattered on the leaves of plum and apple trees sprawling out over the tops of the fences. I tensed at every sound. Perhaps splitting up hadn't been such a great idea.

One of Nicolai's so-called nuggets of wisdom came to mind: *Handle what you're dealt.* I hadn't understood when he'd first said it, but the saying made sense now.

Ash's scent faded, but the stranger's fresh firewood-and-fur smell strengthened. I whirled on the spot, finding no one else there, only me and two parked cars. The thump of footsteps resonated from an adjacent alleyway, and the hairs on my arms stood on end. I dashed forward.

The intruder's smell smacked into me, and a snarl rumbled in my gut.

He burst out into my path, several feet away, from an adjacent lane. I froze on the spot, and his blue, piercing eyes hooked into me. He sniffed the air. "You're wulfkin."

It wasn't a question.

The tall, broad-shouldered man was branded with two gash marks down the side of his face and neck, and blood smeared his cheek. He wiped it away with his hand as his gaze deepened with darkness.

I studied his stubbled jawline, his ocean-blue eyes, and inhaled the fresh blood. It belonged to him.

Wind fanned across my back. It had been a long time since I'd faced off with anyone.

Father had brought me up to use my head, not my teeth.

"What pack do you belong to?" My voice sharpened, and a growl hung off my last word. *Show no fear.*

He studied the path I'd taken. "There's a loose wulfkin in wolf form here, and I think she's wild." His gruff voice raised goose bumps up and down my legs, and I recoiled. "Is she yours?"

My next inhale wedged in my chest. Had Ash been caught or injured? "Where is she?"

"Why would you allow her out amongst humans? Are you trying to reveal us?"

Flames spread over my cheeks. "Who the hell are you? It's not your business what happens on *our* territory."

Since we ran a traveling circus, we claimed any location where we performed, though we rarely stopped in places already taken by other packs. Lucky for us, the majority of them steered clear of cities.

The wulfkin leaned forward, his voice rough and low. "I tried catching her before anyone saw her, but as you can see"—he pointed to his recent wounds—"she wasn't overly friendly." Running a hand through his short, black hair, he stared at me.

When the breeze bathed me in his scent again, his muskiness almost knocked me over, and my eyes dipped south although my brain screamed, "Don't!" This wulfkin should never wear jeans in public unless he wanted every single female to ravage him. And the leather jacket did nothing to hide his muscles.

When I looked up, he wore a sly grin.

Heat scalded my body, and my wolf pressed against my insides, whimpering, demanding we claim him. She wanted this stranger? Working in the circus, I'd seen all kinds, but no one had ever affected my wolf this way.

"Don't flatter yourself." I refused to allow him to openly knock me off my feet with his gorgeousness. Scratch that. With his audacity.

"Why isn't she transforming into human form?" he asked.

My hands curled into fists. "I don't have to tell you anything." Studying the passage ahead of me, I inhaled the crisp air for signs of Ash. "If you remain here, you'll have dozens of wulfkin on your trail, ready to tear you to shreds—"

He narrowed the gap between us, his square shoulders stiff.

"Or, you can help me find M ... the wolf girl, and return with me to the pack to explain yourself."

His ravenous gaze remained on me, searching for who knows what. Every hair stayed in place, despite his bleeding wounds, and a smile was on the verge of breaking the edges of his mouth. Maybe he was only a hungry wolf ready to pounce on his prey.

A train-car-sized load of words bubbled on my tongue, mostly threats, but when a single howl in the distance broke the morning silence, every thought vanished.

My head snapped up. Nicolai. Ash.

Police sirens rang out above the drone of the highway. "We better get out of here," the other wulfkin said.

My heart bounced against my rib cage, and I ran past him. *No! Please, no.*

The rain, now sudden and fast, drenched every part of me, filling my boots and threatening to bowl me over. I rushed along the curve of the backstreet, following my nose, and came to an intersection between two lanes. Cars were parked bumper to bumper near the fences in all directions, but there was no sign of Nicolai. The smell came from my left. I swung in that direction and bolted down the path until I hit a T-crossing, which brought me to an abrupt stop. My insides curdled. The downpour and mist rising from the ground clouded my vision, but what I did see was wrong—very wrong.

Halfway down the lane on my right, Nicolai hunched over a blood-soaked figure sprawled on the ground. A red pool encircled them. Ash? No, it wasn't Ash.

My legs wobbled, and a whiff of the breeze identified the victim as human. Killed by Ash. Of course, I should have known, and in truth, I had but didn't want to believe it.

Where was Ash? And why wasn't Nicolai running away?

"Nic." I walked toward him. He didn't seem to hear me. Maybe it was the sheets of rain, which even made it impossible to hear my own thoughts.

His face was white as paper.

Lightning flashed, and I flinched. What had happened here?

Figures appeared from within the folds of the ferocious downpour on the other side of Nicolai. I stopped.

My brother started convulsing, and in a flash, I realized he'd been Tasered. He collapsed to his knees and rolled onto his side, shaking. His eyes grew wide as they finally found me. "Aleee ... "

"Nic!" I dove forward, but someone grabbed my arm.

I snapped around to find the strange wulfkin had followed me. Water drenched his face, his brows were bunched up, and a snarl warped his lips.

"Let go." Tugging against his grip got me nowhere. "My brother needs me."

"Keep quiet." His words barely registered past the rain splatter. "We have to go." He scanned the area behind us.

"No." I wrenched my arm from him.

Nicolai and I shared a single lifeline. We couldn't die here. Not like this. A whistle blew.

Behind me, three police officers circled Nicolai, who still squirmed from obvious pain, and now their attention was on us.

"On your knees!" one yelled. Two others approached, guns and Tasers pointed in our direction.

My legs refused to move. I couldn't leave Nicolai in the hands of humans who had no idea our kind existed, but I couldn't let myself get caught. Releasing my wolf played across my mind. I could quickly knock out one or two of the men, but maybe not before they shot me a few times.

The wulfkin at my back growled, snatching my hand. I stumbled after him but tore free from his grasp, my leather glove still in his grip.

"Help me save him," I pleaded, snatching back my glove and slipping it over my shaky fingers. Without them, I would put myself into a coma by accidently zapping all my healing energy into anyone I touched. Every nerve tightened as dread coiled inside my belly. "We can take them together. Please." With his help, we could overpower the police and rescue Nicolai in no time.

Over my shoulder, a policeman aimed his gun at us. "Stop, or I'll shoot!"

The wulfkin seized my wrist and dragged me into a sprint, putting space between Nicolai and me. Leaving the alley, we swerved toward the strip of forest for cover. Tears that had beaded in my eyes now rolled down my cheeks in the rain. This wasn't happening. It couldn't be.

Behind me, boots slapped the ground, and voices yelled. Thunder clapped overhead.

The world was crumbling around me, and I was simply running away. Number-one rule—never, ever leave a pack member behind.

I skidded to a halt near the belt of woods, wrenching my grip from the stranger, and turned, surveying my options. Left—two officers ran out from a lane. Right—an empty passage. Ahead—tall fence. Behind—trees. If I could circle back to Nicolai quick enough, maybe I could get past the guard and free my brother.

But the police now had their guns aimed and were too close. "Stop!"

I lunged toward the empty passage. The wulfkin snagged the back of my jacket, trying to drag me into the woods. I tripped and fell onto my backside.

A shot exploded.

I crouched, my arms covering my head.

A crack and then a hollow thump resonated nearby.

No pain meant they'd missed. I leapt to my feet, but the wulfkin now lay crumpled alongside me, blood pouring from his thigh. He pulled himself upright, groaning.

The officers advanced, and more sirens squealed in the distance.

My mind swam in nausea. *Crap.* I forced the wulfkin to lean against me as we hobbled quickly into the woodland. A bullet whizzed by, the heat of it brushing across my lower back, barely missing me.

Charging straight through the strip of woodland, we came out on the other side of the highway, managing to cross before a caravan of trucks. *Safe. Cover. Perfect.*

The wulfkin felt sluggish against me, missing steps and losing blood fast. Thankfully, the pouring rain would wash the blood away and cover our tracks.

My mind screamed to return for Nicolai, but I knew I'd never get near him. He'd be taken into custody. A court date could be months away. The full moon was soon—just over a week away. Then he'd transform into a moonwulf in front of humans, who'd kill him. We were both in so much shit right now. Tears mingled with the rain on my face, but this was no time to cry.

CHAPTER 2

ENRE

Startled awake from a nightmare, my eyes snapped open. My inner wolf was half climbing out of my throat. I hurt everywhere. Shit, even my balls ached.

For a split second, I swore I was back in the cave where my previous alpha, Sandulf, had thrown me in with a dracwulf—the same man-eating, berserk wolf capable of slaughtering entire villages. Instead, I was lying on a bed of blankets, not rocks. Dim light from a window cast shadows across the walls. This definitely wasn't the pack house either. It was a trailer, and my imprisonment with the dracwulf had ended weeks ago, but the raw memories remained. Sandulf had reared the beast that started killing humans.

When I tried to stop the dracwulf, Sandulf offered me to the monster as a potential mate. My insides churned at the thought. But that was behind me, a distant horror I had to forget.

The room spun as I climbed to my feet. Fog blurred my thoughts, strange wulfkin scents smothered my senses, and my legs buckled, dropping me back onto the bed. Around me, elaborate, sparkly leotards and ribbons hung off the walls. Stacks of books nestled on the corner of a table, and a pile of clothes covered the two-seater couch.

Was that a bag of chips on the couch? My stomach growled. When I leaned closer, I realized it was only an illusion caused by the sunlight hitting the sparkling, shiny fabric. *Damn.*

This had to be one of the circus trailers from the Bulgarian pack. The same pack I'd left my family in Transylvania to spy on in order to confirm their alpha was about to attack us. Rumor had it that he planned to slit our throats for our territory. And if that was the case, then I'd strike first. But none of my plans involved getting this cozy with the enemy. Sure, my new alpha, Daciana, had no idea I was here, but sitting back and waiting just wasn't me. She could thank me later, after I saved our hides. And I'd take any punishment she set if it meant I'd protected my family.

Sitting on the edge of the bed, my head hanging forward, I struggled to sort out the multiple wulfkin scents. One in particular overlapped the others—earthy and sweet, with the faintest wisp of lavender—a female. The one I'd saved from the police today. Or at least I thought it was the same day. I shouldn't have gotten involved, especially since it occurred to me she'd be part of the Bulgarian pack. Except, doing nothing when wulfkin were in danger from humans wasn't my style.

A sharp pain coursed through my thigh, and I gritted my teeth. Blood stained the white fabric around my injury. The time I'd spent captive by the demon dracwulf had made me frail, and now the smallest injury took twice as long to heal. Everyone said to give it time. Fuck time. I wanted my strength back.

How was I going to get out of this mess dressed only in briefs and a T-shirt? Scanning the room for my jeans was pointless. They weren't here, and I doubted any of the tights or clothes strewn all over the place would fit me, so I looked around for a weapon. I could smash someone with the desk chair if I had to.

Voices floated in from outdoors, and I pushed myself upright, leaning on my good leg.

Limping toward the door and biting back the growing pain, I slumped against the wall and listened.

"Why bring him here?" a man's voice with a strong Bulgarian accent asked.

"He saved me. I couldn't let him to get captured too." It was the wulfkin girl. Trying to help her had gotten me shot. What trouble had she heaped on me now?

"Yes, you could have." The male's voice grew thicker. "Do you even know where he's from? Let me finish him off before Maxim finds out."

"Absolutely not. The problem is Nic. He—"

"Alena," the man interrupted. So that was her name. "No disrespect, but your brother's an idiot. He can rot in prison."

"Get away from me." Alena's voice quivered as she obviously struggled to control herself. "Never speak about Nic like that again or next time you'll be bleeding before you know it."

Tough girl.

Heavy footfalls faded into the distance. Only one person remained outside.

When the door swung open, a deluge of chilled air rushed inside, and I came face to face with her, the wulfkin I wished I'd left alone. Light from the trailer shone on her features—sharp cheekbones and pale gray eyes the color of clouds after the rain. She frowned while studying me. Behind her, the storm blemished a darkening sky.

How long had I been unconscious?

A breeze blew past, throwing long, dark strands across her shoulders. The temptation to lean in and slide them back tingled in my fingertips. My wolf nudged me, eager to close the distance between us.

"Eavesdropping?" she sneered.

Weakness needled down my thigh, and I jerked toward the wall for stability, but it was too late. My knee crumpled beneath me, and I hit the floor, my ass taking the brunt of it. The suffering, I could handle—fuck, lately I'd become the lord of torment—but limbs that refused to hold me up were a different story. I had made a promise to myself while in the cave with the dracwulf—I'd never allow myself to become immobile again.

Alena lunged forward and offered a leather-gloved hand, but I pushed it away. Rubbing her palms down her pants, she said, "Let's get you back to bed."

Once on my feet, I hobbled farther into the trailer, hissing between my teeth each time I put pressure on the injured leg. I collapsed onto the mattress.

Alena propped her ass against the table, her long legs painted in black denim crossed at the ankles, while her hard gaze homed in on me. Were those reindeer on her sweater?

"Are you hiding my jeans so you can keep checking out my legs?"

One of her eyebrows arched, but her stare didn't falter. "Your wound's bleeding. And you're welcome. I removed the bullet."

A coppery taste persisted at the back of my throat, and a droplet of blood rolled over my knee. I smeared it clean with my palm.

"Thank you." She normally wasn't my type—sleeping with the enemy and all that— but I could make an exception. The fire in her was strong, and who knows, maybe that spunk showed even more in the bedroom. "But if you insist on staring at me, I'm ready to move to the next base."

Alena scooted off the table and crouched behind the

couch. She reappeared with a new bandage, towel, bottle, and a bucket before kneeling in front of me.

"Here." After shoving the already stained towel onto my lap, she proceeded to unwrap my thigh. "Does your cock always tell your head what to say?"

I cleaned the red smudge off my palm with the cloth, unable to peel my gaze off her slightly parted lips. My heart galloped faster at the notion of tasting them. Gorgeous. The light hit her flawless skin, highlighting the few freckles on her cheeks, and the way she'd entered the trailer, shoulders squared, chin high, had indicated a wulfkin with a sense of pride.

"Mostly," I replied.

She peeked out from beneath long lashes and took the towel out of my grasp, drenched it with vodka, and jammed the moist fabric against my wound. Wiping my wound clean, she said, "I see."

I gritted my teeth. It stung, and I had to look to make sure someone hadn't ripped off my flesh and poured acid over what was left. My hands fisted. "Mental note … You're into pain. I mean, causing it to others," I said through my clenched jaw.

She laughed while bandaging the injury again. Her soft tone turned me on more than it should have, and the wolf inside whimpered for a touch, for a connection with this odd character.

Her head snapped up, and those tantalizing eyes widened. Did she sense it too? I'd heard of wolves sharing a connection when they found their soul mate, but not wulfkin. Mainly, I believed the myth was a romantic story created by females. Except, a tornado was whisking through my veins. Before I knew it, I was brushing away the few strands of hair caught at the edge of her luscious mouth. Shivers developed at the base of my gut and spread through me. Every thought vanished from my mind, replaced by one: getting closer to Alena.

Instead of pushing me away, she closed her eyes and leaned into my touch, her curvaceous chest heaving with each inhale. Silence embraced us, and the charge in the room became electric. Following my instinct had gotten me far in life. This felt right.

Sliding my fingers to the back of her head, I drew her into a kiss and parted her soft, warm lips with my tongue. Her lavender scent spread inside me with a blaze while her arms encircled my neck, and she lifted herself to her knees, pressing closer. Our breathing grew heavier, faster, synchronized. I cupped her bottom and squeezed gently. In one swift move, I had her on my lap. Her legs molded around my waist. I ignored the twinge of discomfort in my thigh.

Tugging at her sweater, I tore it off. She took her T-shirt off immediately after. My attention caught on the bouncing tops of her breasts. I slid the bra strap off her shoulder and pushed the lacy fabric lower. A rosy nipple popped out, taut and perky.

I dipped my head and seized her, my tongue flicking the tight bud. The saltiness of her skin danced with my arousal.

Alena's head arched back, a mewling sound escaping her throat. The slow grind of her hips, back and forth, against the bulge in my briefs, had me charged and ready to go while her delicious groans sang in my ears.

She pushed me onto my back and followed, leaving a trail of kisses down the side of my cheek where the wolf girl had scratched me. My flesh tingled, and every hair stood on end.

Grasping her hips, I rolled her over and covered her body with mine, her soft breasts pressed against my chest. Desire purred deep in her chest.

She yanked up my T-shirt, offering me a sultry *do-me* look, and I was all about obliging. My shirt flew across the room. Her gloved hands trailed my stomach, the leather promising kinkiness. Sliding my fingers down the inside of her arm, I started to peel away one of her gloves. She snatched her hand away and leaned against me, licking the length of my neck and earlobe. I drank in her sweet female scent and couldn't wait a second longer, desperate to taste all of her, my hard-on pushing against my briefs.

I popped open the top button of her pants and unzipped them to reveal black lace undies. "Nice."

"Stop talking. Take me." Her tone drowned in desire—gritty and faint.

My fingers curled around the waistband of her pants, eager to pry them off. Her hips raised in anticipation. But when our sensitive hearing caught sharp, male voices outside, we froze. Whoever it was, they were getting closer.

"Shit!" Alena cupped a hand to her mouth, her eyes growing wider. Then she shoved me off her and scrambled to her feet, refastening her pants and tucking the most delicious breasts back into their lacy casing.

Snatching our tops off the floor, she turned and threw mine at me. "I don't know how you made me do that, but stay away from me."

Quick to get dressed, she left me standing in my briefs with the world's biggest boner and the fuzziness in my head clearing. "You seduced me, remember?" Despite the pressing urge to rip her jeans off, lean her over the table, and fuck her hard, I wasn't too sure how we ended up in bed in the first place. I mean, I knew, but … It was as if I'd lost myself in her presence.

She turned toward me with narrowed eyes and parted lips, clearly ready to jump into some rant. The voices were practically outside the window. Thank goodness for curtains.

"Where are my jeans?" I whispered.

Instead of making out, I should have gotten out of there,

kept my distance, and spied on the pack as I had originally planned. Except ... now that I'd tasted Alena's honeyed flesh, I was desperate for more of her. *Too close.*

Damn Alena, and damn my wolf. The lure between us reminded me of taffy: difficult to pull apart and sticking to you, but you always returned for seconds.

She shook her head and drew the blanket up to my waist. The piercing sting in my thigh flared. A quick look under the blanket and I wiped away the droplets of blood escaping down my leg.

The door creaked open. My head shot up.

Alena's cheeks burned bright red, and she bounced toward the entrance. "What's going on?"

An older man with a long face, furrowed brow, and dark brown hair entered. His shoulders shot back, and the scowl wrinkling his features wasn't a great sign.

"Girl, you've brought an intruder into the circus?" The dark tone of his voice screamed with anger. Shaking his head, he glanced at me. "Why are you here?"

I ran a hand across my mouth, still tasting Alena on my lips. "I saved her from being taken by the police ... and took a bullet for her."

Alena's words sliced the heaviness in the air. "He required medical attention, so I brought him back here."

The man's stare bore into her. "You should have known better."

A second wulfkin with long black hair and a matching beard stepped into the tiny trailer, causing it to creak and sway. Any more wulfkin outside wanting to gawk at the newcomer? With each step, this guy's shoulders alternated lurching back and forth. I'd call him Blackie. He shook his head as he approached Alena. Who was he anyway? Her lover?

When the older wulfkin focused his attention on me, he

cracked his knuckles. "What's your name and pack?" His voice was tremulous as he stood, legs planted shoulder-width apart.

My response was instinctive, immediate. "Enre Ulf." I gave my real name but didn't say anything about my pack. If I revealed I'd been living with the Transylvanian pack for years, I might as well cut my own wrists. Maybe I'd claim to be part of a remote European pack with minimal contact, and by the time he verified the information, I'd be gone.

"Ulf?" The wulfkin's nose creased, and he folded his arms across his chest, crushing his violet shirt. "The Varlac Ulf clan?" The furrow in his brow deepened.

That's when my escape plan hit. Why not? Being born into a Varlac family made me a Varlac, and no pack would dare target me without probable cause. Varlac ruled wulfkin, and anyone not following their rules was punished severely. This wulfkin didn't need to know I had left my Varlac family at the age of fourteen, made my own path in life, and now lived with the Transylvanian wulfkin pack in the Carpathian woods of Romania. The part about me still not being an alpha of my own pack, another requirement by my Varlac heritage, was a completely different issue. No need to volunteer that tidbit.

"Yeah. That's me. The clan sent me here."

The older man scratched his cheek as if uncertain whether he should believe me or not. Blackie butted in. "Then you wouldn't mind if we confirmed it."

I shrugged. "Go ahead."

Blackie's chin lifted as he strutted forward and laid a huge palm on my head, forcing it sideways. Inside, my wolf stirred, and my muscles tightened. I bit back the urge to connect my fist to his jaw.

He folded my ear forward, and his clammy touch only fueled my rage further.

The rapid breaths from both wulfkin reaffirmed they'd found my brand. Every wulfkin born into a Varlac clan was branded with a tattoo behind their right ear as a reminder of their royalty status. Two rip marks ran down the length of my ear topped with a crown— exactly how the Varlac reigned over the wulfkin clans in Europe: wrong them and they'd tear your heart out.

I swept Blackie's hand away, stood, and shoved my hands into his chest. A sting crawled up my thigh. He tripped backward a few steps, and when he caught himself, his chest thrust out.

Bring it on. Though trying to stand up to wulfkin in any kind of menacing way didn't quite hold up considering I stood there in my briefs and a T-shirt.

"Satisfied?" My clipped words elevated in pitch, and my gaze stapled both wulfkin to the wall alongside the costumes. The situation had turned in my favor.

While I'd had no initial intention of bringing my Varlac family allegiance into the situation, it might buy me time. From what I'd heard from my ex-alpha, Sandulf, the Bulgarian leader was ruthless, bloodthirsty, and had sworn to personally tear out the throats of every wulfkin in the Transylvanian pack, including me, in order to claim our land. Apparently, this pack had outgrown the circus and planned to relocate. The Bulgarian alpha was also accused of killing wulfkin from other packs each time their circus stopped in different territories. Of course, I suspected Sandulf's stories were stretches of the truth, but I intended to check them out for myself and set things straight. No one would touch my family or take our home, and I was ready to start a war to protect them.

"Girl, fetch him some pants. Where are his shoes?" the older man asked.

Alena inched closer and retrieved an object from behind the sofa. My boots. Perfect. "Thank you," I said.

Lifting her face, she glanced at me for the briefest moment, revealing the fierceness in her expression.

My insides lit. They shouldn't have, of course, but she drove me insane, even when she appeared ready to claw my heart out. I'd forgotten how much wulfkin detested and feared the Varlac.

She tossed the boots at my feet. "Alena," the older wulfkin snapped.

Blackie scurried toward me and set the boots upright.

Alena twirled around in place and dashed out of the trailer, slamming the door behind her.

"Girls." The older wulfkin almost choked on his fake laughter. "Please excuse her. I'm sure you must be famished. Damir, get him some food." He flicked a hand at Blackie, who scrambled outside. This wulfkin held power in the pack. Then reality hit me like a ton of bricks. I knew who stood before me.

"Now, what brings a Varlac to our home?" he asked.

The words I yearned to say went something like, "I'd personally love to show Alena some discipline alone," but donning the Varlac hat meant I needed to act the part, and politics came into play. I took a seat on the bed, glad to be off my leg, which had thankfully stopped seeping blood.

The wulfkin set a chair in front of me. He sat, one leg folded across the other, arms over his chest. "I'm Maxim, alpha of this pack. And the impertinent girl is my daughter, Alena."

I swallowed past the knot forming in my throat. Making out with the alpha's daughter was definitely a sure and quick way to get killed.

CHAPTER 3

ALENA

I stumbled out from behind the huge Moonlight Circus tent, mud splattering my boots as I marched back and forth, unable to cool off. Fairy lights illuminated the place into a wonderland of excitement—far from the truth today.

Enre's kiss still sizzled on my lips. Wiping them didn't help. The tingling refused to leave.

Since the age of five, I'd lived with the memory of my mother's death, along with the many ways I'd get revenge if the killer crossed my path.

Mother's face twisted in tortured agony, her eyes wide. A silent scream hung from her gaping mouth as the disgusting old Varlac from the Ulf family tore her throat out. Goose bumps raked down my arms. His snarly words never left me: "No one denies me."

Now a coward from their clan had returned. What did he want? To take my father from me too? My body trembled.

Thinking back to the way my wolf had taken charge, the way I'd lusted over Enre, made me sick to my stomach. I had never jumped a wulfkin. And definitely not a Varlac wulfkin. The mere mention of the word *Varlac* had my insides driving the air out of my lungs. No matter how much I responded to Enre, or how much my wolf pleaded to connect with him, it would never happen again. Next time, I'd thrust a knife into his neck.

It wasn't as if we needed another reason, but we had to get Nicolai out of prison, and fast. The closer the full moon drew, the more likely the Varlac could accuse us of breaking one of their rules: revealing our kind to humans.

Every part of me shuddered with anger, making the decision to uncover Enre's secrets an easy one.

Thunder crashed overhead. Large raindrops fell, pinging on the metal trailers. I picked up my pace and headed toward the main tent.

"Alena."

I turned around, and Father approached, his spine rigid and hands cramped into his armpits. His wide shoulders hunched forward while water dripped from his short, black hair. For those few seconds, the usual strong statue that was my father appeared smaller, more fragile somehow.

We ducked under an RV's awning, out of the storm. My clothes clung to my body, and a clammy sensation settled over my skin. I caught my breath and stared out into the distance at the red and white stripes of the big top. Numbness crawled over me. Crimson flags tied to the tips of the dome popped in the wind, ropes bounced against metal supports, and clangs resonated in the night as the wind's speed intensified.

"You must have more self-control," Father said. "That Varlac's watching our every move, and I can't have you romping like a teenager. Especially since you didn't seem to have a problem with him before I arrived." He wiped the rain off his face with a palm.

Releasing a long huff, I lowered my gaze as heat flushed my cheeks. "I didn't know what he was." My wolf desired

Enre, and I had offered myself eagerly. *Fool.* "You have to get rid of him."

Father's attention snagged on the marquee momentarily, his mouth thinning, and his strong chin reminded me of Nicolai. What was he doing right now?

"The show will go on tonight as normal."

"What?" I pushed off the RV. "You can't. Not with Nic caught by the police and a Varlac snooping around. Everyone in the pack is in shock."

"Nicolai's the last moonwulf in our pack. Still a baby. But there's only so much I can do if he insists on disobeying our rules and throwing himself under a bus." Father refused to call him Nic, insisting that if parents wanted their kids' names shortened, they would have named them that way.

I frowned. "And yet, if lightning strikes Nic, I'll receive the deathblow too." I remembered Mother telling us that Nicolai and I were mortally linked. She realized it when Nicolai got hit by a car at the age of eight. He was close to death, and I had felt every sting of his pain rising through me. A couple of days later, I fell unconscious when Nicolai had done the same. For three days, we teetered on death's doorstep, and when we finally woke up, our mother said I saved him with my healing. From that moment, I knew I was different, but I refused to let it define me. I healed anyone in the pack that needed it and grew up with a normal life. It was for my own safety, not anyone else's, and sure, after the Lunar Eutine a few pack members went out of their way to avoid touching me, but I'd accepted that not everyone was going to be open-minded to what they didn't understand. And that was fine by me.

Now, Nic and I were bound forever. I learned later this was due to a curse on our family line that had skipped a generation. So I couldn't let anything happen to my brother if I intended to stay alive.

Father embraced me, his chin on top of my head and my hands cradled between our chests. I inhaled the scent of his wolf mixed with perspiration.

"Get him back. Tomorrow. It's *my* fault he's caught." I hated how much my words quivered.

"We bide our time." Father's hands rubbed my back in a soothing motion, which had worked when I was younger, but now, it only irritated me. I nudged him away.

Cross my father and he'd turn brutal, but always for the right reason. Over the past year, he'd been trying to find us a permanent home since our pack had grown too large for the circus. Three to four wulfkin were sharing each trailer now, and the city was no place to transform into wolves and run free. Plus, the councils frequently denied us permits to set up the circus in their towns. Traveling was such a drag. How I'd love us to occupy a forest instead. A perfect place, protected from humans.

"Nic didn't kill the human," I said. "It was Ash."

Father's brown eyes squinted. "Police are swarming the circus, asking questions. With the victim's blood on Nicolai and him at the scene of the crime, he's facing a murder charge. I hope once they test the victim, they'll see his death was caused by animal bites and clear Nicolai. But that might take months in the system." Father couldn't hide the anguish clouding his hooded eyes.

We were in deep shit. My posture softened. "He has to be free before the next—"

"I know." Father shook his head.

The drenching rain increased in speed and ferocity, sheets of water closing us in under the awning. Father leaned nearer. "The police are also searching for two others who were at the scene."

His raised eyebrow sent a twinge of guilt plunging to the

base of my stomach, but it was too late. I couldn't take back the situation or Nicolai's capture.

"The Varlac split us up," I said. "He should be the one to pay for this."

Replaying Enre's insolent smirk and what his father took from us only burned me up with rage. I'd get my revenge, somehow.

"We have enough crap to deal with. Cops in our home, Nicolai charged with murder, Interpol snooping around the circus, looking for Ash."

Ash! Silent shivers climbed up my spine. "Has anyone found her?"

"Yes, Ivan discovered her wandering behind the circus, and she's now locked up." I released the breath I'd been holding. "Thank the moon goddess."

Father stared at his mud-coated boots for a long moment. "Anyway, apparently the Varlac is here to observe us. A regular check-in. I don't buy it. The last time they visited was eighteen years ago. Why now? Especially a member of the Ulf family." He rubbed my arms, a weak smile forcing itself onto his lips. "But I know someone who can help us with Nicolai. We've gotten through worse, and we'll manage this as well. But you need to keep your emotions under control."

I couldn't bring myself to respond. It appeared we were treading water with weights chained to our ankles. Often we'd been chased out of towns, labeled as thieving gypsies, but this was far worse.

"I'll do what I can."

"I'm counting on it. I need you to stay with Enre."

"What? No."

His grasp tightened on my arms, his eyes half closed. "And use your healing ability to get him fixed up so he can leave. See if you can find out what he's up to. And remember who he is."

I hated the notion of spending another second with Enre, and with that, my wolf stretched and prodded against my insides in protest of my thoughts. Why did she respond to him? *Traitor.*

"I know you won't let me down." Father kissed my forehead and stepped out into the rain, darting toward the main tent. He glanced over his shoulder and called out, "I told Enre you'd give him a tour."

A sickness stirred in my belly, and I dropped my gaze to my gloved hands. Father knew I avoided healing anyone. Last time, I had passed out and woke up two days later. A transformation would help me take the edge off, alleviate the tension. Except, the pack had been forbidden from transforming into our wolves for the past few weeks to avoid being seen by the police and Interpol, who now watched us around the clock. My wolf crawled beneath my skin constantly, whimpering for release. I ignored her.

Father was right. We'd get through this. We had to. The night's first performance would kick off in a few hours, and a lot of preparation remained. Behind me, the dark passage between two trailers led to my home, but in Enre's presence, I worried I'd never make it to the show. Though, I wasn't sure if this would be from me trying to kill him or kiss him.

I decided I'd only spend time with him in other people's company. Not alone, whatsoever, and I'd find another wulfkin to house him. I didn't need his scent stinking up my trailer and bringing my wolf into heat.

I sprinted toward the communal dressing room even though the last thing I wanted to do tonight was perform.

*D*ressed up in my outfit, I stood backstage, behind the main curtain, and slid the heavy fabric open slightly to peek out. I inhaled the intoxicating nightly mix of fresh popcorn and peanuts. Voices and laughter filled the area as people moved around, finding their spots in the semi-circle of tiered seating. The dimly lit tent added to the mystery of the oversized golden ball balanced on a lofty red-and-white striped pedestal positioned in the center of the ring. It was all part of the first act, but leaving this prop in full view made the audience extra curious, meaning they sat down quickly.

On the opposite side, two clowns bounced along an aisle, fighting to hold a monstrous umbrella made of balloons. Those two wulfkin adored kids and suited the role of clowns perfectly. Children around them laughed and pointed. An acrobat waving glow sticks rolled the hot-dog cart in front of the ring. Their sales brought in more money than the tickets some nights.

The rain beat against the tent. Terrible weather rarely stopped people from attending the circus. Along the top platform, several uniformed policemen lingered, studying the area. One of them spent time questioning one of our trampolinists. Another officer was speaking to Damir, Father's muscle. My belly ached at the notion of more police watching our every move. Tonight's show should have been canceled.

I released the curtains and joined the rest of the pack backstage. It was organized chaos: wulfkin in every direction, stretching, practicing, or setting up props. Two clowns fitted in blown-up muscle outfits were bumping and bouncing off each other, and I swore one of them would roll out under the curtains and into the ring. Behind them, our twin contortionists scurried in tiny circles on all fours while doing backbends as casually as if they were in wolf form. Our knife-thrower hurled four blades in unison at a wooden board positioned above the male acrobats stretching in the far corner. A backstage crew member who didn't perform was scurrying up a metal ladder to adjust or replace a light.

Several of the male performers released a low burring sound, picked up by the others, and my chest swelled with pride.

We were one family, one team, strong and loyal to each other. We'd get through anything.

Then my sight landed on Enre, and the communal sound ended abruptly, replaced by a few rolling snarls.

His gaze caught on my fishnet bodysuit with a small black strip of fabric across my bust and matching skimpy shorts. My costume always impressed the boys, but I didn't need that kind of leering attention from Enre. He wore his jeans, the ones I had patched up, and his hair was slicked back from the rain.

My wolf clawed within my chest. *Control yourself.*

"I like this side of you." He cleared his throat.

"Best if you stayed in the trailer." I edged behind a small, round trampoline, eager for space between us, though I reminded myself to pretend and be nice to get dirt on him. "Allow the wound to heal." The words tasted bitter on my tongue. In truth, I prayed the injury festered and spread.

"And miss out on seeing you dressed like this?" One of his eyebrows arched slightly.

I sidestepped Enre and retrieved an unoccupied chair from the dressing area in the right wing fitted out with seats and mirrored desks. Offering him a half smile, I pushed the chair toward him. It was all the positive energy I could muster. "Here, take this out into the crowd and enjoy the show."

He set the chair beside him, one hand leaning against the

back for support. "Was hoping to stay backstage and experience behind-the-scenes action." His gaze roamed to the stage around us, then landed on me.

My muscles tensed as my tone dipped. "Really not a wonderful idea."

"Why not?" His head cocked to the side, and his lips pinched. The memory of his mouth on mine sent shivers down my spine. *Remember who he is.*

"Look. We run a legit business here. There's nothing for the Varlac to concern themselves with. Anyway, I've got to go." I strolled to the dressing area, the sensation of his eyes heavy on my back. Moving to stand behind Sonia, our trampolinist, fortune- teller, and my best friend, I grabbed a hairbrush and started combing her dark-blonde curls. Enre remained in the right-wing dressing area.

"He fancies you," Sonia said, staring at my reflection in the mirror in front of us. A slight smirk tugged the edges of her mouth upward. Her eyes were green and huge, reminding me of crystal balls. Even at thirty-eight, she looked ten years younger than her age.

I brushed her locks into a tight ponytail. "You don't know what you're saying."

I glanced at Enre again. Every wulfkin kept stealing peeks in his direction. Father had cautioned everyone from engaging with him, which, of course, made them extra curious.

The solution was for me to drag Enre outside and tell him to get lost. He affected me in the worst possible way. How could I desire and detest someone at the same time?

Sonia craned her neck and leaned past the bodies practicing their routines to better view Enre. "He stares at you as if he's deciding whether you're prey or his mate. That's provocative, Alena. Wish a wulfkin would look at me that way."

Another glance and his eyes were all over me, scanning up and down. Then he turned and limped toward one of our acrobats.

"He's a Varlac," I said. "A viper."

Sonia shrugged. "Imagine getting into his clan. The power you'd have to change life for all wulfkin." Sonia had never been power-hungry but knew my real intention was to help all wulfkin.

"You don't know what you're talking about." Yeah, the power to push wulfkin around and mingle with aristocrats who had their noses up their butts. *No, thanks.*

A chorus of trumpets blared from the speakers, a beat Nicolai had put together. Then the lights dimmed. What was Nicolai doing tonight? Instead of pushing forward with the show, I should have gone to the police station, tried to … I wasn't sure what I could do, but it was better than pretending everything was fine.

The crowd's murmurs silenced. Sonia got up from her seat and clutched my wrist. "Remember what we saw in the cards last week?" She offered me a frown and hurried across the stage to stand behind the curtain with three other wulfkin.

Yeah, I remembered all too well what Sonia's cards had said … That a stranger would emerge and forever change my destiny.

Father was already in position, garbed in his long, fitted red coat, black jodhpurs, knee-length boots, and a microphone in hand.

Tonight, a heavy air tightened around the pack's throats. Plastering a fake smile on my face as Nicolai lay in a jail cell left me feeling dirty and guilty. Father had to rescue Nicolai. Little else mattered, especially not one sexy Varlac who was the manifestation of danger in disguise.

CHAPTER 4

ENRE

I sat among the spectators, staring up at the high wires, and uneasiness settled in my gut. Humans applauded and cheered when the clowns finished their balloon stunts, and I couldn't stop shifting in my seat.

If I failed to stop Maxim from attacking my family in Transylvania, we'd all be slaughtered by this Bulgarian pack.

On top of everything, if Maxim contacted the Varlac clan in Hungary, my web of untruths would turn into a blade at my throat. Father would never back me up or confirm that I was investigating on their behalf. He'd throw me to the wolves and tell them to kill me. Plus, knowing Father, he'd remind me that when I turned twenty-five next week without my own pack and an alpha status, he'd have the right to kill me himself. It was bullshit, but reality.

Fuck, this was why I hated being a Varlac.

A sudden change of music from the playful, mischievous beat to a slow, melodic tune reminiscent of the tango drew my attention to the ring below. The lights dimmed, and a spotlight shone on lush red curtains. A single figure stepped out from behind them— Alena, in her fishnet outfit. With each quick, ballerina-like step, her boobs bounced, and my pulse accelerated. I slid to the edge of my chair. When she twirled on the spot, my breath jammed in my throat. The dip of her waist to the curve of her hips held my attention. My hands tingled with the desire to stroke her long legs, and I remembered how strong those legs had felt around my waist.

With a grumble, I reined myself in and winced from the pain shooting up my leg.

When would this damn injury heal?

From the ceiling, two red silk ribbons cascaded down and dangled in the center of the ring.

Alena wrapped her wrists in the silk and paraded around the ring with her arms stretched outward. She broke into a sprint, gaining momentum with each step.

My eyes locked on her form, her tapered waist, and toned arms. This wasn't great for my self-control, but I couldn't tear myself away. The crowd was silent, and even the music had died. Only the tapping of her feet on the sawdust-covered ground resonated as she picked up speed in her circular race around the ring. The red ribbons twisted over-head and drew her hands upward with each rotation.

On her next step, she lunged forward and lifted several feet off the ground. Her body, straight as a pin, orbited the circular performance ring, and the momentum of the ribbon starting to unwind sent her into a frantic spin.

The spectators cheered, and I found myself clapping in hypnotic awe.

When the spinning finally ended, Alena was lifted higher and dangled halfway up to the ceiling, held by the fabric. In one quick flick, she widened her arms and threw her legs over her head into a handstand. Her strong legs spread into a perfect gymnast's split, and it took every bit of strength to stop myself from lunging for her. The idea of her striking that pose in the bedroom had my pulse kicking into turbo speed. Sure, wulfkin strength made acrobatic stunts easier than they were for the average human, but such resilience wasn't a trait we were familiar with. The way Alena moved and contorted tightened my jeans. I needed to leave the tent and calm down.

With my thigh still rigid from the bullet wound, I carefully eased out of the seat and shuffled along the top row, taking my time and clenching my jaw each time I put pressure on the painful leg. Going down the stairs was the hardest part. I managed to reach the edge of the curtains in great pain. With one last glimpse, I found Alena arching into a backbend, the ribbon wrapped around her tiny waist, supporting her in midair. My wolf whimpered.

Heal, discover what the alpha was up to, and protect my leader and our pack from death—that was my plan. Not Alena.

Behind the curtains, a trampoline sat waiting for the next act. Numerous wulfkin eyes settled on me—blades at my back. They probably contemplated ripping into me. I would, too, if a stranger entered my home. *Get over it.*

I trudged past them. Outside, the rain softened to a sprinkle, but a cold wind slapped against me. Free of the heavy human and wulfkin scents, I contemplated heading to the island of trees near the freeway for a fast transformation, except the change might mess up my injury further. My insides itched, and the wolf within me ached for release. *Soon.*

Night blanketed the land behind the circus tent, hinting at trailer shapes in the near distance. The faint sound of voices reached me from my right. Curiosity and the need to attain insider information had me limping around the tent in the direction of the noise.

The parking lot came into view, lit up by the circling Ferris wheel nearby. Engulfed by shadows, I thanked the moon that the breeze blew in my favor. Mud kept slipping beneath my boots. *I better not fall on my ass.*

Three figures stood several feet away. A flurry of gusts brushed past, carrying the scent of the alpha, his goon, Damir (though I preferred "Blackie"), and a human female I didn't recognize. Pressing my back against the curved tent, I held tight and listened while the trio walked out of view.

"She was seen near your circus the day before she vanished. Both witnesses said she was with a young man who fits your son's description at the time." The female's voice rang through the night. I wouldn't be surprised if her words reached people in the tent. "And today, Nicolai was caught with a dead man. Odd coincidence, wouldn't you say?"

"Like I told you before, I know nothing of the missing girl," Maxim responded, his tone on edge. "Today's tragedy has had an effect on everyone at the Moonlight Circus, and I'm working on getting my son out on bail any day."

That was news to me.

"Now I know you're lying to me," the female said. "You touch your chin every time you lie. Bail was denied. Nicolai is never getting out. Once another warrant is approved, we'll turn this place inside out and uncover every filthy secret you're hiding in this freak show."

The woman had guts, and her words didn't hold a hint of doubt in them. In her mind, she'd probably already stamped guilty on Maxim's forehead. If the authorities denied Nicolai bail, it would have massive repercussions for all wulfkin and Varlac. He'd shift into his wolf form during the full moon, exposing our kind to humans. Not to mention the penalties the Varlac would inflict on this pack when they found out Maxim's pack was endangering wulfkin secrecy.

Shuffling feet sounded, and my muscles tensed, ready to bolt from my hiding place. I inched forward, but they weren't coming my way. Blackie paced in a small circle behind them. I released a long exhale.

"You'll slip, and we'll get you too," the woman said.

The authorities weren't letting go of Nicolai. And for all I knew, he could have killed that human. But was I missing something here? There had to be more to this.

Maxim, shoulders rigid and hunched forward, stared at the human who stood a few inches shorter than him. Neither said a word. Blackie had the alpha's back, his glare piercing into the female. I suspected that if Maxim gave the word, Blackie would rip the woman's heart out in a fraction of a second.

Maxim turned away first. "I'm finished with this conversation." He stormed toward the tent entrance.

Blackie strode by his side, swearing loud enough for the woman to hear. "Fucking pigs."

This pack was in shit.

The female waited in the rain a while longer, studying them, then whirled and trekked into the army of parked cars.

I wiped my face of drizzle—what was left of the storm. Seemed like Daciana's pack, my family, wasn't the only one with colossal issues. Daciana had killed our previous alpha, Sandulf, alleviating some of our troubles, but in this pack, Maxim was sinking in quicksand. If the authorities had already suspected Nicolai of kidnapping, and now he'd been caught with a dead human, I'd say the police would be watching them nonstop.

Footfalls and the squish of mud behind me made me spin in time to spot a figure approaching.

"Who's there?" I asked.

Alena stepped out from a patch of darkness, wrapped in a trench coat, wearing rain boots and stage makeup slightly smeared from the moisture.

My wolf snapped awake.

"What are you doing?" She crossed her arms over her chest, water trickling down her face.

"Getting fresh air." I couldn't nip the grin spreading across my lips, remembering how good she felt beneath me. "Watched you perform. Your flexibility has me intrigued."

"I see past your flirty words." Shadows slid across her hard expression. "Don't think I trust you."

I shrugged. "Most people don't trust Varlac. I get that."

"How can you stand being so arrogant?"

"It's actually confidence. There's a difference."

Her gaze narrowed, and if we'd been in her trailer, I was certain she'd have chucked something at me. Yet, my heart refused to calm down around her.

Before I could stop myself, we were standing a hairbreadth apart, and my arm was snaked around her waist, holding her close. The inner wolf growled in my chest, begging for more.

For a split second, a ravenous hunger slid into her eyes. She felt it too. Part of my brain yelled to ease off, to remember my mission, the danger she posed, and how life between us would never work. But my body had other ideas.

"Shall we return to your room and finish what we started?" I asked.

She shoved her hands into my chest, and I stumbled away from her, barely remaining upright as my knee wobbled.

"Why are you fighting it?" It was my wolf pushing me again. Damn troublemaker.

Her attention lowered momentarily, and when her head lifted, her expression was fierce; fire burned in her pupils, and her mouth remained tight. "Because I can resist what's not good for me. I have self-control. Something you're obviously lacking. Being a Varlac doesn't mean everyone will bend over backward for you."

"I kind of wish you would."

"Shut up. I don't like anything you stand for. Your family members are murderers." Her words were venom from a spitting cobra, striking an open wound.

I didn't know my parents well enough to disprove her accusations, but my father was a bastard of a wulfkin … That, I could attest to. Still, the way she called them killers sounded as if she'd seen their actions firsthand. Despite my curiosity, I couldn't poke holes in my cover. My insides hardened, and my wolf retreated. This was why I had to keep my distance, get the job done, and move on. This wasn't a game, a challenge to chase the prettiest wulfkin, regardless of her lure. I had to protect the lives of my family.

She whirled around and marched away. "I've found another trailer for you to stay in until you heal. I'll take you there now."

What was going on with me? My stomach wrung tight. Was this guilt? Couldn't be. I didn't do guilt.

Driving my mashed-up thoughts aside, I hurried after Alena. She slipped in and out of the shadows, and soon we stopped in front of a trailer, which was two down from hers.

Once inside, she switched on the light. There was a bed, table, sofa, and countertop. "Whoever lives in this trailer has no taste."

"The wulfkin who stay here have simple tastes and don't believe in collecting objects.

You can use it for the *few days* you're here."

That should give me sufficient time to get my plan into action and get further dirt on the alpha.

She broke the silence. "Lie on the bed and take your jeans off."

My pulse charged at her words. I smirked and wiggled my eyebrows at Alena, whose expression remained stoic.

"Father asked me to help heal you, and that's what I'm

going to do," she said through clenched teeth and a forced smile, pulling up the softness of her lips.

In no time, I lay flat on my back in my briefs and T-shirt, again. I threaded my fingers behind my head. After Alena's little confession outside, I wasn't sure what to do with my attraction for her. What had my family done to elicit such hatred?

Kneeling near the bed in front of my injured leg, she wiped the rain off her face with a towel, still wearing her gloves. Perhaps she had a fetish about having sex while wearing gloves—after all, she hadn't removed them while we kissed. I could handle that. And with that thought, an erection was already building inside my boxers. Shit.

Alena placed her small hands above the bullet wound without touching me.

"Close your eyes and relax."

The stiff tone of her voice was anything but calming. An instant heat radiated from her hands, burning into my thigh, drowning my desire. It relieved as much as it stung to high hell. How exactly was she doing this? I'd never encountered or heard of a wulfkin with such a healing ability. To what extent could she heal someone? A bullet wound, a broken bone, or someone on death's doorstep? It had me intrigued because Daciana had recently gained the ability to determine with a single touch if someone was true of heart and spoke the truth. She'd gained it after the Lunar Eutine a couple of weeks ago.

I shut my eyes, ignoring the madness of the day and the corner I'd wedged myself into with the half-truths. My wolf still craved Alena—and she was the daughter of the alpha rumored to be worse than Attila the Hun. So, I was screwed.

CHAPTER 5

ALENA

$\mathcal{P}$ain seared down my arms as I dangled from the branch of a giant oak tree, held by vines around my wrists. Twigs caught in my long hair. No matter how much I stretched, my toes were suspended just above the ground. When I glanced around, my throat seized at the sight of butchered bodies everywhere. Moonlight revealed the tangle of limbs and torsos heaped in a pile. So much blood. The copper tang filled my nostrils.

Then I noticed him … Father's face among the corpses, dead. I gagged. Panic gripped my lungs, squeezing. I tugged against the vines, kicking the air, my body swinging from the tree.

"Help! Someone, please."

Footfalls closed in from behind, and I strained my neck to look over my shoulder— darkness. Turning back around, I found Enre several feet in front of me, standing in the nude. My insides fluttered as my inner wolf snapped awake, whimpering for Enre's touch. Glancing past him, I saw the bodies were gone. Not a single stain marked the perfect, white snow. No footprints. Nothing.

Enre's pale-blue eyes claimed me. All of me. Staring down, I noticed I wore no clothes either.

I kept telling myself this was wrong, but for the life of me, I couldn't remember why it was bad. Especially not when arousal coursed south, burning between my thighs.

Silver light gleamed off Enre's sinewed pecs and the V tapering at his hips.

Shadows conveniently covered his erection, but I knew it was there. The savagery in his gaze promised sex.

Goddess of the moon, help me. I yearn for him. Before I could knock any kind of reason into myself, impulse kicked in.

"Fuck me." My words purred.

At my invitation, his lips split into a smile. He stepped closer as he caressed me with his eyes.

"I'll give you anything you want." His warm breath on my skin had my nipples beaded tight, and his devilish smirk made me wet and breathless. When his hands slid across my waist, I moaned with anticipation.

My legs curled around his hips, and my pelvis rocked back and forth over his hardness. I gripped the vines tying my hands to the branch in expectation of him stretching and filling me. The unrelenting need crashed through me.

"Please, Enre."

The tip of his erection dipped into me, teasing. I pushed forward, every nerve in me focused on that single point of contact.

With hands clutching my hips, he pushed me away. I cried out, arching toward him.

"First," he said in a deep, sultry voice, "promise me." My inhales quickened; I trembled with desire. "What?"

"Promise you'll be mine forever."

A pleasurable ache swirled in the depths of my belly as he

rubbed himself along the length of my sleekness. A half grunt spilled out from my wolf. She'd already claimed Enre as her mate, and I was powerless to contradict her. I felt the connection, deep inside me, threatening to splinter my heart if we ever lost him.

Meeting Enre's lusty stare had desperation surging in my veins, and I pined for him to embrace me and never let go.

"I ..."

The words jammed somewhere between my stomach and throat. My wolf grumbled and rolled for release.

A song of howls broke nearby, startling both of us from our private moment. Wolves circled us, dozens of them, their noses in the air, releasing howling chants.

And suddenly, everything felt right ... Enre's arrival ... my attraction to him ... the coming change.

I woke with a sudden gasp, drenched in sweat, and the sweet, rhythmic pulse from the dream still thumping between my thighs. Throwing the covers off, I slid my legs over the edge of the bed, reached for the water bottle on the nightstand, and gulped half of it without taking a breath. I straightened the lamp and sat there in the streaming morning sunlight. Why had my attraction to Enre seemed so harmonious in the dream? What had any of it meant?

Enre's arrival was a bad omen. It had to be, and he was smack in the middle of the oncoming disaster. Come to think of it, so was I. In my nightmare, the wolves represented the pack. I got that. Perhaps they gathered to celebrate the union between Enre and me. But why was Father dead?

From a young age, most of my dreams had hinted at an event about to happen—such as Ash before her transformation, the police following us into Bulgaria. But there were the many silly ones too—me inside a chicken coop collecting rabbits and hiding them from the other wulfkin who salivated at the idea of eating them. Turned out, the next day, a truck filled with rabbits headed for slaughter had an accident not far from our circus, and the little bunnies got free, bouncing toward our trailers. Let's just say, not many were returned to the truck. So why couldn't I have had a vision about Nicolai and his capture, or Enre's arrival?

Father would get Nicolai out, and soon. He'd have to.

Up on my feet, queasiness swam through my head. I'd spent ten minutes healing Enre last night, and afterward my strength was as drained as if I had run a marathon. A week ago, I'd rushed to a wulfkin who fell from the trapeze and missed the net, landing on her hip. Before I realized what was happening, I'd healed her. That knocked me out for two days. Father was convinced I'd slipped into a coma.

My ability had never been so instinctive, and my reaction time had been immediate. Previously, before I turned into a wulfkin, it usually took an hour to close a simple cut. Now, I had to wear gloves to avoid accidentally zapping myself of all energy. I blamed it on the recent Lunar Eutine when I transformed from a moonwulf to a wulfkin. Something inside me changed.

Once I selected clothes for the day, boots in hand, I was ready for a shower, breakfast, and a visit to the one person who might understand the meaning of my vision.

Outside, the sun gleamed, and only a splattering of clouds marked the sky—no sign of the rain that had drenched us last night. I hurried into the morning wind, inhaling the nippy air infused with pollution, wet soil, and humans.

Near the mess marquee stood two uniformed police officers with Father, who offered me a glance that said to keep moving. After a quick wash, I joined the pack for breakfast.

Around me, wulfkin stuffed their faces, barely saying a word. Usually, I couldn't hear my own thoughts in this place. Considering the lack of woods or secluded parks in Ruse, no one had changed into wolf form, where they were free to run, in more than weeks. The burning itch beneath everyone's skin was getting worse by the second.

A charge permeated the packed mess tent, the kind that required merely a single flick of a match for the whole place to go up in flames.

Enre limped through the entrance.

I stuffed the last piece of meat into my mouth. My pulse hitched to a dangerously high level, threatening to bring my wolf out. Last night, I had struggled to keep calm, but if I had any hope of playing him to uncover the truth of his visit, I had to control my emotions. Those were Father's orders.

Sunlight cast a halo around Enre, though he was anything but angelic. He wore black jeans and a matching T-shirt. The spare clothes I stored in his trailer explained the extra tightness of his jeans and the fabric pulling across his chest. Wasn't he cold?

Glimpses of my dream and how much I yearned for him shoved their way into my mind. Heat crawled up my thighs. Then, images of the bodies and Father from my dream surfaced. Shaking my head, I banished the vision, tucking it in the farthest recesses of my mind. If I stayed away from Enre, the dream couldn't happen.

With his square frame and cocky grin, he didn't care about the way every wulfkin studied him, females were eager to whisk him into their trailers, or the males were ready to tear him apart.

I ducked toward the plate of food when he scanned the room. Varlac were conceited, manipulative, and dangerous.

"This obviously isn't a five-star joint, is it?" Enre asked, his voice flirtatious and loud.

A quick glance up revealed Enre was piling his plate high with meat. He turned and scanned the tent for a seat. No one moved at first. Then three of Father's bodyguards marched toward him, shoulders stiff, spines arched, and expressions fueled by anger.

Enre grinned his stupid smirk. What was wrong with him? Did he know something we didn't? Was the joke on us?

Silence saturated the tent.

"Thanks for offering your seat," he said, using his chin to point to their table.

Damir stood inches from Enre. "If our food isn't to your liking, then you can leave." Electricity sparked through the testosterone-infused air.

Damir's arms twitched, and his posture curled forward. The grumble rolling from his chest revealed the awful truth —he was struggling to restrain his wolf.

I shot to my feet and weaved past the seats and unmoving wulfkin. Not here. Not with police so near. I had to stop Damir. No one else seemed to have any intention to end this.

Damir backhanded the plate out of Enre's hand and shoved him into a food counter, sending cutlery flying off the edge.

Enre caught himself before losing his balance. "Such a waste of food."

Outside the tent, the sound of voices increased, and the shadows of several figures made their way toward the entrance. The police. Father.

My muscles tensed. I pushed an empty chair aside to get closer to the commotion. "We don't want you here." Damir's body trembled as fur sprouted along his arms. His wolf form was breaking out.

Crap.

"Damir, no!" I was by his side, slapping my palms against his shoulder. "Don't do this here."

The silhouettes outside the tent drew closer. No one moved to stop the potential fight.

I shot a glare at two guys as they bustled beside us and said, "Take Damir. Now."

They each snatched an arm and yanked Damir toward the back of the tent, pulling him down to the ground. Half a howl spilled from Damir. One of the wulfkin smacked a palm over his mouth as Father and the officers entered the tent.

I feared my heart would break through my rib cage.

Several wulfkin were on their feet and intercepted Father and the officers at the entrance of the tent. They blocked their view inside, pretending they were done eating. Other wulfkin stood in front of the commotion, collecting their plates in slow motion as if also ready to leave. At least it blocked them from the action of Damir being pinned to the ground.

As if on cue, the crowd broke into loud conversation and fake laughter. "All good in here?" an officer asked.

"My fault," Enre piped up and started collecting the cutlery off the linoleum flooring. "Lost my footing, that's all."

Father's brow creased, his gaze darting in Damir's direction. "Clean up the mess." He shook his head and guided the policemen outside.

Shit.

Two female wulfkin leapt up and cleaned the mess beside Enre, offering him sideway glances. My insides burned. Those girls needed some control.

Damir was on his feet, shaking off one of the wulfkin. "I'm fine. Leave me alone."

I turned to Enre, and tingles spread through my chest as his bright blue eyes landed on me, despite my intentions to resist him. Why was he smiling?

This was my prompt to exit. I marched out, thankful for

the fresh air and the distance between us. How the heck was I going to discover what he was up to if I couldn't be in his presence for two seconds without my body betraying me?

I dashed away from the tent with its smell of steak, bacon, ham, eggs, and Enre. I trekked past the trailers, hearing only the buzz of car engines in the near distance. In the daylight, the fantastical ambiance of the circus no longer existed. Reality was harsh. The striped material of the main tent showed signs of overuse. Stretch marks and rips that were hidden in the darkness were highlighted in the sparkling sunshine. Mud splattered the hem and coated everything in its path, including my brown boots.

When I reached Sonia's trailer and knocked, she answered in a soft voice, "It's open."

Inside, I stepped over a suitcase that had fallen away from the wall. I tiptoed around clothes, scarves, and handbags littering the floor. Sonia waited in one of two chairs at the table beneath the window.

The translucent fabric covering the window pasted a violet tinge across her belongings, reminding me of a night-club. *Sorry, Sonia, it's too early in the morning for discos—unless you're Nicolai.* The thought of him and his love of music turned my stomach into concrete.

He'd spent his first night in prison. Guilt gnawed at my insides; it was my fault.

Despite being a moonwulf, my brother wasn't the fighting type, and in human form, he had no special strength. *Goddess of the moon, he won't last in there.* The other inmates would eat him alive. I understood Father's concern about lying low, but his approach didn't sit right with me at all. We should take action now. Waiting only opened us up to more problems.

"Girl, you going to stand there all day?" Sonia's voice turned loud as she snapped me back to the here and now.

She sat at the table, both hands clasped around at least a dozen twigs, each about half a foot long. Balancing the ends on the center of the table, she let the twigs fall and studied the way the pieces of wood collapsed on top of each other. The majority crisscrossed each other, others rolled away from the pile.

Sonia's dark-blonde curls were pulled off her face with a headband. She wore no makeup or her usual fake gypsy jewelry reserved for the circus customers.

"Have a seat." She spoke without taking her eyes from the pile of sticks in front of her, her head tilting from side to side.

Taking a chair at the table and kicking aside a boot, I reconsidered telling her about my dream with Enre. The more I replayed the vision in my mind, the more I was convinced it was me lusting over him. Heat radiated down my neck at the thought of telling Sonia that I'd turned into some horny nymph.

"What do you see?" No matter how many times Sonia read my future, my insides still fluttered.

"He's at the circus for you."

"The Varlac?" I slouched into the chair, arms folded across my chest, fire scaling my cheeks. "I doubt it." Not the first time the twigs would have been misinterpreted.

"You'll bring a change out in him. How exciting." She flashed me a cheerful smile.

A thousand possibilities swirled in my head, but none of them made any sense, except the one where I hated being paired with Enre. "What does that even mean?"

Sonia inched closer. "The universe has a sick sense of humor. It shows us only snippets of events. You know that." She twisted in her seat and retrieved a pack of tarot cards from the bookshelf behind her. The top card had a brightly colored parrot painted on it. She sighed, stashed it back on the shelf, and continued to fumble through her numerous other decks.

"That's for the tourists." She spoke with her attention still on the bookshelf. "Anyway, what about you? Had any dreams lately?"

I licked my lips, deciding not to share the memory of what Enre had intended to do to me in the dream. "Not much."

"So you dreamt about him? The shake of your head says no, but your tone tells a different story." She giggled, a piercing laugh, as she retrieved another pack of cards, the backs printed with a kaleidoscope of colors in a diamond patchwork design. "Weeks ago, I told you a visitor was coming." Sonia settled in her seat to face me.

"But what does that have to do with me?"

Her gaze drilled into me once again. "I'll show you." With a swift flick of her fingers, she dealt the cards, flicking each abandoned one behind her or onto the floor.

"This one"—she placed a card in front of me and pointed to the man strung upside down by one foot from a tree—"is about being stuck, and this applies to the pack. Our situation."

The memories of me dangling from a tree, the dead bodies, and Enre's arrival replayed in my mind. Words refused to leave my mouth. I longed to tell her everything, but if I said anything aloud, it would make the situation real. Saying nothing kept the vision a silly dream … especially the part about my father being dead.

"And this." Sonia held up another card, showing a great tower crumbling from a fire. "Is change coming whether we want it or not. For all of us."

"What about Nic?"

"I'd say he's part of the destruction, unfortunately."

My body shivered. I didn't like change, especially when *destruction* was used to describe it.

Reclining, Sonia reached across the bed and grabbed a snake-patterned handbag. She retrieved a small mirror and lipstick and painted her lips as if she hadn't just proclaimed an omen hung over our pack. Puckering her mouth, she stared at herself in the mirror, running a finger down the length of her especially large nose.

"When are you going to settle with a wulfkin?" I asked.

She laughed and stuffed the makeup into her bag before flinging it onto her bed. "Oh, I don't need another boyfriend. I have lots of male friends in my life. I prefer it that way. And don't change the topic. Your path and the new wulfkin's are intertwined."

"But he's a Varlac, and I don't want to talk about him." I huffed and pressed farther into my seat.

"He's still a wulfkin, regardless of his family's actions."

I rolled my eyes at the implication that Enre might be here for anything but evil. "Then why doesn't he tell Father why he's really here?"

"Girl." Sonia reached across the table and clasped my gloved hand in hers. "Remember what you told me years ago when I refused Jay's advances? To look past my prejudices, to give the wulfkin the benefit of the doubt." She released my hand and flicked a loose strand of hair caught in her eyelashes.

"Yeah, and you never listened to me," I said. "You ignored him, and he left our pack because he couldn't accept your rejection."

Sonia exhaled, loud and exaggerated, with the bridge between her eyes creasing. "Semantics and irrelevant details. What matters is whether you'll take your own advice."

"But ... " My voice vanished.

"Of course, you'll resist what's coming, and I wouldn't expect anything less from you." She smiled and climbed to her feet, brushing down the fabric of her tiger-pattern leggings. "But don't ignore your dreams. They are trying to guide and protect you as they did your mother and grandmother."

"Little good it did either of them, especially my mother. Why didn't she foresee her death and stop it?" The words had crossed my lips before I could put a lid on them.

Sorrow tunneled behind Sonia's gaze. She stepped closer and dragged me into her arms, squishing my face against her ample bosom. In a strange way, her calm washed over me and reminded me of my mother: her love was fierce and heavy-handed, but soothing and reassuring at the same time. I shut my eyes, and for those few seconds, I pretended my mother embraced me, rubbed her palm down my back, and told me everything would be all right.

I pried free from Sonia's embrace, no longer in the mood for comfort. "Thanks."

"What happened to your mother was tragic, but don't let it dictate your life.

We can't stop the fate of death, no matter how extensive our gifts. Your grandmother died when her twin was killed by another pack. That was also an injustice, but it's life. I love you like my own sister. I only want the best for you."

"I love you too." With that, I made my way toward the door, unable to stop the prickling sensation spreading across my skin.

"Oh, a few of the girls and I are going into the city to pick up some things for the show. Join us. It'll be great to get away for a while."

As I glanced over my shoulder at Sonia, who was plucking an outfit out of her closet, I thought about how shopping was the last thing I wanted to do. "Thanks, but I'm not in the mood. Have fun."

The first trickles of rain fell, and within several steps, it poured. Damn. I ran all the way to Ash's cage to feed her breakfast.

My mind refused to stop replaying yesterday's events and Nicolai's capture. Perhaps it was up to me to do something about his situation since no one else seemed to be taking it seriously.

CHAPTER 6

ENRE

The sign, *Novac Brothers present the Moonlight Circus,* hung at an odd angle from the main entrance to the tent.

Someone ought to fix that.

The front of the circus was the only location empty of wulfkin. Probably because it overlooked a busy, main road.

Shoving my hands into the pockets of my jeans, I kicked an empty beer can and reminded myself I had nothing to prove. I needed to discover Maxim's plans and stop him if they involved slaughtering my pack family in Transylvania. Sandulf was adamant that Maxim planned to take them out. But now the danger of Nicolai in prison weighed heavily on my shoulders. If he transformed while in custody, it spelled catastrophe for all our kind. And I wouldn't sit back and do nothing about it.

Two police cars edged onto the grounds and parked in front of the tent, near me. A third unmarked car nosed in behind them.

Four officers climbed out and ambled toward the tent,

one nodding in my direction. I returned the gesture; it was what humans did.

A female with dark hair emerged from the unmarked car, and I recognized her from the previous night when she had interrogated Maxim about a missing girl. She didn't follow the police officers, but rather scanned the area. When her gaze landed on me, she approached me, as if my presence was an open invitation.

She appeared young, maybe in her early twenties, but a rawness existed in her. Strong footsteps, body as fluid as a panther. If I hadn't been looking her way, she'd have easily sneaked up on me. Even the faint scent of perspiration could be missed on the breeze.

Standoffish, surreptitious, and menacing. No human ever raised the hairs on the back of my neck this way. She prowled closer, arms stiff at her sides. Even the way she wore tight black slacks and a zipped-up leather jacket screamed preda-tor. She retrieved a wallet from her pocket and flipped it open to reveal an Interpol badge and identification: Kalina Watts.

"You're new here." She cocked her head in a way that told me she knew it for a fact. The sun hit three healed scars on her neck, mostly hidden by her jacket collar. She'd been in a few fights. That much was obvious. "Visiting someone at the circus?" Her words flew fast, stating facts with the haziest wisp of an accent I couldn't pinpoint. Maybe Russian.

"I am. Arrived the day before last."

"I saw you last night, hiding in the shadows. Why the need to spy?"

"It was *you* I was uncertain about. But now that we've got this in the open, I'll leave you to your work." I stepped away from her.

She grabbed my wrist with icy fingers—damn strong for a human. "A few more questions."

I shrugged, figuring our talk might provide some insight into the pack and what Maxim had been up to. "Sure."

"Do you have a name?"

"Enre."

"Surname, or do you go by one name?"

"Ulf. Enre Ulf."

Movement flashed behind her eyes, faint and fast, but I caught it. The kind confirming that this woman had a mountain of secrets, and for some reason my last name piqued her interest. Of course, the only ones who reacted to my name were wulfkin, because of their awareness of my Varlac heritage. Except Kalina—a human working for Interpol. And if she and Interpol knew about the Varlac, that was dangerous.

A semitruck thundered down the road in the distance and distracted me, but Kalina's eyes, almost onyx in color, never left me.

"Anything else?" I finally broke the silence. "I have places to be, things to do."

I had nowhere to be, but the way her gaze locked in on me, as if determining the best way to torture, was disturbing.

She retrieved a photo from her pocket. "Have you seen this girl anywhere on the premises?"

The photo was of a young girl in her mid-teens, maybe younger. Blonde, bob-style hair, a tiny nose and mouth, with the deepest green eyes.

"Her name is Ash Antov," Kalina said.

My thoughts returned to Alena and her chase of the wolf girl she had called Ash.

My brief encounter with Ash was enough to confirm she was a wulfkin and still in her teens. It was rare for one so young to turn into a wulfkin. But I had no intention of telling this human a thread of information. Why had Alena been tracking Ash in the middle of the city anyway? How could I use this knowledge against the pack? Meeting her gaze, I shrugged and shook my head.

Kalina shoved a business card into my hand.

"If you see or hear anything related to Ash, please contact me. Her mother is distraught, and with each passing day, our chances of finding her alive diminish." Her face never eased from its hard expression. No hint of sympathy or compassion. The churning words rolled from her lips as though she'd said them too many times and they no longer held any emotion.

"I'll be in touch," she said and strolled toward the tent entrance, her elbows tight against her body.

I doubted it. I planned to keep my distance from the authorities, especially her.

Turning toward the side of the tent for a quick getaway, I caught a glimpse of someone else. A tall wulfkin wearing a wooly cardigan. She reminded me of a polar bear with stick-like legs. She wore tiny white shorts and knee-length boots, and she had somehow managed to avoid muddying them even though everything in the area was coated. A nest of dreadlocks curled around her head in a crown of reds and browns. She flicked them loose over her shoulder, as she strolled in my direction, hips swinging.

She reminded me of Lutia—an ex-pack member from Transylvania. Pleasant to stare at but high-maintenance and ready to stab you the moment you turned your back. After infiltrating our pack in Romania, Lutia had taken Sandulf's side as the alpha female and attempted to kill Daciana. Plus, Lutia had never helped me when I was in the cave with the dracwulf. Add to that the fact that she killed a human to frame Daciana, which broke the number-one Varlac rule and carried a punishment of death if the ruling clan caught her. She ran away in the end, and if I ever crossed paths with her again, she'd wish she were already dead. Gutless weasel.

"I tell you," the woman in front of me said, "if that Interpol woman or the police harm any of our pack, I'll get a machete out and hack them to bits." She spoke with a lisp.

"A bit extreme, but effective." I continued walking away from the front of the circus.

She stepped alongside me, fiddling with a dreadlock. "I've had enough of her kind prying into pack business. The police have followed us for years—" She cupped a hand to her mouth, and her eyes widened.

Years? Why would the police be watching them for so long? "It's okay, you can talk to me. I won't cause trouble."

"You're a Varlac. That spells trouble."

I put a hand on my chest, glancing at the wulfkin walking next to me, intent on not scaring her away while I gathered more information. "We're not above our own rules, and all we want is for wulfkin to be safe. So, this police business, it must be hard for the pack to try and conceal their wolf sides all the time. What do you all do for release?"

Her head cocked to the side, eyes narrowed in my direction. "You tell me first why you're really in Bulgaria."

"Following my father's orders to see how this pack's doing. It's routine business. Anyway, we're not crazy about humans either. We're on the same team." I winked.

She ran a finger across her lower lip. "I'm Eevi by the way."

I stopped and faced her in a quiet spot alongside the big top. The flapping of the tent in the wind echoed around us. "Nice to meet you. I'm—"

"Enre." Her mouth split into a smirk. I rewarded her with a smile, fully aware I'd been the main topic of gossip since I arrived.

Eevi was cute, if you considered chipmunk cheeks and pixie eyes attractive, but not for me. I wasn't seeking any romantic connection, not with Eevi or Alena, or anyone.

She kept silent at first and stared at me, but not in the intimidating way Kalina had minutes earlier. Eevi was sizing me up. I was used to it.

"Everyone's talking shit about you."

I nodded. "What's the wildest claim they've made?"

Her gaze traveled upward momentarily, while she chewed on the corner of her lower lip. "So many to choose from. Hmm." Her eyes settled back on me. "That you're here to steal all the females and force us into mating with you so you can spread your seed."

I choked on that one. "Wow. I didn't expect that." Running a hand through my hair, I inhaled the cool air.

"Another claim is that you're here as a scout so the Varlac can take over," she said. "Trust me, neither of those is true." I couldn't attest to the second claim, but the first option had me intrigued.

Eevi studied me with hooded eyes. "Why were the police here?" I asked.

She shook her head, releasing several of the stiff dreadlocks from their pins and sending them swirling into a merry-go-round. They smacked into the sides of her face, and she slid them away with fingers that blinked blue from the chipped paint clinging to the tips of her fingernails. She glanced quickly behind us. "They told me not to go talkin' to you." She fluttered her lashes in my direction.

Reaching over, I caressed her shoulder and ran a hand down her arm.

Her breaths hiccupped. "The police found another body several blocks away."

"Yeah, I know about the one that got Nicolai caught."

"No. This body is apparently a couple of weeks old." She shook her head, her dreadlocks grazing the back of my hand.

I picked one up, turning the knotted lock of hair between my fingers, using it as a distraction while my curiosity was heightened by the body they'd found and its connection to the circus.

Eevi's posture softened, and her eyes smiled at me. "So, you're not here to terrorize us?"

The next inhale stuck in my chest, and my words refused to come at first. I released her dreadlock. "Of course not." I'd do whatever it took to avoid any wulfkin getting hurt. "*Another* body then?"

She shrugged. "No matter where we are, Germany, Czechoslovakia, Serbia, the bodies turn up around the circus."

"Who does Maxim think is responsible?"

She ran a hand down my bicep, squeezing lightly. I didn't flinch. Her gaze focused on my chest. "Well, many of us think—"

"Eevi, I do hope you're not feeding our visitor with your wild stories?" Alena's voice made Eevi recoil. The wulfkin's cheeks colored, and she pulled one of her dreadlocks across her lips.

I glanced over my shoulder. Alena approached with a firm expression planted on her face.

"What were you going to say?" I reached for Eevi's arm, but she pulled back, sidestepped around me, her chin low to her chest, and then rushed away.

Damn.

"I know what you're doing." Alena's accusation was direct and aimed for my throat. Her expression matched her tone: tight mouth, creased brow, and a look on her face that would have anyone running for the hills.

I admired her style and couldn't resist grinning. Or the sprint my pulse leapt into. Every part of me yearned to drag her into my arms and make her forget the hostility building in her body language.

"You plan to seduce every female until you find dirt against us, don't you?"

"Never took you for being the jealous kind."

"This isn't jealousy." The sexy black corset tapering down to her thin waist snagged my attention. The cargo pants and boots she wore had me picturing her wearing only the corset. My wolf, now roused, rolled inside me. Did Alena realize how much sexiness she radiated, especially when angry?

She arched an eyebrow.

"We chatted. Most of the pack isn't overly welcoming. It was nice to have someone to talk to, but if you insist on keeping me all to yourself, then I suggest we spend a bit more time in your trailer." I winked.

Her frown and thin lips broadcasted her rage. "Eevi's dated nearly every wulfkin in this pack. And she's always searching for her next victim. Anyway, I'm sure you're getting what you want with the police here. You'll be returning to your clan soon to report us. It's what Varlac do, isn't it? Make shit up and punish the innocent"

"Harsh. You really hate us, huh?" I slouched on my good leg, waiting for a comeback.

She offered none. "Haven't seen any behavior worth reporting yet. Unless there's a sin *you* wish to share." Unintentionally, my voice dipped low and gravelly.

She pursed her lips. "Father wants to speak to you later, once the police leave."

Alena turned away. I stepped after her. "Any chance of getting more of your magical healing?"

Her limited time healing me last night was enough to make a difference. I imagined if she did it for an hour or so … I'd be strong again in no time.

Glaring back at me, a crease captured her nose, as if I'd asked her to my trailer for casual sex. Well, I had, but still.

"I don't have time today." She stomped away.

Unable to tear my gaze from her round butt and thinking what I'd love to do with it, I reminded myself to rein my wolf in. The short time I'd spent in her trailer had intensified how much I desired her, which meant I had to cut the strings. What could I offer a wulfkin like her anyway? I potentially threatened her father and concealed the real reason for my visit to Bulgaria. I could ask her to accompany me to the Transylvanian pack, except I wasn't even their alpha. *Fuck.* That reminded me that soon my father would have every right to finish me off if I didn't have my own pack. Maybe this pack was my chance—once and for all—to be rid of my father's threats.

I'd only been at the circus less than two days, and already my situation had become more complicated. Though, the dead bodies connected to the circus intrigued me. What if Maxim was protecting someone who was on a human-killing spree? Then he would have broken the number-one rule: Never kill a human. And it was punishable with a swift death at the hands of a Varlac.

CHAPTER 7

ALENA

"Alena Novac, this way, please." A detention center guard opened the metal door in the visitors' room. My stomach had knotted the moment I stepped onto police grounds, praying no one recognized me.

I trailed behind the guard into an area four times the size of my trailer. The stink of urine and old sweat saturated the air. The visitors' room was underneath the police station, and the dim bulbs barely lit the place.

Two of the three small tables were occupied. Sitting at one table was a young man, and at a second was a business-man, or maybe a lawyer there to visit a client. Their heads turned in my direction without so much as a smile, but their gazes trailed down my body and reminded me of the way certain spectators at the circus stared at me.

A second officer stood in the far corner, a baton in one hand, and the other resting on the butt of a gun strapped to his waist. His gaze lingered on me long enough to cause chills up my spine.

I took a seat at the empty table to my left. The guard dumped the parcel of beef jerky I'd brought Nicolai in front of me. Wrapping my gift back up with shaky hands, I sat with my brother's heavy jacket across my lap and waited. Would he forgive me for leaving him back in the alley when the police turned up? I'd done the only thing I could at the time —run away. *Goddess, give me strength.* The incident had been little more than a day ago, but it seemed as if a lifetime had passed since then.

I noticed another metal door across from me, no doubt where prisoners emerged. My gaze caught the Gestapo-like guard in the corner, wearing a twisted smirk. I'd been stupid enough to wear leather pants sitting low on my hips and a tight, V-neck top. He gawked at me and licked his lips.

The concrete walls were covered with peeling paint, and the fluorescent light overhead flickered, threatening to go out. If it did, I wouldn't hesitate to strike the leering pervert before he reached me.

The clock ticked away, and my knees refused to stop bouncing beneath the table. The lawyer's client came and went—twenty minutes. My butt ached and turned numb from the uncomfortable wooden chair. I'd been promised forty minutes with Nicolai, so this waiting time better not be included. I shifted in my seat for the hundredth time. Then the door in front of me creaked open. My pulse sped up threefold. A tattooed inmate shuffled into the room, his ankles and wrists chained. He grinned at me, and I lowered my gaze.

Then he sat in front of the young man at one of the other tables.

I angled myself sideways on my seat and strained for any sign of Nicolai. The door shut.

What's going on? I glanced around, hoping to meet gazes with one of the two guards, but neither looked my way. If Nicolai didn't show up soon, I'd throw this table at someone.

The grating of metal against cement had my head snapping up. My insides melted at every hobbled step Nicolai took in chains. No shoes. He held up his pants with one hand, but he smiled when he spotted me.

He slid into the seat across from me; a layer of dirt coated his face. The side of his mouth was swollen and bruised.

My next breath hitched. "Oh, Nic." I slid out a slice of dried meat, but he shook his head at it, his eyes never leaving mine.

"I'm sorry I left you with the cops. I wanted to come back for you, but—"

"Then you'd be in here too. Am I getting out on bail?"

"It got denied." Nicolai's expression fell. It twisted my stomach. "But Father knows someone who'll get you out soon."

"Thought you were the Interpol woman again."

"Kalina, the one who's been at the circus?"

"Yeah, she paid me a visit this morning." He lowered his voice and leaned over the table toward me. "She accused me of murder but said if I told her where Ash was, she'd ensure I didn't get the death sentence and maybe even shorten my term." He snorted and struggled to wipe his mouth, handcuffs clanging. "She asked a million questions about Father and you, why the circus never returned to a town twice, and why we've stayed in Ruse so long. She even said something about human trafficking. Hell, where are they getting this bullshit from?"

Father was aware the police had been watching us for years, but now Interpol too … This meant they'd been studying our every move because of the dead bodies. A shiver rippled down my back.

"The way she stared at me was like"—he did a quick scan of the room and lowered his voice further—"like she knew what I was." He shook his head. "That's crazy, right?"

"You're paranoid."

His eyes widened, and his fingers gripped the edge of the table. "I can't stay here. I have no right to a phone call, no heat, no hot water, not even two meals a day. The damn guards took my shoelaces and belt. An inmate took my shoes. It'll be a full moon in a week. They'll kill me."

I reached over and clutched his hand. It was frozen beneath my touch. My throat constricted. "Father has a plan. He knows someone inside the prison system. Just hold on."

"No. I want to leave now." His words resonated, drawing the officers' attention in our direction.

"What did Father teach us?" My voice strangled as I attempted to hide signs of my unease. Every part of me yearned to break him out right now, regardless of the consequences.

Nicolai's terrified gaze swept the room.

"He said never show your fear. Be strong, and he'll come for you. Hold it together." I squeezed his hand in mine, never wanting to release him.

"Not sure I can. I'm in the cell for twenty-three hours a day and get only one hour to go outside. I'm going insane. And there are so many roaches. If the prisoners don't kill me, or the police during the full moon, the roaches will." His chest heaved with each strained breath, and again his stare darted around the room. "I want out. It's a tomb in there."

My insides quivered. I wasn't sure how I'd survive in his place, and it killed me to know I couldn't take him home today. Plus, all this talk of roaches had my skin crawling.

"Please." His eyes glistened, and his stomach pressed against the table. "Please, take me with you. Don't leave me here. I'll die if I stay another night."

Dread crawled through every inch of my soul. Words jammed in my throat. Nothing I could say would ease the terror he was living. The last time I'd seen Nicolai this distraught and on the verge of crying was at the age of five. A bear had cornered him in the woods. It took him months to get over the trauma. The more drawn-out his stay in prison, the more likely they'd break his spirit. He wasn't a fighter, or a leader. But he was my brother, and I loved him.

"I'll ask Father if he can speed things along, but it's tricky. The police are everywhere at the circus, watching us."

Nicolai wiped his cheeks, streaking dirt and tears across his skin. He kept silent for a moment, his gaze lowered. When his head lifted, so did his shoulders. "How long?"

"Several days." My voice quivered.

He licked his dry lips and slouched into his seat. "You're cutting it pretty close to my next change."

"Father promises to have you out."

Leaning closer, I confirmed the Gestapo were a fair distance across the room and whispered, "Another body was found. That makes it eleven. Father is convinced it's the Varlac, especially now that one of their clan has arrived at the circus to supposedly *check in*." I rubbed my palms up and down my thighs until I felt the friction and sagged back in my chair.

"Shit," was all Nicolai said.

"Double shit." Triple that if you included the way I couldn't keep my damn libido in check near Enre.

"I've screwed everything up, haven't I?"

"No, don't say that." I reached for his hand, but he pulled away.

"If I hadn't tried to save the man from Ash, we could have already moved across the border." When he spoke, his voice was barely audible. "I tried to run away, but I couldn't. So much blood. I wanted to save him."

An invisible fist tightened around my throat. "I know you did. We'll get out of this, you'll see."

"But," Nicolai began, "you could break me out. Because if I die, so do you."

Ignoring his reminder of our linked souls and predicament, I said, "Where do you think the police will check first?"

"I won't return to the circus. I've got places to hide. Maybe I'll cross the border, make my way into Romania, and wait for the pack to arrive."

"The moment you escape, they'll put a manhunt out on you and send your photo to every law enforcement office and border in the country."

His shoulders hunched forward, our faces inches apart. "I'll hide out in the national park. No one will find me. Then I'll cross the Danube River into Romania when things quiet down."

"You're not making sense, Nic. That's reckless and stupid."

"Swap places with me and see what it's like in here, then tell me you wouldn't do anything to get out." The dip in his trembling voice terrified me.

"I'd swap with you in a heartbeat." And honestly, I wished I could.

The creases on the bridge of his nose softened, and his mouth opened, but his words were lost to the loud bang of a baton striking metal.

"Time's up."

"What? No, it's only been fifteen minutes at most. You said forty."

Nicolai stood, the meat parcel clutched in his hand. His mournful expression said more than his words ever could. *Get me out, please.*

The creepy prison guard grabbed my brother by the arm and heaved him toward the back door.

"Hurry along."

I was on my feet and ready to rip the man's hand off, but the Gestapo yelled my way, drawing his baton. "Седни." *Sit.* He gestured to my chair with his weapon.

Nicolai's jacket lay on the ground near my seat. I grabbed it. "Wait, he forgot his jacket."

The guard nudged Nicolai inside, but not before my brother peered over his shoulder with a look belonging to someone being escorted to a guillotine. The door smacked shut. My free hand rose to my chest, and my heart ached.

For a few seconds, my legs refused to move. They'd frozen on the spot, and the lingering thoughts of rescuing Nicolai chiseled inside my mind. If the guard hadn't prodded me to leave the room, I might have done something stupid. That's all Father needed. Both of us locked up.

By the time I'd picked up my handbag from reception and emerged into a day that had no right to be glorious, I'd made up my mind.

Nicolai had a point. He could hide out in the national park, and who said Ash couldn't join him? She appeared to listen to him. The police could check the circus, and when they found nothing, Father could organize our transfer into Romania. All part of the circus business—moving from place to place.

The more I contemplated my idea, the more I liked it. Father refused to tell me much about his scheme for rescuing Nicolai and only reminded me to be patient. Anything I said to Father would fall on deaf ears while the police were involved. But I'd been brought up to take action when I believed in something strongly enough. And there was nothing more important than the life of my brother.

CHAPTER 8

ENRE

I hurried down the cracked and aged footpath that ran between train tracks on one side and homes on the other. A streetlight overhead flickered, and the stench of garbage floated on the air. My wolf, clawing at my insides, whimpered for release, urged me to find a forest, to run free, to hunt. But after three hours of limping around Ruse, it seemed this city didn't believe in reserving woodland. The occasional park, sure, but they were close to houses and too open. I could never hide there. No wonder Maxim's pack was desperate to leave.

Once my wound healed, I'd have to make a call regarding Maxim. One option was to reveal my true identity with the intention of negotiating a way for both packs to share the Transylvanian land … if Maxim didn't murder me instantly for lying and infiltrating his pack. And if he didn't, it still didn't guarantee he'd agree to my proposal. Then there was Daciana, who'd be furious at me for making decisions on her behalf.

Another option was to play the Varlac card further and raise my concern of Nicolai, a moonwulf, in custody a week before the full moon. But how would that solve my issue with them not taking over Transylvania?

Or, as a Varlac, I could announce I was privy to Maxim's plans. But what issue would the Varlac have with them taking over territory? Alphas did that all the time. No, that wouldn't work either.

Perhaps I was going about this all wrong. My focus should be on convincing Alena of my plans. She might understand … *Yeah, right.* She'd made it pretty clear I was the devil in her eyes. I had no other choice but to make her see me as a decent wulfkin. Add to my to-do list the need to get Nicolai out of prison—and quick.

The night's cold chilled me to the bone. I drew the collar of my coat tight to my throat and hurried onward, despite the fire consuming the bullet wound in my thigh. The injury caused stabbing agony through my leg, and then some. With the next step, my wolf pushed forward. A half howl grunted at the back of my throat, and my body trembled from the forced change.

"Not here." My words were a hiss as I stumbled into a shrub. Shoving my wolf back sliced at my insides. My breaths accelerated; my hands shook.

My wolf was getting stronger. After I had accidentally attacked Daciana years ago, I promised myself it'd never happen again, but even after so much time suppressing the beast within, I was struggling with him again. The urgency to change itched beneath my skin, but I resisted the building pressure to scratch like some fleabag. Somehow, I'd make it to the strip of woodland outside the city.

The circus lights beamed from behind the train terminal ahead. A conductor blared words I didn't understand, and the screeching of wheels sounded. Soon enough, a train rattled down the tracks and stopped at the platform.

Swerving around the rear of the building, which smelled

of urine, I emerged from the entrance to the station, greeted by late-night commuters hurrying off the train. A whole herd of them.

My wolf whimpered, inhaling their perspiring odors. When I sidestepped an older gentleman, a familiar scent teased my nostrils.

I stopped amid the commuters brushing past. The air was stained with oil and burning train brakes. There it was again —wolf and lavender.

Sniffing the breeze, I wove through the moving river of humans and nudging elbows, scanning the area. A lone figure in a jacket and hood rushed onto the platform and hopped into one of the train cars. The height and slight wiggle of her backside confirmed it was Alena. What was in her arm? Looked like a rolled-up rug.

Before I could think about it, I darted after her and slipped into the car behind hers.

The door slammed shut within an inch of snagging my coat.

Of the three passengers, only the blonde female closest to me wore a smile. I didn't do blondes or humans, so I broke our stare and kept an eye out for Alena.

The city train lurched forward, and I gripped the metal pole for balance. My reflection bounced off the dirty windows: stubble desperately in need of a trim, wind-messed black hair, pupils so pale one could easily mistake them for wolf eyes. Wrapped up in a coat and jeans, I reminded myself of a stalker. All I was missing was the hood drawn over my head.

Brakes screamed as the train slowed, my body stumbling sideways. I clutched the pole tighter, and the doors squealed as they opened. Two other passengers exited. I stuck my head outside. The wind chilled my bones. No sign of Alena. I ducked back in.

Seven platforms later, Alena exited the train and hurried along with a handful of passengers onto a shadowy footpath heading away from the station.

I kept a wide berth. The cluster of humans thinned out until it was only the two of us. Curiosity made me focus on the rolled up object tucked under her armpit. She was up to something, but what?

The occasional car zoomed down the lonely road, and every second streetlight was out. The trees lining the path in front of cement blocks of buildings reminded me of Romania in many ways, along with why I hated leaving the woods.

Dimness encased this part of the city, encouraging muggers and stalkers to track their prey. I had no intention of harming Alena, but someone else might be lurking.

Farther ahead, on the corner of the street, stood a three-story structure with the sign Police on it. Every window lit up the road. Alena was marching toward it, probably visiting her brother, except who would allow visitations so late at night?

Another gush of freezing air shoved into me from behind, flaring the ache in my thigh. Alena halted and turned around. She spotted me. *Fuck.*

Even from a distance, I recognized what the crease across her brow and down-turned mouth meant. Her arms tightened at her sides.

I closed the distance between us. Wind blew the hood off her head and tossed the neat ponytail into a wild mess. She greeted me with a scowl, red blotches on her cheeks from the cold.

"Why are you following me?"

"What are you doing here?" My gaze dipped to the gray carpet fraying at the edges under her arm. "And why are you carrying a carpet?"

She licked her lips. "I don't answer to Varlac stalkers."

"Love it when you get feisty. But seriously"—my gaze fell to the rug again and back—"you planning on decorating someone's place with that?"

"Look." She glanced down the empty street where the breeze howled. "I'm only going to say this once. Get lost and leave me alone. Go pester someone else. I'm not interested in being a Varlac's fling." She spun on her heel and stormed away.

"I know what you're doing," I called out. "Sneaking about, dressed like a ninja, rushing to the police station."

She glared at me over her shoulder, her gaze tossing poison in my direction.

"It has something to do with your brother," I continued, intending to strike a nerve. "Something illegal." Damn, I admired her courage, because I'd do the same for my pack family.

Her boots click-clacked as she blazed toward me and whacked a fist into my arm.

"Are you stupid? Don't blurt that stuff out. Can't you see where we are?" She glanced at the police station. Her shoulders curled forward in a classic I'm-going-to-attack-you posture. "What do you really want?" Her voice grew gruff.

My response gushed out before I could make sense of what to say next. "I'll help you get your brother out."

A nervous giggle crossed her lips, and her flickering gaze was a dead giveaway of how much this was out of her comfort zone. "I don't know what you're talking about."

I wiped my mouth and moved to stand beneath a great tree stripped bare of leaves by the winter winds. The branches deflected some of the light off me. Alena didn't follow at first; then, with a loud sigh, she trudged closer, standing the carpet roll on its end in front of her.

"Stop pretending," I said. "I know what you're up to, and I

have no issues with it. I won't breathe a word to anyone. I'd save one of my pack members from the police too." Though, in truth, I'd leave my real brother in prison to rot. Throw my father in there too.

She didn't respond at first. "Why would you care if I rescued my brother or not? It has nothing to do with you."

"You're right, it doesn't." I should have walked away and tracked down a place to transform and release my wolf instead of getting involved in Alena's business. Instead, my response spilled out. "I feel partly responsible for his capture. If I hadn't distracted you, he might not be in this mess. I want to help."

"And then the Varlac would have an excuse to kill me, like … " Her words vanished, and her gaze dropped.

What was she about to say? Like whom? Who had the Varlac taken from her?

"I give you my promise. This will be our secret. No one shall ever hear of it from me."

"A Varlac's promise is like planting an underground mine," she spat out in haste. "It sits there for years, until one day, it explodes, stealing your feet out from under you."

"Well, it seems you have me figured out. That was exactly my plan." I circled Alena, needing the movement to add heat to my frozen body.

She shrugged. "Well, I'll go home then."

"And I'll follow you tomorrow and the day after."

Her eyes narrowed as she studied me. "Why do you care? Our pack means nothing to you. Nic will turn into a moon-wulf in just over a week. Time's running out for him. This is my problem, not yours. I'm the one who left him behind with the police." A frozen gust blew past, ruffling Alena's ponytail. Her eyes glistened. I considered taking her into my arms to warm her, though I figured I might be pushing my luck.

My hands curled in my pockets, fingers frosty, and my

chest tightening. "Believe it or not, Varlac don't want our kind revealed to humans and would do anything to stop that from happening. If Nic gets caught, it's a problem for every wulfkin."

Alena stared at me with narrow eyes. I knew she blamed herself for her brother's capture. Living with guilt like that would eat anyone up. She didn't deserve this, and neither did her brother. My whole life I'd fought to protect wulfkin from humans discovering us, and I wasn't going to ignore someone in need of help, especially when one of them was Alena.

"Are we going to stand outside and turn to ice, or get the job done?" I asked. "You'll need me to keep an eye out as you rescue Nic, or as a distraction to get him away if the authorities spot us."

In her gray eyes, thoughts swirled, and her constant scan of the area told me she was considering my offer.

"Why would you do that for us?"

"We're on the same team here. Shall I carry your carpet?"

She responded with a frown and tucked the rolled-up rug under her arm.

I took that as a no. "Let's move." I didn't wait for her response and slid into the shadow alongside the cobblestone buildings, slinking closer to the station. Faint steps fell into a rhythm behind me.

She brushed past me, turned, and pressed a finger into my chest. "Fine, but try anything, and I'll rip your heart out. We're doing this my way. And I'm going first." I nodded, resisting the urge to draw her into my arms and kiss those purse lips.

She frowned and continued onward.

I followed her. Before we reached the entrance to the police station, Alena sneaked down a side alley and disappeared around the corner into the dark.

Closing in from behind, I curved right into the murky passage, my shoulders scraping the brick enclosure. I hurried in an awkward and angled walk-hop, trusting Alena knew where she was going. Against my better judgment, we were about to break into a prison. This was the police we were dealing with. But I doubted I'd have any luck in stopping Alena.

She halted and shifted my way. Within the cloak of the night, I barely distinguished the outline of her body.

"We'll scale the wall and land in a small courtyard. Stick close. There are cameras, but since it's only a holding cell, there's a few spots to hide."

Looking up, I stared at the circular barbed wire lining the top of the brick wall, and now the carpet made sense. *Clever girl.*

"Use the spot here." She tapped the stone barrier. "There are a few broken bricks that should be easy to grab and step on while climbing. Anyway, make yourself useful." She handed me the carpet, which was starting to unravel.

Her ascent appeared effortless, scaling the wall as quickly as a squirrel dashing up a tree. A tasty squirrel, for that matter. Reaching the top, she stuck her arm toward me. I handed her the carpet, and in slow motion, she placed it on the barbed wire. Testing her device a few times by pushing down on the carpet in several places, she climbed higher and carefully lifted one leg over and then the other. Soon enough, she'd slipped out of sight.

Following suit, I used the irregularities in the wall as Alena suggested, but my progress was slower since my thigh quivered each time I pushed myself off it. After two attempts to get my wounded leg over the barbed wire and slicing my jeans near the knee, I took a deep breath and tried again. I clenched my jaw, ignored the pain, and threw my leg onto the other side. Straddling the wall with only an old carpet between barbed wire and my jewels, I slipped my other leg over and hopped down on the other side. The stinging pain of my injury throbbed, and I rode the wave of agony for a few seconds until it eased. Why was I doing this again?

A pile of wooden crates lay near, and it reeked of cabbage.

From our shaded area, concealed by a ledge above us, I stared out into a courtyard empty of guards. A spotlight from the police building swept in a semicircular motion across the yard, which was at least double the size of the great circus tent. Directly across from us stood a small concrete block with no windows, only two doors. A metal one in the center and a wooden one directly across from us.

A discomforting feeling churned in my gut. I rarely shied away from breaking rules, but when it involved the possibility of turning into a wulfkin in front of humans in order to save us, I had a problem with it, especially since there would be cameras around. That single action provided the Varlac with the right to execute wulfkin, whether I was their family or not, and I was pretty attached to my head.

"What's the plan?" I whispered.

She inched forward, taking a peek up at the structure behind us. "As I thought. No one's there." She tugged her hood lower over her head. "Only one camera. I don't think there are any in the cells from what I saw," she whispered. "I'm going to break into the storeroom. I've done some research, and someone online said he used to work there when he was an inmate. It's connected to the cells. Plus, there's apparently no security alarm on the door."

"Apparently? You're basing this on what a dubious ex-con said online?"

Her gaze met mine, and her whisper was louder than it should have been. "It's a risk I'm willing to take."

"Maybe we should work on this some more and return tomorrow?"

Refusing to acknowledge my suggestion, she hurried toward the wall. When the spotlight finished spraying light on this side of the courtyard, she bolted straight down to the other side, vanishing into a location too far for the light to reach.

My turn came. I lunged ahead and limped to Alena, who huddled in the shadowy corner. Our sides pressed tightly together.

I whispered, "What's the plan now?"

She dug into her pocket and retrieved several lock-picking tools.

"Seriously?" I asked.

"Trust me. Father used to get me to unlock old trailers. He'd buy them cheap after they were dumped by their owners. He's a closet junk collector."

I scanned the yard and counted the seconds when the sweeping light steered away from the storage entrance.

"You have about eight seconds to open the door."

When the moment came, Alena pounced forward and hunched over in front of the lock. The beam returned, and her head jerked up. She sprinted back, crashing into my side.

"Might take me a couple more tries."

After her fourth attempt, she said in between rushed breaths, "I think I almost got it."

My insides jittered. I hobbled toward the entrance and threw my shoulder into the wooden door. It groaned and snapped, but it didn't open.

"What are you doing?" Alena prodded my back. The floodlight was returning. "I'm helping," I said.

The sound of voices and jangling keys reached us from within the police office across the courtyard from us, silencing Alena's words.

My pulse pounded beneath my skin. I pitched my weight

once more into the door. I stumbled inside as a metal piece of the lock clanked to the ground.

Then the rear door to the police station across the courtyard flung open.

I snatched Alena's wrist, hauled her in, and shut us inside. The broken lock meant the door against my back wouldn't stay closed on its own. Pitch-darkness surrounded us, and the stale funk of rotting vegetables fouled the air.

Only a thin sliver of illumination filtered into the room through the gap under the door every few seconds.

Listening to the footsteps in the yard, I tried to imagine where the police were headed. If they chose the door I was leaning against, we'd be caught. Then what? Take them out and make a getaway? My stomach refused to settle, and adrenaline pumped so quickly, my wolf threatened to pour out of me any second.

A loud *crack* drew my attention into the dark room. "Alena?"

Light flashed across the floor from outside, revealing Alena's legs dashing into another room. "Alena, we have to leave," I whispered.

No response.

If I went after her, the door I was holding shut would swing open, revealing us to the police. Fuck. What now?

On the other side of the door, the footfalls on concrete receded, but their voices didn't disappear completely. They were loitering in the courtyard by the sound of it. We'd wait until the guards left the yard, unless, of course, Alena turned up with her brother and set off alarms. I hoped that wasn't the case.

Where did Alena intend to stash her brother anyway?

My insides twisted, and there was still no sign of Alena. I didn't function well with waiting. You might say patience wasn't one of my virtues. It was get in, do the job, and get out. Or attack, if needed. But my hunting skills didn't apply to humans.

The police hadn't returned inside either, and their stomping boots marched and shuffled outside at regular intervals. With each passing second, my nerves intensified. The wolf rumbled in my chest, whimpering for release, and I contemplated transforming. It'd make for a swift escape, but what were the chances of not being caught on video footage in my wolf form? Should I risk it? It was insane, and I couldn't leave Alena behind.

A siren blared.

I jumped, my whole body shuddering, and my heart stuck in my throat. They'd found us.

Outside, the stampede of boots escalated. *Holy shit. Alena?*

Two options: turn and run, or dash into the prison and attempt to find her.

The slapping of shoes echoed from within the building. Were the guards coming?

The other door inside the storeroom creaked open. *You better be Alena.* My breath accelerated, and I fisted my hands.

Movement closed in, then crashed into me. Alena's scent hit me like a brick wall.

"Crap, crap, crap." Her voice trembled. "We need to get out. Now."

"Where's your brother?"

Behind her, more stomping feet. "I couldn't get him."

I snatched her wrist and ripped open the door just as the strobe light flashed our way.

Fantastic. Gaze low, I hustled Alena toward the wall where we'd entered.

"Stop!" Two officers with guns pointed approached from across the courtyard. My wolf was already pressing for escape. Terrible timing.

In one rapid motion, I grabbed Alena by the waist.

"Jump." I pitched her up. She latched onto the wall and carpet and scrambled over it with no problem.

A bullet whizzed past my ear, the cold rush of wind raising the hair down my arms.

Way too close. No time to think about it.

More voices.

I leapt onto the wobbly crates with my good leg and jumped up with all my wulfkin strength. With my torso across the carpet, I pushed forward in a roll. Another bullet whizzed past my backside. Barbed wire caught on my jeans and tore the fabric along with flesh. I tumbled down, landing on my side. A whimper flashed past my throat. Fuckin' hell, it stung. Every part of me was inflamed.

Alena was there, pulling my arm, dragging me away. No time for pain. I'd suffer later.

Together, we hurried down the alley, my leg and hip on fire. On the street, I spotted officers pouring out of the station, one of them yelling for us to halt.

Alena glanced at me, shadows smearing her delicate features. "Start unbuttoning your shirt and pants."

Didn't take her for the kinky kind, but then again she wore those gloves. "Really? You want to do this here?"

She offered a scowl as she hauled me by the hand across the road. I cringed each time I put pressure on my leg. Stars danced in my vision from the pain lancing through me.

Police ran after us.

Sirens howled in the night, and we burst into a side street as Alena's plan fell to shit. I drew on my wulfkin strength, ready to transform, well aware I'd pay for it later.

CHAPTER 9

ALENA

*E*nre and I ducked into a dark alleyway overshadowed by tall buildings. The sound of my boots clicking on the asphalt sent bolts of terror through my body. Police sirens and voices escalated around us, and my heart somersaulted. Father would kill me if he found out I'd attempted to break Nicolai out of jail.

"This way." Enre snatched my wrist, yanking me into a lane surrounded by looming buildings, murkier than the last. It carried the ripe stench of rubbish. We huddled behind a dumpster. I gagged and pressed my hand over my mouth. A wall, icy on my back, sent shivers up my spine.

Two police officers turned down our alley, and I prayed they wouldn't spot us. Enre drew me under his arm, his body tense, as if he'd strike out at anyone who threatened me. The scuffle of shoes grew louder. I froze.

Enre inched forward, ready to fight the police. My muscles tightened. This wasn't going to end well.

A radio crackled, and an officer answered it, mumbling about spotting someone on another street. They retreated from our alley. When I exhaled, I realized how long I'd been holding my breath. Enre and I waited a few minutes before stripping out of our clothes. It was the fastest I'd ever undressed, despite the nerves crawling under my skin.

Enre's chest heaved with each inhale as he gawked at me.

"You going to keep staring?" Despite the dread pressing my insides, facing a naked Enre had my pulse racing to an entirely different beat.

He didn't respond.

Thank goodness for the darkened lane, or there would be no way I'd be able to control my gaze from roving everywhere south of his waist. The silvery aura of moonlight bouncing off his shoulders was enough to reveal his sculpted arms, firm pecs, and toned stomach. My fingers burned with the need to touch. He appeared larger, even taller, in the nude, if that was possible.

"Like what you see?" he whispered, his voice suddenly caressing my skin.

My eyes narrowed and met his shameless smile. I swallowed the thickness in my throat, unable to find my voice.

He grabbed our clothes and disposed of them in the dumpster, careful not to make a sound as he set the lid down.

Inside, my defenses crumbled, but I lifted my chin, determined to show him I wasn't a pushover.

"Follow my lead. I'll get us out of this." Without another thought, I called to my inner wolf, giving her what she'd desired for the last few weeks. The ripples from the transformation vibrated across my flesh, and the freedom of unleashing her washed over me.

I convulsed and fell to my hands and knees, my limbs stretching and contorting. A thick fur coat of white and gray sprouted from my body, and the recent heaviness I'd harbored from keeping my wolf at bay for weeks vanished. It was the most stupendous sensation in the world ... Okay, maybe not the ultimate feeling, because the idea of Enre bringing me to orgasm pulsed through my veins. What was wrong with me? This was no time to get hot and steamy.

The world appeared different. Muted colors, clearer sounds, and sharper smells telling me we were near an Italian restaurant.

Enre had also transformed and was shaking his back leg. Probably feeling pain from his wound. The faint moonlight gleamed off his brindled, gray pelt and whitish ears.

Voices drifted our way from a side street. We lunged back behind the garbage bins, our bodies pinned together. I peered out and spotted two officers vanish in the direction of the police station.

A howl was dying to roll free. Not the time for that either.

Next to me, Enre brushed his head along my ribs. My whole body buzzed. He trotted out from behind the bin toward the alleyway.

I hurried and sidled up to him, his heat pouring into me. He glanced over momentarily with his huge, blue wolf eyes, and my legs weakened. With his fur touching mine, I leaned into him, sniffing his musky scent, tempted to affectionately nip his ear.

The street in front of us was clear of humans, so I bounded out of the alley and entered another road. Enre darted ahead of me. We passed more tall buildings.

When I spotted three policemen scanning the area ahead, I suppressed a growl. Enre halted several paces in front of me. Thankfully, they hadn't looked our way … yet.

I retraced my steps. Enre followed. We hurried past an auto repair shop on the edge of town and entered a residential part of the city. Single-story houses with tiny front yards lined the road, along with the occasional tree and streetlight. The air was still foul with oil and grease. I hurried forward, nails scraping the road.

Wind combed through my fur. My pulse accelerated. An engine groaned behind us.

White, red, and blue lights flashed in our direction.

Enre snarled. I turned as he leapt over a brick wall, and I followed, clearing the barricade. Together, we huddled against the inside of the wall. Enre laid his chin on the nape of my neck, partly concealing me. His heavy breaths parted the fur on my face, and his muskiness filled my nostrils.

I wiped away that foolish idea as the patrol car drove past us, prompting several dogs from neighboring homes to bark. Were they barking at the car sounds or the scent of us on the air? The porch lights at the house behind us switched on, and a feminine squeal instinctively made us both leap over the fence. We bolted down the street, past parked cars and trash cans, and jumped into the shrubs at the end of the road.

We emerged on the other side of the bushes just as a train rattled past. Its blasting air collided with us, pushing us back a few steps into the hedge. My adrenaline galloped too fast, and for those few seconds, I lost my sense of direction toward home. Everything happened too fast.

Side by side, we darted beside the rail line, away from the platform and police, and stayed in the shadows.

Running free with the cold air in my face, I refused to consider my messed-up life and focused instead on how liberating it was to be in my wolf form. Exhilaration seeped into my veins. We were headed along the train tracks, houses on either side of us, but they were far enough that we'd be nothing more than a shadow if someone spotted us. I stopped and finally released the howl from deep within my throat.

Enre did the same. The moment was perfect. This was how wulfkin should live—in freedom, not trapped amongst humans. And this was why our pack had to move to Transylvania sooner rather than later.

When Enre nipped playfully at my leg, I pounced on him, but he recoiled and ran. His back leg buckled each time he landed on it. I'd offer him more healing once we arrived at the circus.

Taking the bait, I gave chase, my gaze on his rump. If it was a race he wanted, he got it. Adrenaline raced through my veins, and the sense of freedom pushed forward, every other worry tucked to the back of my mind. Not now, not in wolf form. I only cared about being a wolf, nothing else.

My paws pounded into the soil as I passed him, leaping away from his snapping mouth. He played dirty, the scoundrel. Houses, trees, and metal fences on either side of us flew past in a blur, and a concoction of humans, rubbish, and earthy scents flooded my senses.

The next station loomed ahead. We slipped into the shrubs near the tracks each time a train approached. Seven platforms later, I'd barely caught my breath, though the familiar smells of Ruse filled me: burning wood from nearby homes, smog from the trucks heading out of town, and the faint but distinct waft of wet dog fur.

After waiting for Enre to catch up, I burst left into a line of bushes and emerged into a blackened street; I recognized it by the grand oak trees lining the road. We weren't far from the circus.

Enre tore out of the bushes several paces from me. Scampering onward, I swung left into an alley between two houses with high wooden fences and mailboxes, and even a cat sprinted out of our way. At the end of the lane, I crossed a path and entered the unkempt empty lot behind the circus.

I plunged forward and blended into the overgrown grass with the halo of the circus in the distance.

Enre crashed into my side, my legs collapsing from his weight. Each breath thundered fast and heavy. He slumped down alongside me, panting for air.

It'd been a long time since I'd run in wolf form to the point of exhaustion. Lying there in the earth's embrace, caressed by moonlight, and cooled by the breeze, life somehow seemed to stand still. The strange sensation of being in Enre's company was familiar and offered me the kind of safety I'd only previously sensed with my pack.

At that moment, I didn't want to leave my perfect cocoon and deal with pack issues, Nicolai in prison, the police searching for us, or how I'd keep this a secret from Father. Those problems were a world away, at least for those few seconds when my wolf reveled in the way Enre's body pressed against mine, warmth radiating off him, and the soft brush of the breeze in my fur.

Utter bliss and silence surrounded us. Then another screech of brakes flooded the quiet and brought with it reality. Police were probably still watching the front of the circus. We were safe from view for now, and with that single notion, I transformed into my human form with the ease of ripping off a coat. A gust of wind struck, making me tense as the freezing cold sunk its fangs deep into my flesh.

A rumble of disappointment rolled from Enre's throat, but he changed too.

Sitting upright, I hugged my knees to my chest, and Enre sat so close, the scorching fire of his skin leapt onto me. I welcomed the warmth.

Enre tucked his legs close to his chest, arms draped across his knees. My gaze dipped to the blushing bullet wound in his thigh. It wasn't bleeding, which was a healthy indication of healing.

"That looks painful. After all that running, I probably owe you lots of healing."

"That would be nice." He smirked his stupid smile. Strange how it was growing on me.

"You know, I never expected a Varlac to help anyone but himself. You surprise me."

He shrugged, moonlight gleaming off his stormy blue eyes. "Maybe we're not all the same. So, why is your healing so powerful?"

"At the last Lunar Eutine, I changed from moonwulf to wulfkin, and since then, I've been able to heal wulfkin quickly. I've always worked with healing, but not like this.

Father said my transformation happened during a strong matriarchal moon, meaning only females changed, so my abilities were somehow upgraded, or something. Also explains why Nic didn't change over from a moonwulf. Though, I honestly don't really know."

Enre nodded, and his gaze rolled to the crisp sky full of stars. "What happened back in the prison?"

I sighed. "After I left the storeroom, the next door was easy to break through, but the main entrance to the prison took ages. And when I finally opened it, I must have tripped a perimeter alarm. I hadn't even reached Nic." I cut a glance to Enre, his expression solemn, without a hint of cheekiness. "It was too late."

"You did the best you could, and it's probably good you hadn't reached him. The officers won't associate him with the attempted jail break."

I bit my lower lip, well aware I could have done more. I choked back a hiccupped breath. "He won't last in there."

"A risky break-in. Maybe we should have planned better before just charging in there, but at least we didn't get caught." He placed a hand on mine, the heat spreading up my arm, but his words slapped me in the face, and I pulled away.

"It was my idea. This isn't about you judging me." Up on my feet, I rubbed the cold out of my arms, the sway of the long grasses scratching the skin around my thighs. "Nic only has over a week until the moon makes him shift. And then what? I have to get him out."

A shattered expression hooded his eyes. "I'm not judging, but you've got to admit you didn't put enough thought into it."

I offered him a wry smirk. "I don't want to talk about it anymore. Let's get back before someone sees us." I turned and headed toward the line of trailers, regretting my decision to allow Enre to join me. What was I thinking? All I'd managed to do was give him evidence to hold over me. A silly mistake I'd never repeat.

Over my shoulder, Enre remained seated in the grassy field, the night easily veiling him if anyone scanned the empty lot where he sat. My wolf urged me to return to his side, or better yet, invite him back to my trailer. After all, he'd helped me tonight.

"How about some healing?" I asked.

"Do you mind if I take a rain check on that until tomorrow? I'm exhausted tonight." His voice sounded far away even though he sat only a few steps from me.

"Of course, no problem." It wasn't like him to turn down an invitation to my trailer.

Why was he so distant?

"Good night then." When he gave no response, I trudged toward the trailer, my belly in knots. *Forget him.*

The fairy lights from the big top remained lit, as they did every night, whether we performed or not. I hurried onward, my arms tight against my chest as the cold prickled across my skin, before anyone saw me and asked where my clothes were.

Worry for Nicolai overtook my thoughts. Worse yet, if the police knew someone from the circus was trying to break him out, they'd come to Father and me.

I climbed into my trailer and slammed the door shut.

For the rest of the night, I didn't sleep a wink. When the morning sun glared in through the window, I was still lying in bed unable to get comfortable. My brother was a softy and didn't have a hard bone in his body. I'd never seen him fight or snarl at anyone. So how was he supposed to last in a cell with inmates who'd probably chew on him for a snack? Not to mention his upcoming moonshift.

A knock at the door instantly brought me to my feet. My hands trembled at the notion of who'd be visiting me this early. Part of me hoped it was Enre.

"Alena." Damir's voice boomed from outside. "Your father wants to talk to you.

Now."

My mouth dried. Had Father found out about last night? I got dressed in jeans, a hoodie, and stepped into my boots while my body remained numb of feelings. On the way out, I grabbed my windbreaker.

A ferocious wind folded around me, promising the onset of snow despite clear skies. With fists stuffed into the pockets of my windbreaker, I dragged my feet behind Damir toward Father's RV.

Inside, Father stood near his table, his weighty gaze drilling into me. Oh, I was in so much shit.

"Take a seat, Alena. Damir, please wait outside until I'm finished here."

I slipped into the chair while Father watched me, shaking his head. "I know it was you."

"I … I don't know what you mean." My gaze scanned the room and across numerous books on the shelves. Even my voice betrayed me, shaking and high-pitched.

"When the police told me about the attempted break-in at the detention center, my thoughts flew to you. No one else would try such a stupid stunt." He paused and narrowed his eyes. "I want to know who helped you."

My head jerked up. "No one."

"Ah, so you admit it was you." *Shit.* I sucked at lying.

"The police told me there were two people involved."

I sighed. "You should have seen Nic yesterday when I went to visit him. He was already broken. I couldn't stand seeing him that way."

"I already told you I'm taking care of Nicolai, but—"

"Then why haven't you done anything yet?" My voice climbed an octave. "You keep telling me to leave it to you, but I don't see you doing a thing to help him."

He huffed and shook his head in my direction. "You don't know what you've done." The tone beneath his words rumbled. "I had plans in place to rescue him, but now they're useless. There'll be police everywhere near the station."

I curled into my seat, shoulders slouched, hands in my lap, suddenly feeling like I was five years old again, when I'd brought home two bunnies and a guinea pig I'd "borrowed" from a neighbor because I wanted a pet. The police had been on our doorstep within the hour, and Father had to apologize on my behalf.

He kneeled in front of me, taking my hand in his. "You need to trust me when I tell you I've got your brother's interests at heart. And you can't break the rules and expect me to look the other way. It tells the rest of the pack that I'm a feeble leader."

"Then punish me." I deserved it and so much more. I'd stuffed up his plans, and now, because of me, Nicolai would remain in prison a while longer.

"Not until you tell me who helped you." Creases marred Father's brow. "If you don't, then the whole pack suffers."

"What?" I drew my hand from his.

He stood up and paced to the door and back. "Breaking rules has consequences. The police come sniffing around our circus more than they should. If you or your brother are accepted to lead this pack when I die, you need to understand that your actions impact everyone."

"That's not fair."

"Life isn't fair." Father frowned. He licked his lips and stopped several paces from me. "Once Nicolai gets out, we're doing what we should have done a long time ago. That monster, Sandulf, killed two of our scouts. So I'll return the favor and eliminate the Transylvanian pack and claim their land for us. But until then, we can't lose our heads."

My voice failed me.

Father shook his head and marched to the door, pushing it open. "Damir, call a pack meeting in the mess tent, now."

He glanced back at me. "Last chance. Who helped you?"

My gaze dropped as my hands fiddled in my lap. If I told Father it was Enre, he'd probably have a stroke knowing I allowed a Varlac to join me. Plus, Enre would end up getting kicked out and reported to his clan. As much as I hated his family, he helped me last night. How could I turn him in?

CHAPTER 10

ENRE

*P*ressed up against the back of Maxim's dilapidated RV, which had dented bumpers and sun-bleached yellow paint, I listened. Maxim and Alena talked about last night's attempted breakout. She told Maxim it was her but not who helped her. Still, my muscles tightened.

Maxim claimed he'd kill the Transylvanian pack in Romania. A part of me had hoped it was another of Sandulf's exaggerations. Apparently not.

The crunch of footsteps on the other side of the RV forced me to step away in case someone spotted me. I curved around two other trailers before limping to the mess tent with every other wulfkin headed that way. I'd hardly slept that night from the pain in my leg. Running from the police could cause that. What was I thinking?

Fuck, I didn't get to hear whether Alena had outed me in the end.

Once inside the mess tent, I wove past the glaring pack members, toward the back, and stopped near Eevi. The scorched stench of breakfast meat permeated the air and soured the back of my throat. I ignored the hateful frowns thrown my way. Tough crowd.

"I think they found another body." Eevi nudged my arm.

"Have you heard something?" I asked, sweat rolling down my back despite the cold. "N-nope."

Her hands twisted one of her dreadlocks in a nervous way. "More police came to the circus this morning."

I was in a pit surrounded by wolves looking for any excuse to eat me alive. If Maxim suspected my involvement last night, then I might finally see the Bulgarian pack as Sandulf had described them: bloodthirsty monsters.

A sudden sting pinched my leg, and I hissed through my teeth. The transformation and last night's run had aggravated the bullet wound, and instead of getting better, I now limped worse than before. I should have taken up Alena's healing offer last night, but after the ruined break-in and Alena's worry over her brother, I couldn't bring myself to ask any more of her.

Maxim and Alena entered the tent. My pulse kicked up a notch. The chatter around us died. *Showtime.*

Alena slipped into the crowd, taking an empty seat at a table without a glance my way.

Maxim moved to stand at the front, facing the pack, his legs parted to match his wide shoulders, fists by his sides. A quick glance had his gaze landing on me for a second or so. What did he know?

I swallowed the knot forming in my throat and held the dread on the inside. If the alpha had any inclination of my involvement in the attempted breakout of Nicolai, I'd already be locked up somewhere, or worse. But a Varlac breaking their own rules would have him suspecting I wasn't Varlac.

"I appreciate everyone coming here on such short notice. First, I must apologize to our guest for not giving him a proper introduction earlier. He's traveled all the way from the Hungarian Varlac family to visit us." He offered me a terse nod and waved a hand at me.

"I'd like to welcome Enre Ulf. He'll be staying with us a few days, so please pay him the respect he deserves."

Every head turned in my direction, their glares sliding across every inch of my body. I forced a smile.

"Events have been unusually strange," Maxim continued, "and I had hoped to return to our usual routine, forget our past, and move on. But this morning, the police have brought unfortunate news to my attention." He paused, his gaze sweeping the group who'd fallen deadly silent.

"Last night, two people tried to break into the city's detention center."

Yep, here it comes. My muscles tensed.

"The police came to ask me whether I believed the culprits could be from *our* circus. I might have dismissed their accusations, except that one of the suspects confessed to me this morning."

I struggled to swallow past the unmoving boulder in my throat. "I have yet to identify the second person involved."

A long breath spilled past my lips, and my shoulders relaxed.

"I want to extend the opportunity to the one responsible to come forward and explain themselves." Maxim rubbed his stubbly chin. "I promise I will be understanding, and I don't expect you to reveal yourself here. Come and see me today in private." He shrugged, though his narrow eyes and thin lips were anything but casual. "If not, I can't promise I will be as forgiving when I eventually come for you."

A few murmured voices rose from the masses. Somehow, I doubted his generosity extended to me.

"So, until the perpetrator steps forward, I am putting the pack into lockdown." His words elicited groans and whispers from the pack, steadily growing louder.

Someone said, "Force the wulfkin who confessed to tell you who it was. Don't punish all of us."

"No one is to leave the circus grounds without my permission." Maxim's voice boomed louder. "Anyone caught doing so will be punished. No excuses."

"This isn't fair," someone else called out.

Everyone quieted down, waiting for the alpha's response.

Fuck, Alena. You've thrown me to the wolves now.

The cacophony of angry words, sighs, and the shuffling of seats against linoleum escalated.

"You're killing us," Eevi piped up, drawing attention our way.

Wonderful.

"We haven't released our wolves for weeks, and I'm feeling it. How much longer do we wait? My wolf wants out, and you want us caged in the circus? Why aren't we moving? You promised we'd be gone by now to—"

"Eevi," Maxim said, a heavy growl hanging off her name. The alpha's gaze slid across to me for a smidgen of a second. The crowd fell silent. "Watch your words carefully.

Once the situation with the police has settled, which should only be a few days at most, I promise everyone a trip to the national park. Until then, stay strong and support each other. This is a difficult time for our pack, but we will get through it *together*." With one last look my way, Maxim turned and strode outside with Blackie.

The tent became a whirlwind of activity, a chorus of whispers, and a few wulfkin stormed out.

I leaned toward Eevi to ask a question, but she shot forward and blended into the crowd, vanishing.

Alena glanced my direction, worry marring her expression, and she took a step toward me. I was eager to settle a few details about last night. She did a quick sweep of the room and then spun around before dashing outside.

I lunged after her, groaning from the ache gripping my thigh. Pushing past wulfkin who refused to move out of my way, I ignored their grunts and exited the overheated tent. A chilly but refreshing breeze greeted me outside.

Alena's blue windbreaker and dark hair vanished around the corner of a trailer. The mid-morning sun beat down on my back as I hobbled after her.

Near the far side of the large tent, Alena sneaked past three trucks parked in a U- shape. Inside the formation lay a huge wooden container the size of any trailer. Except it was positioned on a platform with wheels, most likely pulled by one of the trucks. The worn paint on the sides of the container had mostly faded away, but the bleached turquoise color used for the name *Novac* remained, even if in the form of washed-out streaks.

Alena was nowhere to be found, but a familiar scent hit, the same one I'd inhaled when I'd first encountered Alena. It was the wolf girl.

Climbing the steps up to the old trailer, I stood outside the door and knocked.

I listened and heard a shuffling sound, like feet dragging hay, along with a low rumble. My spine stiffened. I lifted my hand for another knock. The door swung open, and the barnyard smell mingled with wolf wafted out.

Alena greeted me with a scowl. Behind her, a black curtain with rips in it concealed the rest of the room.

"We should talk," I said.

Her brow creased. "Nothing to talk about. Keep your mouth shut and there'll be no problem."

"Why would you cover for me?"

"You helped me out, and I'm repaying the favor, that's it. Isn't that enough? Unlike the Varlac, I—"

"Would you lay off the Varlac insults? Unless you're going to tell me why you detest us, stop judging."

Her cheeks colored. "Doesn't stop you from assuming things about us." She folded her arms, and her eyes pierced me.

A loud thud behind Alena made the platform beneath our feet quiver. My response stuck to the tip of my tongue. "What have you got in there?"

"Just leave me alone. Please. After last night, it's best no one sees us together." She turned around and hurried back inside.

I entered the darkened room and closed the door. The whiff of wet dog fur flooded my senses. Light seeped out around the corners of the curtain, and I pushed it aside to find two cages taking up the length of the container. The cages stood at least six-foot-three in height. The metal bars were peeling … probably from many years of use by this pack, though at least they'd invested in new locks for both cage doors. Fresh air blew in from the line of small holes along the tops of the walls.

From the first cage, a familiar wolf pounced at me, her brow smacking into the metal frame, her height easily reaching my waist. A whimper rolled off her tongue. Ash.

Alena sidled up the narrow passage between the bars and wall. She glanced my way. "Happy now?"

I shrugged. "What's wrong with her?"

Alena slid closer. I backed into the curtain, giving her enough room to pass.

"A couple of weeks ago, Ash was chosen to transform from a moonwulf to wulfkin at the recent Lunar Eutine. Except she's remained in her wolf form ever since. I've been trying to help her change into human form, but nothing's worked. I think it's got to do with her age, maybe stress."

Ash prowled inside the cage, more cat-like than canine, bronze tufts of fur gliding past the bars. Her nose lifted and inhaled the air, then the wolf slumped onto her belly, a great breath gushing from her nostrils. Kalina, the Interpol woman who was searching for Ash, came to mind. This whole time the pack was trying to help Ash. No foul play.

"She's only fifteen," Alena continued. "The youngest moonwulf I've ever heard of transforming into a wulfkin. And she wasn't even part of our pack. We sensed her when she came to the circus here in Ruse with her human mother. No father in the picture. I don't think her mother even knew the species of the one who got her pregnant. Weeks later, the full moon hit, and we found her in her wolf form on circus grounds, lost and terrified."

"That's why she's here."

"We want to help her." Alena nodded. "And I think she likes you."

"Really? Wouldn't have guessed."

"Well, she hasn't attempted to bite you yet." I retreated a few steps. "Good to know."

Back on her feet, Ash paced the cage in a circular motion, a low grumbling sound rolling from her chest.

"She misses Nic. He used to visit her daily, spend hours with her." Alena's words were barely audible.

"I'm sorry we couldn't free him."

Alena shook her head, keeping her gaze on Ash. "Can't do anything about it now.

Father is watching me, and with the lockdown, we're all stuck."

"Still brazen of you to try to rescue your brother."

She turned my way with an expression I couldn't quite pinpoint. A cross between intrigue and biting back an insult. I guessed the latter.

"I would have done the same for my pack," I said.

Her brow pinched, and she looked away. "You're not really what I expected from a Varlac."

"Did you just give me a compliment?" I covered my heart with a hand. "I'm floored.

Maybe Varlac aren't as terrible as you think they are?"

When her gaze jerked my way, I realized I'd pushed my luck. "I know exactly how terrible they are. You seem a bit different. That's all."

I changed the topic. "Who gets the privilege of enjoying the second cage?"

"Nic, since he's still a moonwulf and changes once a month at the full moon." Alena knelt in front of the occupied cage and threaded an arm inside. Ash was sniffing her hand, licking it, and dropped down onto bent legs.

Leaning against the wall, I studied the way Alena carefully placed both gloved palms above Ash's back and shut her eyes. The same way she'd used her healing energies on my bullet wound. I could've used a bit of her mojo right now … and a bit more, too.

Peace fell over the trailer. Only the rush of wind beating against the walls sounded and the occasional grunt from Ash —or was she snoring? Alena laid her forehead against the metal cage and stayed there.

I couldn't help but admire the devotion Alena showered on Ash, never giving up on the poor child. And the way she'd risked almost getting caught for her brother—these weren't the actions of a bloodthirsty wulfkin. Perhaps my way of dealing with her father was wrong. I needed a diplomatic approach, a proposal Sandulf obviously hadn't been able to pull off. This option meant either revealing myself, or enticing Maxim to open up about his intentions to take over the Transylvania land and how he planned to rescue Nicolai. Except, either way, I'd draw unwanted attention, and my situation could turn ugly in a hurry.

CHAPTER 11

ALENA

One bruised shoulder and a deflated ego later, I dragged myself off the makeshift soccer field at the front of the circus. Bright lights lit up the yard that would otherwise be drowned in the darkness of night. I tagged Sonia to reenter the game in my place. The pack could have their soccer game. I couldn't get Nicolai out of my head, so I turned against the icy winds and hurried toward my trailer.

Two stir-crazy, uneventful days had passed since Father announced a pack lockdown.

The police hadn't left their posts from across the main road. Father might as well have gotten a bed to sleep at the police station or his legal aid's office while attempting to get Nicolai out on bail before the encroaching full moon.

Enre had been keeping his distance from me. And then there was Kalina, the Interpol lady, who visited us three times a day asking about Ash. She dropped hints about other missing kids. Her words about human trafficking and the idea of us being framed swirled in my mind.

Father was still pissed that I wouldn't tell him who had

accompanied me to break out Nicolai. He didn't need to know. I owed Enre that much for risking his life to help me rescue my brother.

A part of me hoped my instincts about Enre were right—that he was different from his father. Mother had once told me about the riches the Varlac stole from other packs, the girls they kidnapped and forced to work for them, and how easily they disposed of anyone who stood in their way. What if they weren't all the same?

The night howled around me. Reaching the rear of the big-top tent, where only the moonlight bounced off the trailers, a chill crept through my bones. The sudden awareness of being surrounded by shadows played on my nerves. I kept checking over my shoulder. The night never worried me, but tonight the darkness felt heavy on my shoulders.

Wulfkin voices shrilled in the background as I reached for the door handle to my trailer. Grass crunched in the empty lot behind my trailer. I wasn't alone.

More steps, fading quickly.

Too many wulfkin and human scents mingled in the air to distinguish any particular one. I crept around my trailer and peered out. A silvery tinge lay across the field where overgrown grass swayed in the blustering winds. In the distance, a black, human figure slipped away. Whoever had been there was barely a blip in the night.

Before I had time to debate whether it was a great idea or not, I was in the greenery, zipping behind the stranger, curious to uncover who was spying on us.

The figure stopped, and I dropped to the ground, nestled in the grass. I peeked out through the blades. The breeze blew the intruder's hood off and revealed Enre. A Varlac who broke rules. What a surprise.

My wolf whimpered with longing for Enre. Total

betrayal. But then again, the past two nights, I'd had the same horny dream with me tied to a tree and Enre teasing me. Aside from leaving me desperately unsatisfied, I suspected change was coming soon. If the premonition involved Enre satisfying me, then I was all for it, but if it had anything to do with the dead bodies in my nightmare, I didn't want an inch of it.

Why was Enre sneaking away from the circus anyway?

He hobbled away from the empty lot. His limp had improved, though I'd never seen a wulfkin take so long to heal. Perhaps he'd had a critical injury recently. Someone might have attacked him before he arrived at our pack. A pinching sensation squeezed in the pit of my belly. Was that pity? No way.

Up on my feet, I tracked him, keeping a safe distance. Father told me to watch the pack, and … well … I wasn't sure if Enre was included in that. I'd pretend he was.

He slinked through the streets, hurried through any lit areas, seemingly returning to the strip of woods where Ash always escaped. A couple of times Enre peered over his shoulder, and I hid behind trees, fences, or cars, thankful the winds were in my favor.

Up ahead, he crossed the major highway and vanished into a narrow passage of dense trees. Why was he coming back here?

A black mutt the size of a cat ran after me, growling as I waited at the curb for a truck to zoom past.

"Shoo." I waved a hand at the dog. "Go away." He barked in response.

I snarled, and the little critter scampered back the way I'd come seconds earlier. At least he wouldn't get hit by a car.

Tiptoeing to avoid the clicking of boots against asphalt, I darted across the road.

Once in the cover of forest, I couldn't see Enre anymore. I traveled through the woodland, sniffing the air.

A twig snapped behind me. I spun and spotted Enre standing several paces away. He raised an eyebrow. "You should practice your stealth skills."

"You left the circus, and we're on lockdown."

"Doesn't apply to me." He rubbed his lips, staring at mine. "It seems you've broken the rule though, following me."

A police siren blared in the distance, and we turned in unison toward the sound.

"We should head back," I said, my gaze locked on the shadows over my shoulder, convinced I'd see the blue and red lights at any moment. Except, it wasn't against human law to be outside at night. They had no idea it was Enre and me who'd broke into the prison, or we'd have been arrested by now.

Enre strolled deeper into the woods, away from the freeway, his head low and his body already blending into the night.

"Hey," I called out, following him. "What are you doing here?"

He cut me a side-glance from hooded eyes, and if it weren't for the occasional spray of moonlight amid the canopy of leaves, his grim expression would have been lost.

"Getting fresh air."

"Right, and I'm a fool."

He released a chuckle, and the tone made my wolf squirm, clawing at my insides for release. She'd claimed him as her own on no basis other than pure physical attraction. It didn't mean I agreed.

"Why are you following me?" he asked, not slowing his pace.

I kept up with him, pushing low-hanging branches out of

my way, twigs snapping beneath my boots. "Why won't you tell me where you're ?

He didn't answer.

"While you're on our territory, Father has a right to know your whereabouts and what your intentions are. I can easily go back and tell him about your little stunt here."

He halted and turned my way. "And how will your father react when he finds out you allowed me to help you attempt to break out Nic?"

My next inhale came with a gasp, but I reined it in. "Go ahead. You'll be the one questioned for breaking your own precious Varlac rule about not doing anything to draw human attention to us." The beat of my heart escalated.

Only the breeze and occasional car noise passed between us. "Touché."

His response crawled up my spine. What was I doing anyway? Playing with the devil, a Varlac I knew nothing about. I shouldn't be here but at home, listening to Father. I'd already ruined his plans to free Nicolai once.

"What's really going on in this pack?" he asked, his tone authoritative and direct.

I tucked frozen hands into my jeans pockets. "I don't know what you're talking about."

"Why have the police been finding dead humans near the circus in every city you visit?"

"Who have you been talking to?"

His bluntness and knowledge squeezed my chest. So that's what he wanted— information on why the pack was drawing human attention. And who killed them.

"Doesn't matter," he responded.

"Speak to the alpha about such matters, not me." I resisted the urge to step away. "I can never get close enough to your father for a simple conversation."

I inhaled an icy breath. "Is that why you're visiting us?" I asked. "To get dirt on the pack so the Varlac have an excuse to kill us?"

He shook his head. "Believe it or not, Varlac care for the well-being of wulfkin."

Right then, I wished I could peel back the night, see the lies on his face, and ask him why one of his family had killed my mother if their clan only wanted to help us. But Father had told me to never mention it. The Varlac would kill us before admitting to their atrocity.

"Like I said, speak to the alpha." A snarl hung off my last word.

He stepped closer. "You can speak to me freely, Alena. I won't share anything with the clan if you don't want me to. What are your father's plans to deal with the police? Will he cross the border and leave the country?"

I retreated, hating where this conversation was going—interrogation-style. "I'm starting to see the real you here."

His lack of response said it all. I was a complete and utter fool. I turned away. My pulse raced, and sickness coursed through me.

When I glanced over my shoulder, Enre had vanished into the forest. I blinked back angry tears.

Varlac didn't care about anyone but themselves. Part of me yearned to chase Enre and force him to tell me everything. Why he was really in Bulgaria, and what were his intentions? I should have known better. Varlac *were* cold-blooded murderers.

As I entered the camp, I stomped between the trailers. Shame crawled up my neck and cheeks, and my stomach ached. The little doggy from earlier in the night was now sitting outside my trailer. If I wasn't burning up with embarrassment, I might have considered it cute. I flung open my trailer's door, not caring that the doggy jumped in or that I slammed the door shut so the whole place trembled. Enre had made me believe he might be attracted to me, and I was stupid enough to fall for it. Flopping onto the bed, I pulled a pillow over my face and screamed into it. Crap, I'd *fantasized* about that monster.

Flames burning orange and red crackled in the wind, licking at the limbs of a grand oak. A thick, sooty column of charcoal spiraled upward, blotting out the bright sky. No other tree in the forest was lit. Then I noticed someone tied to the trunk, arms pulled tight behind them and around the tree.

"Alena."

They were calling me. My feet were now running, and the heavy stench of smoke pitched to the back of my throat, stinging. Fire captured the canopy of the great oak, crawling downward. Then I recognized him. Nicolai. Tied to the flaming tree.

Suddenly, a bucket was in my hand. Except there was no water in it. No well anywhere nearby. I threw it away.

Shudders snaked up my body, and I ran faster, but the tree was moving away from me.

"Alena."

I tripped over a root and fell forward, striking the earth face-first. "Alena."

The roar and snap of flames grew louder. Jumping to my feet, the tree with Nicolai was now even farther away, and the fire almost upon him.

"Hold on, I'm coming." My heart drummed against my rib cage, and tears blurred my vision. "Please, don't go." I bolted closer, jumping over dead logs, not caring for the scratches from shrubs. I had to save him.

"Alena. Hurry."

The crash of timber collapsing echoed around me, and the burning branches of the tree plummeted, striking Nico-lai, engulfing him.

I screamed.

When I bolted out of bed, sweat coated me, and I swore the faint ashy smell of fire filled my nostrils. Tears flooded my cheeks, and my body shook. Moon goddess, I never wanted to dream again.

CHAPTER 12

ENRE

*B*loody streaks tarnished the morning sky.

No wulfkin prowled the circus grounds this morning—most were probably at the mess tent having breakfast. I didn't have the stomach for food today, or to be gawked at. On the main road, a police car remained parked. The police had been watching the circus as they had been doing ever since they'd apprehended Nicolai. I stood between the parking lot and the big tent and rubbed my eyes.

Last night, I'd returned to the detention center in the city, hoping to break Nicolai out. His incarceration posed untold danger of exposing us to humans. But once I arrived at the station, I'd spotted a problem. More specifically, multiple problems. Police had been posted outside, and some even lingered a block away. The passage Alena and I had used to sneak in was blocked off. And the back alley had been crawling with officers.

Disappointment wormed its way into my thoughts. Getting in there was going to be a real chore now.

A car door slammed from the parking lot, bringing me back to the present. The Interpol lady—Kalina—weaved through the cars and nodded to someone in the parked police vehicle. She was one determined woman. It surprised me the authorities had enough staff to spend this much time on one missing teenager, but what would I know?

She glanced over and nodded at me. I sauntered in the opposite direction, toward the rear of the circus, avoiding her in case she decided to chat.

Halfway across the grounds, Maxim rushed out from the mess tent, his gaze low as he weaved between the trailers. No goons. Time to act.

I sprinted after him. For days, he'd been out of sight. This was my chance to discuss his situation and somehow force him to admit he had a real problem with Nicolai. Plus, I'd make him reveal his plans to move to Transylvania. If I got him talking, I could offer him a different solution than killing Daciana's pack, including me.

Fists clenched, I curved around the line of trailers and emerged into a narrow path behind them. No sign of Maxim. I darted left. Blackie stepped out from behind a trailer right in front of me. I skidded to a halt, inches from smacking into him. His palms collided with my chest, and I reeled backward.

The wolf clawed at my insides, attempting to climb out. "Why are you following Maxim?"

The alpha reappeared from behind Blackie and set a hand on his shoulder. "It's okay, Damir. I need to speak with Enre." Maxim stared my way. "Come with me."

I nudged past Blackie, our shoulders grazing, and trailed after Maxim into his RV. Inside, shelves transformed his walls into an overflowing cascade of books. Not a single spot remained bare, and I wondered how he removed a book without the whole lot of them coming down on top of him. Yet his bed was neat and tucked. Did he even sleep there? No clothes on the carpet, unlike Alena's place.

"Unfortunately," Maxim said, taking a seat at a small, wooden table, "it's a bit hectic right now, the busy time of year." He scratched his chin. "I apologize for not giving you more time when you first arrived. I hope everyone has been courteous and helpful to your every need?"

Maxim wasn't a fool, but I went along with his act.

"I've never met a friendlier pack." I slipped into the seat across the table from him.

Hands planted on the table, back pressed to his chair, he stared at me. "What do you want to discuss?"

The very moment my mouth opened, a loud knock on the door resonated. What now? Another of Maxim's goons trudged inside the already small space, the RV swaying.

"Two humans from the Ruse council are here, insisting it can't wait. Something about us needing to vacate the location this week. They've cut our permit short."

Maxim sighed, his posture shrinking forward. Then the crease in his brow returned, deeper this time.

"Should I tell them to return later?" the goon asked.

"No." Maxim focused his attention my way. "Sorry, but we'll have to reschedule our talk for later in the day."

Already on my feet, I figured if the city council of Ruse were reneging on their permits early, it meant Maxim might decide to move into Transylvania this week. After his chat with the council, he might openly reveal his plans if he grew desperate enough. It also meant he'd need to make a move to free Nicolai soon.

"No problem." On my way out, Blackie made sure to knock his shoulder into mine, hard enough to sting. His face would meet my fist before long.

Outside, two humans in business suits and with slicked hair waited. One hugged a briefcase to his chest. I wondered if the guy had a million euros in there, considering how tightly he gripped the case.

I hurried past them and away from Maxim's RV. Annoyance stuck to my insides.

Then a swarm of voices and hoots caught my attention.

Emerging into the empty lot behind the circus, I found the source of the noise. At least fifteen wulfkin crowded in a tight circle around two in the center. They hooted and snarled.

I should have ignored the commotion, but curiosity got the better of me. A bit of entertainment sounded inviting.

Standing at the edge of the mob, I peered past heads blocking my view with no success. Someone cheered from within the fold. I shifted to the other side for a better vantage point. That's when I spotted him, and my insides iced over.

Radu, one of my pack members from Transylvania! Why was he here?

Blood trickled down his cheek. He was the only one I had shared my plan of coming to Bulgaria with, and I couldn't imagine why he would follow me. Had something happened to the pack?

A wulfkin, smaller in stature, laid heavy punches into Radu's torso while my friend covered his face.

Fire catapulted through my veins. If Radu revealed his true alliance to the Bulgarian pack, we would both be skinned alive. This was a disaster in the making, and I had to get him away from the pack. Radu received another blow to the gut, and I threw myself into the hoard.

Elbows and bodies whacked into me. Forcing myself into the impromptu boxing ring, I tackled the wulfkin who was beating my friend, despite my aching thigh. We fell to the ground with a thud, me on top of him. The crowd cheered.

I climbed to my feet, as did my opponent. Before he lifted a hand, I swung a fist and sent him back onto his ass. This wulfkin might've been skinny, but he was damn fast too.

To my side, Radu met my stare with silvery eyes, and a nervous smile inched up his mouth.

A second wulfkin jumped onto my back. My knee buckled, and I reeled forward. The crowd retreated as I landed face-first, eating a mouthful of dirt.

He delivered two punches to my head. My pulse had morphed into a charging bull. I bucked him off, and already my wolf clambered for release. Every part of me yearned to rip into anyone who stood in my way.

Back on my feet, I located my rivals behind me. Two attackers, ganging up on me. Such babies.

I cracked my neck, rolled my shoulders, and cocked my chin toward them. "You both ready to choke on your own blood?"

A sudden torrent of water splashed my side, drenching me and my opponents. One of them tripped backward, dragging his buddy down with him.

I laughed and wiped my eyes clean of water, the chill extinguishing my rage.

Several paces away, Alena held an empty bucket in her hands. "You're all a bunch of wild dogs."

Practically every onlooker booed.

I stuck out a hand to Mr. Skinny to help him up. The other wulfkin had already left. "We good?"

He made a short guttural sound and accepted my hand.

Facing the crowd, I said, "Nice to know I'm not the only newcomer who's welcomed with such open arms."

"What are you talking about?" a wulfkin I recognized as Ivitka asked. He had a square, shaved head, successfully achieving the intimidating look. "He intruded on our territory"—Ivitka pointed his chin toward Radu—"and refused to give us his name. Gives us the right to force the answer out of him. Since when are you against Varlac rules?"

I closed the distance between us, my breathing fast and

rough. "When the wulfkin you're ganging up on is a Varlac." The lie flew free too easily. I hoped no one asked to verify Radu's authenticity. He had to leave, and damn quick.

A few in the crowd gasped, and others retreated to the big top.

Radu exhaled, loud. A side effect of nerves getting the better of him.

A semicircle of gazes locked onto me. "If you have an issue with not attacking a Varlac," I said, cracking my neck, "I'd gladly change your mind."

"We didn't realize you were organizing a Varlac convention," the meathead said. "How many more should we expect of your kind?"

Someone behind him chuckled.

"I'd be very careful with that sharp tongue of yours," I said.

"Perhaps you should have informed the alpha of your visitor beforehand." Alena sliced through our staring match.

"This is Radu of the Varlac Clan, and he's my father's advisor." The whispers flatlined.

"And unless anyone else has an issue with this, we're out of here." I waved for Radu to follow me.

Wulfkin parted, creating an easy path for us to exit. The stares burned into my back, and I kept up the act, my spine stiff and chin high.

With Radu on my heels, we hurried inside my trailer.

"Varlac?" Radu asked. "Are you insane? The laws about impersonating one could get us—and your father's advisor —killed."

"Quiet." I turned up the radio, which was playing a random soppy song, and checked the window. All clear.

Radu's flaxen hair was a mess, and blood was smeared into one of his sideburns. At least he'd shaven off his awful beard.

I retrieved one of my unused bandages from the cupboard, along with a bottle of vodka and a towel, and pushed them into his grasp.

Radu collapsed onto the bed. "I could have died out there."

"They were playing with you. This is why you should have taken my offer to train. It wouldn't hurt to learn how to punch and defend yourself." I dragged a chair closer. "Why are you here?"

Radu's shoulders hunched, and sweat bubbled across his upper lip. His shaky hands fiddled with the bottle cap and filled the room with the stink of plum vodka. He drenched the fabric.

"Daciana sent me."

I leaned forward in my seat, my breath caught in my chest. "You told her."

He shrugged, his gaze low, and patted the wound on his cheek with the soaked cloth.

He winced. "She's very persuasive."

I rubbed my mouth, knowing firsthand how pushy Daciana could be. At least she had sent Radu, rather than arrive herself, which would spell disaster. I told Radu about my disguise, the situation with the council, the police, dead bodies, Ash, even Nicolai stuck in jail where his turning would show humans that werewolves were real. I left Alena out on purpose; it was not the time to discuss how my wolf desperately claimed her, or how I'd contemplated making her mine when this mess was resolved. Though I doubted she'd open her heart to me if I challenged her father and took his place.

"This pack's done a spectacular job of digging its own grave. I see why you claiming to be a Varlac wouldn't be suspicious." He reclined on the bed, resting on his arms.

My forearms pressed to my thighs. "The alpha, Maxim, isn't quite fitting the image Sandulf painted."

Radu's eyebrows climbed his forehead. "Hard to believe, considering the mess they have at their doorstep."

"Something else is going on, and I'm not convinced Maxim's at the center of it," I said.

"Yeah, but we didn't suspect Sandulf either, and look how he turned out. Fathered a brutal dracwulf, tried to sacrifice you to it, and attempted to kill Daciana. Everyone hides secrets. The better one can conceal it, the more horrendous the crime."

I straightened. "Since when did you become such a cynic?"

Radu shrugged. "Must have been when Sandulf beat me up and left me for dead."

A rock song bellowed from the radio. I stood and glanced out the window, expecting a bunch of busybodies. I spotted no one.

"So what did Daciana say?" I asked, still staring out at the large circus tent in the distance.

"Levin Ulf … uh, your father … he rang up looking for you." I snapped around. "What for?"

"Daciana kept lying about you not being there, but on the third phone call, she finally broke down and admitted you were in Bulgaria. He said he's coming to Transylvania in a few days, and if you're not there, he's coming for you in Ruse."

Fire slammed inside my chest and crawled up my neck. Was my father turning up to serve his punishment for still not being an alpha? My twenty-fifth birthday was a few days away, and I still had no pack of my own. This couldn't come at a worse time.

"Daciana wants you to return home immediately."

Pacing to the door and back, I kept my voice low. "And then what?" I spun to face him. "Wait for Maxim to come and kill the pack? My being here will solve all our troubles. Plus, Nic's still in prison. If he turns wolf inside the jail, our kind will be revealed to humans. We'll be hunted down and killed. I can't leave until Nic is out." Surely, my father would understand the importance of this delicate situation. Then again, maybe not.

Radu patted his bloody cheek with the towel.

I slumped onto the bed next to him, the mattress bouncing beneath my weight. "I want to take over this pack."

He gasped, making a girly sound. Of course, I wouldn't call Radu masculine to begin with.

"Don't you get it?" I asked. "If we unite our packs, we will be the biggest pack in Europe, and the Varlac will be forced to overlook Sandulf's rule-breaking and spare the pack from punishment. We'll achieve a level of immunity against the majority of wulfkin rules." Plus, I'd finally get Father off my back about this alpha bullshit. I shot to my feet, pacing in a small circle.

It was the only way. The more I thought about it, the better it sounded.

Since arriving in Bulgaria, I'd intended to avoid a fight, but I was an idiot for being so naive. With the strength of his large pack, the only approach in our favor was for our two packs to merge. Maxim would never agree to this, and would mean killing him. I'd have to find a way to deal with that.

When I pivoted toward Radu, his cheeks had paled. "Risky move," he said. "What other options do we have?"

"Daciana wants to talk to Maxim and negotiate an agreement."

"Not going to work. Maxim openly admitted he planned to kill the Transylvanian pack because Sandulf killed two of their scouts. They'll kill us the moment they discover who we are."

"We should head home then. Come with me. Forget this suicide mission."

I huffed an exhausted breath, my shoulders sagging. "We'll die if we do nothing. And I can't leave before I get Nic out of prison for the sake of every wulfkin."

Radu fiddled with the corner of the blanket on the bed, and for a long moment, he remained silent. Only the tunes on the radio filled the space between us.

With Maxim in desperation mode, he'd make his move any day, and I wanted to be here when it happened. Better to be within the enemy ranks. I'd have easier access to the alpha.

Thoughts of Alena fluttered in my mind, and I drove the images of her away. Not when so many lives depended on my decision. I'd help the Bulgarian members with their troubles, too. With me in charge, Daciana and I would come to an agreement between our packs. It had to work.

Radu broke the silence. "I guess there's nothing I can say or do to convince you otherwise?"

"Nope. But I promise to return before my father arrives."

Radu's silvery eyes glinted in the sunlight pouring in from the window. "I'll stay and help you."

I choked on my next inhale and coughed. "I appreciate it. But your presence will only get us caught. I am a Varlac by blood. You're not. It's best you leave before someone comes and demands you prove your heritage."

His eyes widened, and I hated freaking him out. Instead, I changed the topic. "Any news on Matias or Lutia?" Yeah, I despised Lutia for turning our old alpha,

Sandulf, against our pack, but I hadn't given up on tracking her down.

He shook his head. "Since they fled, neither have been seen or heard."

Matias was my friend, but he had left when the difficulties arose with Sandulf. I worried he'd run to Hungary to report the dracwulf incident to my father.

Radu continued to explain how Botolf, the elder in our pack, had officially declared his retirement, and it made me laugh. Botolf had been threatening to give up work for years.

"And Daciana's human lover, Connell, spends nights at the house now."

My laughter subsided. If my father visited Transylvania and found a human living with us, he'd explode. Unfortunately, Daciana wasn't a wulfkin who took anyone's advice, no matter how sensible. A year ago, I'd thought Daciana was meant to be my mate, but I'd accepted her choice of a human partner, and now it seemed my inner wolf had claimed Alena.

On his feet, Radu brushed bits of loose dirt off his jeans. "I'd better go."

I stood and gave Radu a quick hug. A selfish part of me wanted him to stay for the simple reason that I missed my family. But he'd be safer at home … for now.

"Tell Daciana to trust me," I said. "I won't let her down. And for the moon's sake, tell her to get her lover to stop visiting the house until this crap is over." Last thing we needed was my father scenting the human all over Daciana and the pack house.

Radu smirked. "Yeah, right. You know her."

Holding back the frustration bubbling in my throat, I said, "I know."

I walked Radu in a wide circle around the outside of the circus to avoid bumping into anyone. At the main road out front, I hailed a passing cab. "Go straight across the bridge to Romania. Take care of Botolf and Daciana until I return."

Radu's creased brow screamed worry and naivety. "I'll see you soon." He climbed into the taxi. I shut his door, and the cab drove away.

Time to escalate my plans for the alpha. I started my trek back to the circus but froze.

At the entrance to the main tent, Maxim stood, watching me, arms folded tightly across his chest. I wasn't sure if relief or dread coursed through my body, but perspiration rolled down my spine. With Radu gone, Maxim couldn't unravel the lie about my father's advisor paying me a visit, but my lack of formally introducing Radu to Maxim before entering his territory might prompt a phone call to the Varlac in Hungary, who'd quickly reveal my lies. I was fucked.

CHAPTER 13

ALENA

*E*nre was a hazard beyond being a nosy Varlac spying on us. His danger burrowed under my skin like a thousand parasites scavenging for blood.

He hadn't been able to get his father's advisor away from me fast enough after the fight, and since when did anyone have to stand up for a Varlac? They were notorious for their ruthlessness and their battle accolades, and this applied to their advisors and staff. Their clan was a war machine. So why was that Varlac Radu cowering?

Inside the center ring of the big-top tent, the acrobatic ribbon hung from the ceiling, the ends wound around my wrists. My feet were still on the ground. Concentrating on the practice routine wasn't working. Behind me, wulfkin bustled around for their stunts and performances.

"If you're going to just stand there all day, can we have the ring to practice our motorcycle ball of death?" Ivitka's thick Serbian accent echoed from backstage. Dressed in his leather bodysuit, he stood there with his hands on his hips.

I unraveled my arms. "Sure, go for it." Not like I was making any progress.

Heading toward backstage to wrap my red performance ribbon up, I spotted Damir entering from the rear of the tent. His frame was solid, every bit resembling the bodyguard. Even on stage when he performed his weight-lifting act, he remained stiff. I wasn't sure I'd ever seen the wulfkin in relaxed mode.

He scanned the area and stopped searching when his sights landed on me. "Your father wants to speak to you."

Sonia approached from the dressing area. "Go, honey, I'll roll up your ribbon."

"Thanks." I touched Sonia's arm for a few seconds and offered her a grateful smile. "Come and see me later," she said with an arch of her eyebrow.

I nodded and left with Damir by my side, but I was curious what Sonia had seen in her divining sticks this time.

"He's in his trailer," Damir said, stepping into the sun. "You trimmed your beard?"

He shrugged. "Needed it."

Not a talker. He never was, but still, today felt off. Fire boiled in my stomach, and my muscles tensed, but I couldn't work it out. The prickles rushing down my spine refused to quit, and the air grew heavier. My wolf sensed it, too, whimpering for no particular reason. I yearned for some alone time, preferably in an open forest with the wind in my hair and lots of rabbits to chase.

Father's raised voice shot out from my right, at the front of the circus, about ten feet away, not his trailer. Damir sprinted ahead. I hurried after the large wulfkin.

At the front of the main tent, Father was in a heated discussion with Enre. Father's shoulders were forward in a boxer's posture, head low, arms by his sides.

Enre was slightly taller, back stiff and arms folded over his broad chest. He threw a glance my way before he spoke.

"Like I said, my parents sent their advisor for a quick update. The intention wasn't to panic your pack."

"That's no excuse." Father's voice deepened, and a drawn-out growl rumbled from his throat. "When anyone enters *my* territory"—he thumped a fist against his chest—"I should be the first to be told. I shouldn't hear it from pack members." Father circled Enre, his hands tight by his sides. "Why are you really here?"

Enre's straight stance gave little away, though his darting gaze took in where everyone stood, which emphasized his hunter instincts.

Father nudged Enre's shoulder with his own as he stepped around him.

Enre's response came fast. "Nic's incarceration is a disaster in the making. If he turns, he'll reveal we exist to all humans, and you'll bring the entire power of the Varlac down on your pack. We need to work together on this and get him out." His hooded eyes pinned Father. "And *I* ask the questions. What are you doing about Nic? Who's killing the humans?" Enre's expression pinched, and his gaze locked onto Father for several deadly silent moments.

"I will get Nicolai out. I don't need *your* help." Father's glare never left Enre.

"Absurd." Enre broke into a laugh, loud and for show. "You've got issues *here*. This is why I intended to speak to you about this earlier in *private*, but if you insist on airing your dirty laundry, I'm thrilled to oblige."

"I realize I can't tell you to leave my pack, but you are not welcome here." The viciousness in Father's voice startled me.

Enre studied Father intently and spoke through clenched teeth. "I'm here to help." I choked on my next breath, drawing Damir's attention. He shook his head.

"If that's the case," my father said, "tonight, after the show, you will accompany the pack to the national park." He looked my way. "Alena, you are in charge. Plan to leave by midnight, and take Ash with you."

"No problem," Enre said, too quick and eager to comply. "What's going on?" I asked.

"The police are getting a warrant to search the circus tomorrow. I want most of the pack gone." Father's orotund tone gave me goose bumps.

"But they've already searched the circus."

"They aren't convinced." Father tossed his glare at Enre before continuing. "And if I weren't already buried in this shit, I'd drag you to my trailer and force you to tell me the truth. Then I'd call your clan to confirm it. And I'll do it anyway *once* I deal with our current dilemma. So, you can either play along and pretend to help us, or be a hindrance."

The tension enveloped me, strangling my lungs.

Finally, Father broke the staring match and turned toward me. "I have a meeting in the city with the council. Prepare the pack for tonight." A flick of his head toward Damir, and the pair circled Enre without a word and stormed toward the parking lot.

Yep, the day was officially nasty.

Icy winds numbed my face, tugging on my jacket and tossing my hair. I tightened the collar around my chest, unable to force my legs to move.

What else could go wrong? A noose was strangling the pack, and with each passing day, it constricted. If only Nicolai hadn't been caught, then we would have left Ruse by now. It was my fault for not sticking by Nicolai that morning. And I wasn't strong enough to break him out of prison. I'd made our situation so much worse.

Nearby, Enre remained, jaw clenched and his focus on the main road. He looked ready to launch an assault on someone's throat.

Technically, if he hadn't shown up, our pack's situation

might have played out differently. Ever since his arrival, our troubles had been exacerbated, and yet, staring at him, a part of me fancied inching closer for all the wrong reasons. No wonder my life was in such a knot. I should never allow my wolf to take charge, especially not when it involved my emotions. While my mind scolded me with lectures about staying away from Enre, my body deceived me, burning for a touch.

Enre turned my way, his cheeks red from the cold, his blue eyes piercing and broody. "It's going to snow."

Words tangled on my tongue. What could I possibly say? Since arriving, he'd been playing me to get information. So why couldn't my wolf and the heat between my thighs back off?

He dropped his gaze and vanished behind me.

Ahead, several cars drove along the main road. One of them pulled into our parking area. Probably locals eager to purchase tickets for tonight's show. Father should have canceled it.

A snowflake caressed my cheek with its icy touch, and another landed on my nose. I stuck out my gloved palm. Around me, a curtain of tiny, white flakes floated down. They melted the moment they landed. My mother had once told me that getting caught outside on the first day of snow was a wulfkin's blessing—a chance to cleanse and purge yourself of any wrong intent or doings. Letting the feathery crystals find me, I closed my eyes and pretended my life wasn't a desperate patchwork of bittersweet feelings. Never again would I jump for the first wulfkin who showered me with attention. I visualized every last piece of desire I held for Enre being washed away on the breeze. *Please, Mother. Please help me forget him.*

I whirled around and ran to the big top to organize the pack's outing.

The show flew by without a hitch. Every wulfkin's anticipation to run free in the national park spiked their cheery mood. For weeks, we'd all been eager to release our wolves. I smiled to myself as I sat in the pack bus with other wulfkin and pulled aside the curtain at the window. Night clung to the circus tent. We'd switched off the fairy lights for concealment, and after the customers had left, everyone had jumped into action. Our plan came together perfectly; we'd leave the circus grounds through the back to avoid being seen by the police out front.

Damir and a few other wulfkin Father had asked to stay behind grumbled for most of the performance, but nothing could be done about it.

The bus was loaded with eager wulfkin, chatting and laughing like the happier days before the complications of dead bodies and land restrictions. Most of us filled up the front three-quarters of the vehicle, but I sat on the second to last row of seats with Ash, who crouched in the aisle near me. Her leash chained her to the back exit doors. There was no need for a cage. Once we reached our destination, she'd be free to run as much as she desired.

Ash grumbled at other wulfkin climbing onboard. When Enre entered, she shot to her feet and wagged her tail. *Really?* She'd fallen for his charm, too.

He strolled down the center aisle toward me. A few wulfkin snarled as he passed. Yep, he'd managed to become even more unpopular.

Please don't sit next to me. Please don't sit next to me.

A shiver slithered in my belly and moved farther south the closer he got. It shouldn't have. I'd purged him out of my system. *Goddess of the moon, help me.*

He slumped into the seat in front of me and pressed his

back to the window, staring at me with a flat expression. Despite the lack of light, even with the curtains pulled shut, his pupils gleamed.

"Can't say I've ever been on a group trip," he said.

His soft voice was silk against my skin. What was wrong with me? "From what I've heard, Varlac aren't much into family gatherings."

He cocked his head and studied me.

I shouldn't have said anything. *It's better if I ignore him.*

"And what exactly have you heard?" He draped a bent arm over the back of his seat.

"Oh, you know, the usual. How you spend most of your time cutting off wulfkin heads, dine on our blood, and bathe in the riches you steal from packs."

He chuckled. "We sure have a terrible rap, and such exaggerated stories. How can you bear speaking to me?"

"It's difficult."

Ash raised her muzzle and bellowed out a howl. A few wulfkin joined in, including Enre. The sounds vibrated through my body, rousing my wolf to attention. When more wulfkin jumped into the chant, I couldn't resist the lure to release a howl too.

It was liberating. When Enre glanced my way, I scowled. How dare he make me enjoy myself in his company!

Ivitka, our designated driver, climbed in. Everyone broke into a cheer of excitement. "This is more like it," Ivitka said. "Time to go."

Ash brushed past my leg, strangling herself in the process, to reach Enre. Her tongue dangled out of her mouth, her front paw stretching toward him.

I rubbed her ear and attempted to draw her backward by pulling on her leash. Enre scratched her head.

When Ash whimpered, I asked, "Want to swap? She might settle down."

He shrugged, stood, and then inched closer. But Ash refused to budge from the aisle in front of my seat, trapping me in. Ash gawked at Enre with huge, adoring eyes. He stepped over her, and I scooted against the window.

The vehicle's engine groaned and grunted awake, and the pack clapped and cheered. Enre flopped down beside me. Ash leapt onto him, her front paws on his shoulders, her sticky tongue licking his cheek.

I chuckled but stayed in my corner, trapped by Enre endeavoring to throw off a two- hundred-pound wulfkin. Soon, he succeeded, and we sat shoulder to shoulder. Ash was there too, her chin resting on Enre's thigh. He scratched her head.

"Looks like we're stuck," he said, giving me a sly grin. "She only behaves this way with Nic."

"I do have a way with the ladies."

"Well, considering Ash is still in her mid-teens, I'm not sure you should say that out loud."

He glanced at Ash and rubbed her ear. "She's lonely. And I'm sure I remind her of your brother."

Ash barked once.

Enre shifted and stretched his arm across the seat behind me. "Wake me up if I snore." He shut his eyes.

Despite us sitting mostly alone and in the dark, Enre didn't make one move. Not that I craved it … Of course not. It was what I expected from him. Still, the niggling fire from where his thigh touched mine spread through me. Stealing glances wasn't helping matters, no matter how much I studied the sharp edges of his cheekbones, the stubble covering his square jawline, or the lusciousness of his lips. How would he react if I kissed him? His scent was hypnotizing, tingling my insides.

Ash stared at me, her pointy ears up.

Enre had made it obvious that he was only here for insider information on the pack. I was his stepping-stone.

I settled into the seat and hugged my arms across my chest.

My nose tickled. Knowing my luck, it was probably a persistent mosquito. I swatted it away, but it returned. Grumbling, I twisted to hide in the pillow. Wait, why did my pillow smell of musky wulfkin?

My eyelids flipped open, and my face was buried in Enre's chest.

I straightened in the seat and wiped my mouth, praying I hadn't drooled on him. From the aisle, Ash watched us.

Enre wore a stupid grin. "Knew it wouldn't be long before we slept together."

"Real funny." I scanned the empty bus, with exception of the bus driver who sat there, watching us with an arched brow, and my pulse ran two notches too fast. "Where is everyone?"

"They got off."

I grabbed my bag off the floor and shot up.

He made a swiping motion with one hand, stopping in the middle of his chest, and glanced down at his shirt. "You drool?"

Fire claimed my cheeks. Thank goodness for the dimness. "You going to just sit there?"

Enre got up and took a step past Ash, giving me space to pass him. "I feel dirty now, violated." Amusement laced his words.

Refusing to meet his gaze, I unlatched Ash from the back doors of the bus and hooked the leash on her collar. We hurried off the bus, Ash taking the lead, dragging me behind.

Outside, the cold, damp air soaked my clothes, but once I changed into wolf form, I'd barely sense it. I couldn't wait.

Lights from the vehicle lit up the blanket of snow coating the narrow parking lot. No other cars were there. Farther ahead, the enormous fir trees towering over us had to be at least one hundred feet tall. Lush foliage with long branches, laden in snow, hung low around the trunks, resembling the perfect Christmas tree. To my right, a white clearing between the spectacular firs revealed footprints leading into Rusenski Lom Nature Park. My insides jumped with excitement to be free. The park was protected and owned by the Ruse council, meaning people were forbidden from living in these woods. If this weren't the case, Father would have set us up as rangers to live here years ago.

Enre emerged from the bus. "What happens now?" He hugged himself, rubbing his arms for warmth.

"This is your chance to go and have a bit of fun. Release your wolf, run wild, and enjoy, but you must return here just after dusk tomorrow."

"Why? What happens? We turn into pumpkins?"

I rolled my eyes. "We return to the circus. That's what."

The bus started up, a great backfire exploding. We didn't need humans suspecting anyone of trekking into the woods during the night. It might spark a massive search and reveal monster wolves in the national park.

Ash tugged at her leash and dragged me into the clearing. I stumbled over a dead log and kept slipping on the freshly fallen snow while I stared behind at the bus leaving. No sign of Enre. Hadn't taken him long to jump into action … but who could blame him?

My flesh already rippled with the urgency to transform. After a short stint of running and finding the familiar huge tree, I yanked on Ash's chain. "Stop."

Her jaws snapped at me, but she stopped, though she continued to whine.

"Calm down. Give me a few seconds to get ready. Geez, impatient much?" I unlatched the leash from Ash's neck. "Now, stay."

The bright moon revealed her ears, rotating like a radar dish, taking in the crunch of footsteps from other wulfkin running wild in the distance.

In a rush, I stripped and stashed my clothes, shoes, and backpack inside the hollow at the base of the tree, stuffing them deep. The snow wouldn't reach them. Before I stood, my wolf flooded me, pushing with urgency and flowing free. Silver fur covered and embraced me, and I dropped on all fours with a howl roaring past my throat, echoing through the dark.

Ash's voice joined in with the chorus of several other wolves in the area. My heart drummed against my rib cage.

My muzzle grazed Ash's side. Together, we launched into a fast romp, dodging trees and letting the wind sideswipe us. This was living, and I couldn't wait until we moved to Transylvania in the Carpathian woods forever.

The whole night and day had passed too quickly. During our run, we'd crossed paths with a few of the other wulfkin, but surprisingly not Enre. I wondered where he'd gotten off to.

Now the sun was vanishing behind the horizon of trees as the second night closed in. Ash and I, in wolf form, squatted near shrubs several feet from the parking lot, watching the wulfkin emerge from the woods in human form, climbing onto the bus, chatting, and laughing. Father had demanded I remain in the forest with Ash for a second night in case the authorities were still snooping. They'd pick us up the next morning. The other wulfkin had been told so they wouldn't make a huge deal about our absence.

The snow on my belly cooled the adrenaline. We'd run for most of the day and chased endless rabbits. Ash's heavy breaths steamed against my side, and the scent of her last meal of wild boar floated in the air.

When the bus engine started, and the side door clanked shut, I became aware of a problem. Enre hadn't boarded the bus.

CHAPTER 14

ENRE

I leapt out from behind an overgrown shrub and released a short, sharp snarl. My paws sank into the snow.

Alena spun to face me. The backpack dangling from her mouth dropped to the ground, and her lips peeled over fangs. Her jaws snapped in my direction, her nose wrinkled with anger.

Ash pounced and crashed into my side, and then rebounded off me, stumbling. In wolf form, I overshadowed her, but who didn't love rough play? I nudged her aside and approached Alena, who scooped the belongings back into her mouth and trotted away, head high.

Alena's unblemished silver fur glistened each time the radiance from the waxing moon pierced the canopy.

She wore her stubbornness as armor. Didn't she realize donning her animal form meant letting the wolf take charge, being wild and free? She reminded me of Daciana, pushing me away. I should keep my distance, considering how my situation with Daciana had ended. She'd chosen a human over me. I'd accepted it, even congratulated her, but the rejection stung.

I'd come to Bulgaria for a simple task, no matter how much my wolf protested and demanded we claim Alena instead. I hadn't had sex for months, so that was the real problem.

With Ash by my side, I soon caught up to Alena, and the three of us ran deeper into the woods. The snow had stopped, and a light breeze blew. Alena's scent—earthy and sweet with lavender—wafted to my nose.

To my right, movement. I froze mid-step.

A rabbit?

I lunged after it, Ash on my tail, and captured the delicious morsel in seconds. New record.

Ash prowled close, snarling for her share. I dropped the dead animal into the snow, and Ash snatched it. Within a few quick bone-crunching bites, it slid down her throat.

We walked for another hour, maybe more, and Alena finally halted, near a small clearing. If I were alone, I'd have run halfway across the woods by now. Instead, we traipsed around like girls. Okay, fair enough, I was with two girls, but lucky for them, they were two females I enjoyed, and I wouldn't change our time together one bit.

Alena scanned the area encircled by pines with low-hanging branches. Only a thin layer of white covered the ground. She dropped her backpack near a tree, then shimmied out of her wolf form, and stood on two feet, completely nude, shivering and hugging herself.

My pulse drummed as my gaze traced the curved lines of her delicious breasts and the ruby, erect nipples. Her tapered waist and flat stomach led to stunning hips and long, firm legs. I craved her body wrapped around mine.

She reached for a coat from her bag, folded herself in it, slipped on her gloves, and stepped into boots.

No matter how much I told myself to keep a distance, I struggled to listen to my own advice. Not when the most gorgeous creature with admirable determination, loyalty, and courage stood a few paces away.

"Why didn't you get on the bus?" she asked while retrieving a leash from her pocket.

I can do bondage if she insists. "Come here, Ash," Alena said. Ash's whines tugged at my heart.

Alena's voice rose. "Ash, please. I can't lose you during the night." Ash retreated, her back legs bumping into a dead log.

I slipped out of wolf form, and the sudden iciness of the night slapped against my skin. "You don't have to tie her up. She'll stay with us."

Alena's head jerked in my direction, her gaze dipping south.

Oh yeah, she likes what she sees.

"How would you know? She's under my protection. I can't risk losing her in the park." She blew hot breath into her cupped hands.

I rubbed my arms, the cold settling into my bones. "Where's she going to go? The three of us can warm up together. I'll keep an eye on her. She's a wulfkin."

Alena shook her head. "You don't know what you're talking about."

Ash dashed behind a tree, and Alena chased after her.

"Wolves should be free, not tied up. She'll stay with us."

My teeth chattered. Ash slipped past Alena and scurried across to me, her body heat and fur a blessing. I crouched low and hugged her as both a show of protection and for warmth.

Alena shot me a glare and stomped back to the tree where she'd left her backpack. She rummaged in her bag and tossed a folded blanket my way.

I caught it with one hand. Animal fur—nice. "Put it on or you'll freeze."

I threw it over my shoulders and tugged it around my chest, figuring I should have been smart and grabbed my stash of clothes, too. Not that I planned to stay in human form for long anyway. Transforming heated our bodies. Despite the frostiness, our wolf forms were more resilient than our human ones, and a bit of chill wouldn't kill us.

"Why didn't you get on the bus?" She proceeded to collect branches, snapping them to check if they were dry.

"Why didn't you?" I knelt in the center of the clearing and flattened a circular patch of snow with a rock I found nearby.

Ash huddled next to me, her paws also stomping the ground in front of us. "Father told me to stay in the woods for another night with Ash, in case the police

were still searching the circus. The bus is coming for us first thing in the morning. What's your excuse?" She set an armful of branches by my side.

I constructed a small platform out of the branches, and then arranged the remaining sticks like a teepee.

"Spotted you two hiding from everyone else and was curious. No rush to return to the circus anyway, especially without you there."

"You ignored me for several days and now you miss me?" Snow crunched underfoot as she approached. "You should keep your lies straight."

"A bit harsh."

Alena stopped next to me, her coat slightly open across her chest. A glimpse at her cleavage, and my adrenaline spiked.

"Well, you weren't exactly honest with us," she said. "Like, why would you send your Varlac friend away so quickly?" She retrieved several pieces of scrunched-up paper from her pocket and strategically placed them in and around the pile of wood. With a quick flick of a lighter, she touched the flame to the paper.

I placed my cupped hands on either side of hers to stop the breeze from snuffing out our fire.

"No lie. I'm a Varlac, watching over your pack."

The papers lit, and soon the flames engulfed the sticks.

She turned to face me. "Why? Varlac always have ulterior motives, and don't give me that crap about how you don't."

It was generally the truth. She had me there. Except it wasn't what she thought. "Don't hate me because some other Varlac upset you."

"Even when their blood runs through your veins?" Jumping to her feet, she stormed into the forest. "I'm going to find more branches."

What had my family done to her?

I warmed myself by the swelling blaze, and Ash settled closer. The fire's reflection bounced off her patchwork fur of dark and light bronze. It was better if I kept away from Alena and finished what I came here for, but the heaviness in my gut demanded a different outcome.

I scratched Ash's ear. "Listen. I know you can understand me. Please, don't go anywhere. I'll be back, I promise. Stay."

Ash lifted her head, holding my gaze with her dark eyes, then settled her chin back down across her outstretched front paws. Her eyelids shut.

"Thank you. We won't be long."

Up on my feet, I hurried into the woods, following Alena's scent, determined to uncover her reasons for hating my family.

The wind velocity increased, and my feet were ice. I tightened the blanket around my shoulders, which did little to keep me warm, so I summoned my wolf. A great breath gushed from my lungs, misting the air in front of my face as I fell on all fours. Fur spread over my torso and limbs, and the cold vanished, replaced by an adrenaline rush to hunt down Alena. I released all human appearance and became one with my wolf. *This is how it should be.* Snatching the blanket in my mouth, in case she accused me of losing her property, I ran free through the woods, following her lavender scent.

Trees were easily dodged, colors muted, and the occasional spray of moonlight shone on the tree trunks and white powder coating the branches. This was life. The breeze carried Alena's sweet aroma, propelling me forward.

Swinging right, I pounced through knee-deep snow. A silhouette appeared in the distance. My target.

Alena turned toward me. Night stole her features until I got close, finding her arms filled with branches. Her wild, huge eyes held another emotion behind them. A familiar wildness—her wolf.

I dropped the blanket into the snow and shook my fur, climbing to my feet as a man. She stumbled backward into a tree, the sticks falling to the ground.

"You shouldn't have followed me." Her voice wavered.

I adored the effect I had on her. Smirking, I shortened the gap. "And why not?"

"Because you left Ash alone."

Less than a pace between us, I shoved some of the wood on the ground aside with my foot, ignoring the cold and welcoming the fire coursing through me.

"You don't give her enough credit. She'll be fine." A guttural tone resonated from inside me. My wolf nudged against my insides, insisting we take Alena now.

One of her eyebrows arched. "You always so reckless?"

"It's not recklessness to put trust in Ash."

Her breaths deepened, and her gaze dropped, checking me out. I could deal with that. "Why are you mad at me all the time?" I asked, rubbing the frostiness out of my arms.

Her mouth opened, but no words came out. For a long

moment, she remained there staring at me, and only the hoot of an owl sounded around us.

"So." I broke the silence, trying to fight a horrid shiver engulfing me. "You going to share that coat or let me freeze to death?"

"Turn back into a wolf if you're cold, or grab your blanket." Alena turned away, but I grabbed her elbow, adrenaline coursing through my veins.

"I know you feel it too," I said. "Our wolves call to each other."

She responded without looking my way. "If I gave in to her all the time, I'd be a wild wolf. We're wulfkin. We can't do that."

Those words sounded familiar, as if I'd heard them somewhere before. I lost my train of thought. My fingers buzzed. I scooped an arm around her back, bringing her tight against my chest, forcing her to face me. Every part of me yearned to strip her down and run my hands over her flesh.

She softened in my embrace, and her warm exhale unfurled over my face. A labyrinth twisted behind her pale-gray eyes, the same look she'd carried back in her trailer when her wolf took over and we made out. I was ready to dive in and get lost.

Lifting her chin, she pressed her lips to mine, stealing my breath.

I cupped the back of her neck and kissed her. She sucked on my lower lip and let out a tiny cry. Her taste had stayed in my mind since our last kiss, and now my arousal stood on end.

Pinning her between me and the tree, I leaned closer, a blaze raging inside me. She tugged open her coat, welcoming me.

My arms snaked around her tiny waist, her bouncy breasts against me, and I drank in her scorching heat.

The breeze shifted, flapping the edges of the coat we shared and sending a chill across my back, but I was drowning in the inferno between Alena and me, loving every second.

Her gloved hand slithered down between our chests and wrapped around my cock. My lips broke from hers; a groan echoed in my throat.

A sly grin split her pouty mouth, and I was lost. "Turn around," I said.

"What?" She released her grip. I wanted her touch back. "Bend over."

Her eyes widened the same time as her mouth.

I nudged her shoulder away from me, and she now faced the tree. She stared over her shoulder at me with a raised eyebrow but never told me to back off.

Pushing the coat away from her butt, I uncovered the most delicious backside and long legs. I grasped her hips and heaved them toward me. Sliding my hand down her ass and to her inner thigh, I parted her legs. Her breath hitched.

"How much do you need me?" I asked as I stroked the gorgeous curve of her ass, sliding lower to the burning passion between her legs. So temptingly wet. My wolf stretched inside me, commanding we claim her this very second.

Alena's response was a whimper, and gravelly moans, which I took as her ferocious desire to accept me.

Kneeling in the icy snow behind her, her beauty overtook me, her sexiness, her fire. Her seductive, feminine fragrance filled my senses, fogging my thoughts. I grasped her hips and tasted her with long licks. Her quivering beneath my touch had me so hard it ached. Clasping her sweetness around my mouth resulted in her purring and twitching beneath me. I tongued her until her knees wobbled and threatened to collapse.

"I'm dying to sink into you." My body pulsated with desire.

I inserted two fingers inside her, sliding them back and forth. Her pelvis ground back and forth, her breaths louder, quicker.

Her body trembled, and the escalating screams were driving me insane in anticipation.

Fuck, she had me wound tight.

Taking mock bites out of her butt, I withdrew my hold and stood. Hard as steel, I was ready to party.

Without notice, she pulled her gorgeous ass away and turned to face me. Her cheeks blushed bright red, her eyes still caught in the elysian pleasure, and she dug a hand into her coat's pocket.

Never saying a word, she stood there, her voluptuous breasts rising and falling with each fast breath, nipples taut. She held a leash.

"You dirty, dirty girl." My words lowered. "Give it here."

She shook her head and wore the grin of a wicked temptress about to get her way.

I skimmed a hand around the back of her head and drew her closer, my lips taking hers. Our tongues entwined, and her kisses matched my hunger and ferocity.

Sliding the leash out of her grasp, I broke our kiss and threw one end of the leather over the lowest, thickest branch of the tree alongside us. Most of the snow remained on the ends of the branches. We were unlikely to be showered in snow.

Alena didn't hesitate to jump up and snatch the ends, one in each fist, her feet suspended off the ground. A sexy, tormenting grin captured her mouth.

Kicking her boots off, her tiny feet reached out for me, the tips of her toes on either side of my waist, curling inward, pulling me closer. Every nerve ending in my body suddenly focused on those points of contact. My eyes focused on her delectable body.

I grabbed both of her ankles and spread her legs wide, getting hornier by the second at the view.

"You just going to stare?" Her voice was as engorged with lust as were her breasts. "Oh, babe, I'm going to fuck you like I've fantasized since we first met."

My fingers inched up her toned legs toward her hips. She extended her legs wide open for me … Oh, her acrobatic ability was coming in very handy. I gripped the underside of her thighs, positioning my tip into her entrance. The sensation of her heat against my cock sent shivers down my spine.

"Kiss me," I begged.

Wildfire burned behind her eyes. Her lips brushed mine, soft, warm, and inviting. I slid inside of her, spreading her clenching walls.

She mewled.

Grasping her hips, I rocked into her, back and forth, our movements simultaneous, our rhythm quickening. My pulse drummed, and with each delicious smacking sound, my balls tightened.

I hammered into her as her legs tightened even more around my waist. We moved together, gasps escalating, our bodies covered with a thin layer of sweat despite the cold.

She arched backward, echoing passionate screams. I slid my fingers between our bellies, dove deeper to her melting bud and rubbed it ferociously with my thumb.

"Come for me, Alena."

A charge streamed through me, and I wrestled to take another breath. We were both on the brink of exploding. And suddenly her body shuddered. The constriction on my erection tipped me over, and my body throbbed into her.

My arms entwined around her as she released the leash,

falling into my embrace. Her face snuggled into the nest between my neck and shoulder, her inhales loud and fast.

As I fought for my next breath, we stayed that way, my heartbeat matching her racing pulse.

Our gazes met.

"I could do that every day with you," she whispered.

"Just once a day? Not enough for me, babe." I withdrew myself as her feet dropped to the ground. She drew the coat tightly around her body, rubbing her arms.

Placing a kiss on her nose, I said, "I'd love to steal you and take you away forever."

Softness caressed her expression as she stared at me without a trace of hatred. Was it her or her wolf who looked at me with such desire?

A whimper sounded in the woods. Alena's head shot up, her expression transformed into concern.

"We should go to Ash," she said and grabbed the leash, slipping it off the branch. She stepped into her discarded snow-covered boots.

"Then maybe we can continue?"

She offered me a deliciously wicked wink and trudged ahead in the snow, passing me. A few trees behind me, Ash trotted in our direction, her ears low.

"I'll take her back and stay with her," Alena said, already at Ash's side, scratching her head. "The bus will be coming for us before daylight."

"I'm going to get us some food." I slipped into wolf form, embracing the sudden warmth, while the exhilarating excitement of having had sex with Alena had my arousal resurfacing and clinging to me like a straitjacket. Sprinting in the opposite direction, I was determined to take down the first animal I encountered and impress Alena with my hunting skills.

CHAPTER 15

I slumped in my seat at the back of the bus, my legs stretched out along the seat. Our driver, Ivitka, blared a rock song on the radio as the bus rattled down the freeway. The tiny lights running down the aisle of the bus cut through the four a.m. darkness.

"The wild boar you caught was so sweet." I eyed Enre, who reclined in the seat directly across from mine. He wore the wrinkly jeans and jacket he'd stashed in a dead log while in the woods.

Ash's head popped up from her spot in the aisle between us, ears perked. Her long tongue extended, and she licked her nose. If we offered her more chow, she'd gobble it.

Enre studied me with his fiery, blue gaze and blew me a kiss.

My first instinct urged me to go to him, crawl across his lap, and ride him. It had been on my mind since we woke up in the forest, huddled near the dwindling fire. Yesterday, my wolf had taken over again, and before I'd known it, Enre and I were having sex. But I didn't regret a single minute.

Enre had stayed in the woods for me, kept me warm, and

hunted for our food. Why would he bother unless he had feelings for me? Had I been wrong the other night about him using me? What if he was here to help our pack?

Since arriving at the circus, Enre had helped me attempt to break out Nicolai and connected with Ash, and our wolves had bonded. The rest of the pack trod with care around me because of Father, but Enre didn't, and I liked that.

Enre shifted in his seat, arms folded across his chest. "If you keep staring at me, I can't control what I'll do next."

"When have you ever held back?"

"If you want me, say so. I'm yours." He returned to slumber mode.

How do you respond to that? My body quivered, and I didn't trust my voice. I'd likely invite him to my place, and the cogs in my head whirled. He'd return to Hungary soon enough, and hopefully with me on his mind, he'd have only good news to report back to his clan.

I couldn't believe I was even contemplating spending more time with him, considering his family and their purpose.

Ash whimpered. I leaned over to scratch her ear. "We're almost home."

"She doesn't want to return to her cage," Enre said, reminding me of Nicolai.

My stomach churned at the thought of my brother. How could I be enjoying myself when Nicolai remained locked in a cage? Shit, the full moon was tomorrow night, and instead of helping my brother, I had followed Father's instructions to stay in the woods. He kept me at a distance on purpose.

I'd visit Nicolai in prison this morning and bring him more food and clothes, but not before I insisted that Father tell me his plans. If he didn't … then I'd go against his wishes and rescue Nicolai tonight. This time, I'd succeed. Whatever it took. Maybe Enre would join me again, and we'd create a foolproof plan. It would have to work this time.

"No one likes being locked up." Enre's voice snapped me out of my thoughts, and for a smidgen of a second, I swore he referred to Nicolai. But he spoke of Ash.

"When we move to a new place," I said, "Ash can roam free in the woods. We'll all be free."

Enre stared at me with a hooded gaze, the sexiness replaced by darkness. "Freedom always comes at a cost," he said.

Agreed. Father had made the final decision to take the lives of the few wulfkin who occupied Transylvania after Sandulf killed two of our scouts. It never sat right with me, but it was the way of the wulfkin. No pack would openly accept another onto their land.

An ache spread behind my rib cage. Too many emotions tugged me in different directions. I couldn't deal with this now. Not with the worry in my stomach for Nicolai. It was as if my insides were a coliseum with warriors tearing each other to shreds.

I hugged my knees to my chest, focusing on the grunting engine of the bus and the crunch of the chains on our wheels against the snowy asphalt. The detention center would open at nine. I'd be there. My gaze focused on the trees we passed outside, their hypnotic sway in the breeze.

When the front doors squeaked open, I stirred awake, as did Enre and Ash. The lights inside the bus were off, and the first hints of orange streaks lit up the horizon outside the windows.

I tapped Ash on her back, and she bounced to her feet, snarling in protest. Enre stretched his arms and released a yawn.

I took the lead with Ash at my heels.

Outside, a blustery wind blew, and the snow fell as a thick

covering through the dark, making it difficult to see. Perfect coverage if the police were nearby.

My boots sank in snow with each step, and I waved for Ash to follow. "Let's go."

Parking at the rear of the circus concealed us well. I tugged the hood over my head and hurried amid the trailers buried beneath the blanket of night. We soon reached Ash's trailer. I hated locking her up too, but it was for her own good. I couldn't put her in jeopardy at the hands of the humans. After unbolting the door, I knelt next to her.

"I'm sorry. It won't be long until we move and you can be free. Maybe before that, you'll change back." I wrapped an arm around her neck and hugged her. Ash pressed against me, her warmth flowing in waves. "Nicolai should be home soon."

Her head jerked up, her snout brushing my chin.

She missed Nicolai almost as much as I did. But I couldn't leave her outside for long.

Not with police snooping around. Footfalls crunched behind me.

Enre. He moved closer and patted Ash on the head. "Come on." He climbed the steps and pushed open the door to her trailer. "I'll return and spend the day with you. How does that sound?"

Ash grunted at first, then leapt toward Enre and past him. Rushing inside, I led her into the cage, shut the door, and snapped the lock.

Soon enough, I trudged toward my home, figuring with the sun still lingering on the horizon it'd be too early to bug Father about Nicolai or to find out the results of the police and their search warrant. Enre remained by my side.

"Your place is in the opposite direction," I said. Despite my intentions with Enre in the bus, now that I'd arrived at the circus … Reality had an odd way of zapping the fun out of life.

"Thought I'd walk you home."

I hugged myself for heat. Enre wrapped an arm around my shoulders, drawing me close to his side.

"It's promising to be a cold day," he said. "Let me know if you need extra heat." I didn't pull away but soaked in his fiery warmth.

The response *yes please* danced at the front of my mind, but that wasn't going to happen. Today, I had to get Nicolai out of prison if Father hadn't made progress. "My place has plenty of insulation and heating. Anyway, you promised to spend the day with Ash. I appreciate that, but you don't have to."

"I want to. She's a nice kid who's scared and lonely. I can relate."

"Really? You, scared and lonely? Never. I picture you with girls hanging onto you.

You've yet to show fear of anything."

He chuckled. "No one is fearless. And the only girl hanging on me is you."

We stopped near my trailer. The wind whistled between the buildings, and winter settled into my veins. Shadows from nearby trailers cast a heavy mood; except, with Enre by my side, I felt invincible. That was ludicrous, but the way our wolves connected eliminated my dread, my vulnerability. It was as if I sensed his emotions before he showed them, and they affected my wolf. His confidence poured through me. Earlier, in the woods, my arousal had been beyond control. I wouldn't change that moment.

The lights to the mess tent lit up. Someone was awake.

Enre tightened his hold on my waist and pressed my back against the trailer, his mouth inches from mine. His muskiness and timber scent had my breath sprinting.

"Are you certain you don't want company?" His lips grazed mine ever so slightly, weakening my knees, but I pulled back.

"Tease," I said.

"No teasing. I'm offering everything I have—me. We could run away and never return."

His words offered a haunting appeal. I suspected if I agreed, he'd insist we leave that very second. But what, specifically, did he want to run away from? Was his life as a Varlac that bad? I imagined him living in Hungary with servants who probably filed his claws and provided him with the finest foods on a silver platter. No worries. How could that be difficult?

"Don't people usually run away to *join* the circus?" I raised an eyebrow. A scratching sound from inside my trailer jerked our attention to the door. Enre sniffed the air. "What's that?"

I reached for the handle. I'd forgotten about leaving the stray dog inside. He'd had plenty of water and snacks while we were gone.

The moment I opened the door, the doggy leapt out and turned to face us several paces away. My magenta leotard dangled from his mouth. Was that a rip?

"Bad boy." I crept closer. "That's my favorite outfit. Drop it. Now." He growled and bolted for the mess tent.

"I'll get him." Enre laughed and broke into a run, chasing the pooch.

I was hot on their heels. If Father saw the runaway, he'd make me take him to the pound.

The rascal raced under trailers, across the grounds, making it hard to keep up with him. The dog scrambled into the mess tent.

"Crap."

Enre also vanished inside.

When I entered, a wall of tension smacked into me. I froze, my inhales bottlenecking in my chest.

Four wulfkin turned toward me: Enre, Father, Damir, and Lutia.

Lutia was one of our undercover spies and scouts who had obtained valuable information. She'd infiltrated the Transylvanian pack for over a year and gained Sandulf's trust. Her reconnaissance party must have returned from searching for potential territories in case Romania didn't work out.

She snarled, and her glare threw knives in Enre's direction.

He stood close to the entrance, my dog locked in his embrace. His expression resembled someone who'd just witnessed his own death.

CHAPTER 16

ENRE

*L*utia's lips twisted. A snarl rolled through her gullet, and her shoulders hunched forward.

I'd had no idea the bitch was from the Bulgarian pack this whole time.

For close to sixteen months, she'd lived as a member of our family in Transylvania, shared meat with us, and pretended to care, before attempting to kill Daciana, framing her for a human death, and leaving me to die in the cave with the dracwulf. If Lutia and I were alone, I would have snapped her neck. And that was me being nice.

The mutt in my arms whimpered, and I set him down. Three other wulfkin stared my way. Fog blurred my thoughts. I'd gotten myself wedged in this corner real tight.

After Daciana had taken over as my pack's alpha, Lutia ran away. So, was she playing the same game with this pack, or had she been providing insider information to our enemy all along? The latter notion had my muscles knotted.

For those few seconds when no one said a word, only Lutia and I knew the severity of my situation. She held my life in her hands.

"Lutia," Maxim said, "what's wrong?"

She flicked strands of blonde hair over her face, and movement behind Lutia's narrow eyes showed panic.

"Why's he here?" Her shrill voice irritated me as much as it had back in Romania. Alena stared at me, the dog now in her arms.

If the earth were to ever open up and swallow me, this would have been the perfect moment. But I refused to give Lutia satisfaction. I stepped closer.

She recoiled toward Maxim. She had encouraged Sandulf to toss me to the dracwulf and even had the nerve to pay me a visit in the dracwulf's cave, feigning care while she gave me food. My jawbone twitched with the expectancy of sinking my fangs into her jugular.

"How long has she been in your pack?" I addressed Maxim, who wore a slack expression.

"Lutia's been with us since she was a child. Why?"

Lutia cocked her head in Blackie's direction. "Take Enre to a cage, now."

"Wait. What?" Alena approached, a grimace capturing her delicate face.

I hurried toward Lutia, eager to shut her up, but Blackie tackled me. Breaths gushed free, and my face hit the dirt floor with a thud. The size of a rhino, Blackie sat on my back, his muddy scent and perspiration choking me.

"Get off him!" Alena called out.

"Hey, Lutia told me to take him, and I've wanted to do that since I met this bastard." Blackie sniggered and climbed off me, but not before his boot sharply connected with my ribs.

A gush of air caught in my lungs. "Enough," Maxim said.

I winced and took a few deep inhales. He'd get his chance to feel my fists. I climbed to my feet.

"What is going on?" Maxim's voice pitched several deci-bels too high.

"Lutia killed a human, and for that I will gladly issue her punishment now." I shook myself, my legs tense.

Lutia huffed and glared my way, her posture rigid. I wouldn't be surprised if she burst into her wolf form, and perhaps that would make her keep her trap shut.

She brushed a blonde strand behind her ear. "Who are you to dish out anything?

You're—"

"He's a Varlac," Alena interrupted, her eyes fixed on me, packed with uncertainty. "How can you be sure she killed anyone? Was she reported to the Varlac? Is that why you visited us? For Lutia?"

"No," Lutia butted in. "He's from the Transylvanian pack. He followed Sandulf's orders."

The hairs on the back of my neck bristled, and cement filled my stomach. I stepped toward the exit. The lies were tightening around my throat. With her accusations and Maxim already suspecting me, continuing to live would be pushing my luck. *Fuck.*

"Did you even love Sandulf?" I asked. "Or were the tears and anger fake too?" Lutia's left eye twitched.

I continued, ready to take her down with me. "You were ready to leave Maxim's pack for Sandulf's, weren't you? I overheard you and Sandulf conspiring. You butchered a human to frame Daciana. You insisted Sandulf let the dracwulf kill me. And you told Sandulf you'd personally sneak him into this pack so he could murder Maxim."

"Shut your mouth!" A snarl followed, and her fists knotted by her sides. "You'd do anything for your opportu-nity at female alpha."

"Quiet," Lutia spat. "You chased Daciana, but she didn't want you. I bet that stung. Then she took a human lover. *She's* the one who revealed us to humans, and then she killed *my* Sandulf. The Varlac should come for her."

Maxim placed a hand on Lutia's shoulder, and she retreated, her gaze locked on the ground. Her fingers were twisted against her gut, and silent words dribbled from her mouth.

"What's going on?" Alena stared at me as if seeing me for the first time. "Who are you really?" Maxim asked.

Blackie lunged toward me, and my muddled mind made me slow to react. He shoved me into the center of the mess tent.

I stumbled forward. The wolf rippled beneath my skin, demanding release. There was no doubt which reaction was required here. Flight was out of the question. This was fight time. Except the odds weren't in my favor. I doubted Alena would attack, but I didn't put it past the other three wulfkin to have a go at me.

Maxim's brow creased. The word *die* might as well have been inked on Lutia's forehead. Blackie was still a meathead. And then there was Alena. Her cheeks paled, and the way her body stiffened, waiting for a response, sent a spasm of guilt through me. She held her breath. Her pain was the hardest to swallow. I'd let her down.

"What are you waiting for?" Lutia growled. "Get him before he runs." I'd never realized I could hate Lutia even more. *Fucking bitch.*

Facing the alpha, I knew any further secrets would kill me quicker. "Maxim, you've only been fair to me since I arrived, and I respect you for that. Give me a moment to explain this to you. Varlac to wulfkin."

"So you admit you're from the Transylvanian pack?" Maxim asked.

My spine hardened. "I am a Varlac. Lutia did slaughter a

human to frame Daciana, and it will bring the Varlac ruler to your pack. And yes, I am from Romania, but—"

Maxim waved a hand and shot a glare to Blackie. "Get him out of here. Lock him up." He turned to Lutia. "You," he shouted, "tell me what you've been up to!"

The air in the tent thickened, and my wolf clawed harder for release. Blackie stomped near, his lips peeling back over glistening teeth.

Fuck if I'd allow him to lay another hand on me. He charged again. I jumped out of his path at the last moment, spun, and kicked his backside, propelling him headfirst into a table. He crashed to the ground.

"I don't need an escort," I said.

Maxim was at my side. I hadn't sensed him move. "You lied about which pack you were allied with and why you were here, giving me the right to punish you as I see fit. It's a Varlac rule, which I'm sure you're well familiar with. It seems your family has a knack for breaking them." His low, scratchy voice reminded me of Sandulf when he had admitted I was dead to him.

Blackie collided with my back. My head whacked against the ground, and my vision danced for those few seconds. He grabbed my ankles and dragged me out of the tent and onto the ground, now snow mixed with mud.

My last vision was of Alena, a hand plastered to her mouth, her head shaking.

I never should have come to the circus. Falling in love with the enemy always got you in trouble—or killed.

---

*B*lackie thumped his palm into my shoulder blade and pushed me into the second empty cage, alongside Ash's. He slammed the bars closed behind me.

Ash eyed Blackie. The tiny slits high on the wall threw shards of light across her flattened ears and creased nose.

"Enjoy the few hours you have left, *traitor.*"

I easily could have taken him on the way to the cage, but then what? Return to Transylvania and wait for the forty or so wulfkin to attack? That would be if my father didn't get to me first. We didn't stand a chance. Somehow I had to turn the predicament in my favor and avoid dying in the process. Until then, I'd play prisoner.

My wolf thrashed inside, eager to give this wulfkin the beating he deserved. I turned to face Blackie, who stood outside the cage, his arms crossed.

"When I get out, you're the first person I'm coming for," I said.

The wulfkin huffed, thrust out his chin, and burst into a wail of hyena-like chuckles. "Can't wait. You may have tricked Alena into believing you were someone else, but I saw through you from the start. Right through your shifty eyes."

"Shifty eyes? Didn't realize you were checking me out, but you're not my type. Try the local zoo, I believe they have a gorilla that might interest you."

A scowl crossed the wulfkin's face. He marched out of the trailer and slammed the door.

Ash grumbled.

"Agree, he's a dimwit. Good to know I'm not the only one who doesn't like him."

Shadows filled the enclosure. The wind whistled outside, some of it finding a way indoors through slivers of cracks in the walls.

I paced in circles around the enclosure, straw crunching beneath my boots. Every hindsight in the world wouldn't help me. My situation had derailed fast. All I had was the minuscule hope that Maxim wasn't the alpha Sandulf had portrayed him to be.

It might explain why Maxim hadn't delivered his punishment the moment he found out I was from Transylvania. I was a traitor, like Blackie put it. If that had been Sandulf, he would have killed me on the spot, no hesitation. But considering how Sandulf turned out, perhaps his methods weren't a great example.

I sat on the floor, near Ash's cage, and she joined me. Her fur poked through the bars and against me, along with her radiating warmth.

"You're probably wondering the same thing." I scratched her head. "How did we end up in here?"

She whimpered at a low pitch. I took that as agreement.

"Wish I could work out how to set you free from your wolf form." I rubbed her ear, and she slid onto her side, giving me easier access. "Looks like we're both stuck for now."

We sat for who knows how long. When I'd lost feeling in my toes, I contemplated stripping and changing into wolf form. Up on my feet, I unbuttoned my coat. The creak of the door unlatching stopped me.

Ash jumped to her feet, sniffing the air, and released a throaty growl.

I shook my legs and arms to boost the blood's circulation, ready for the unwanted visitor.

Lutia entered. The faint light from outside highlighted her face. A fresh bruise on her cheek, a dash of purple under her eye, and a cut on her lower lip said it all.

"Is that all you got for betraying this pack? Perhaps Sandulf was wrong about Maxim, after all."

"Why did you come to the circus?" She fiddled with her blonde hair, wrapping a strand around a finger. "I might get kicked out because of you, and only if I'm lucky will they not report me to the Varlac. If I go down, I'm dragging you into hell with me."

"You're not going anywhere until I make you pay for the shit you caused in Transylvania. You seem to forget I am actually a Varlac."

"Yeah, yeah, a Varlac who has no standing until he gets a pack of his own." She rolled her eyes. "Big threat when you're behind bars. Now listen, I'm a fool for even considering this, but I'll help you save your pack."

My thoughts froze. Had I heard her right? "Why would I believe you?"

She strolled along the narrow passage between the wall of the trailer and our cages. "Because there are wulfkin out there right now deciding on how to best finish you off. Damir seems intent on using his hands to rip your head off your shoulders while Maxim is leaning toward several pack members ending you with an old-fashioned fox hunt. Yeah, you're the fox."

Lutia sauntered closer, her fingers running along the metal bars as she passed. "Mind you, there are several others who have suggested more creative ways to eliminate you."

I refused to pay attention to her exaggeration, despite the boulder expanding in my gut.

When Lutia passed the next cage, Ash leapt forward, teeth exposed. Lutia yelped and flinched, her back pinned flat against the wall.

Ash threaded a paw through the bars and reached for flesh. "Pesky mutt."

Ash snarled, drool seeping from her fangs.

"Good, Ash. Tear her leg off," I said, just as Lutia lunged to the side in front of me, her cheeks flushing and inhales quickening. "You're not any safer over here." I cracked my neck and approached the bars.

Her retort flew fast. "You've always been an idiot. Maybe

the dracwulf should have finished you off. And to think Sandulf actually contemplated giving you his pack when he retired. But I convinced him you'd be a threat because of your Varlac lineage."

Every part of me vibrated from the fury pumping in my veins. "You're doing a wonderful job of convincing me to give a shit about your plan."

Her posture straight, Lutia said nothing at first. Silence fell between us. Only Ash's occasional low growls resonated through the trailer.

"That's the thing." Lutia broke the stillness. "Everything I did was for Maxim. His orders were to cause disarray in the pack so he could attack without being detected.

Fewer casualties on his side. But after spending more time with Sandulf, I started thinking differently. I decided to join him, help him fend off the Bulgarian pack. But then that bitch, Daciana, ruined the plan." With a flick of her hand, she flung loose strands of ashen hair from her pinched face. "Why can't anyone see that Daciana caused the pack's problems? She was dating a human, exposing us to him. It led to Sandulf's death."

"I bet *not* being appointed female alpha aided in your decision."

She blew warm air into her cupped hands. Ash yipped in her direction.

"That had zero to do with it. But now Sandulf's dead, and … " She shrugged. "I want to do the right thing. Give him what he wanted—protect his pack. But I can't do it on my own."

I struggled to respond. Every fiber in my body screamed to escape from the cage and make this squirmy weasel pay with her own life. Wulfkin who betrayed their family on a whim were more dangerous than your worst enemy. They followed no logic and had only one instinct—to protect their own ass. Without a doubt, they had to be stamped out.

An icy breeze whistled under the trailer's door, shaking it against its hinges, and doing little to cool the inferno in my chest.

My arm snapped through the bars, and I snatched a handful of Lutia's jacket, jerking her forward, whacking her face into the metal cage.

She yelped and squirmed in my grip.

Ash made a jumbled whimpering noise. She wanted in on the action. I leaned in. "Why shouldn't I kill you right now?"

"Because I can convince Maxim to spare your life."

I softened my grip. She recoiled. I yanked her back again, banging her chest into the bars again. "I'm still waiting for a reason not to kill you."

"Don't you listen? I just told you. I'll tell Maxim that if he doesn't free you and forget Transylvania, I'll turn myself in to the Varlac and tell them I murdered a human on his command. He'd be targeted by the Varlac and punished."

She had a backbone, I'd give her that. Except, I suspected her threat to the alpha would be empty and she'd somehow manage to drag the Varlac into this mess without bringing any attention to herself. Then hell would break loose on everyone else.

"And what do you get out of this?" I mushed her face against the bars. "I get to be part of your pack again?" Her eyebrows lifted.

I fought the urge to laugh at how ridiculous she looked.

"We start fresh with you as pack leader. It's what you need to gain your parents' approval."

Her response caught me off guard, and I loosened my hold. She slipped free and leapt from my reach, rubbing the red line indented into the side of her nose.

Ash gnashed her jaws at Lutia, whose scowl could have

scared a field of crows as she made for the door. It slammed shut behind her.

Lutia was broken in the worst possible way, and next time I laid my hands on her, she wouldn't walk away.

The door handle creaked again. Ash leapt toward the entrance, a whine at the back of her throat.

Maxim strolled inside, flanked by two goons.

My throat dried up, and I couldn't help but be reminded of Lutia's threat about the alpha deciding how best to kill me.

I retreated into the corner, convinced I would die today. But then again, I'd been wrong before.

CHAPTER 17

ALENA

I sighed in the chair across from Sonia, her divining twigs and tarot cards splayed out on the table between us. After Father had brushed me away, saying he didn't have time to talk right then, I'd shuffled to Sonia's trailer.

"I'm an idiot."

The faint smell of sandalwood drifting through her trailer didn't settle my nerves. "I thought my dreams were a prediction, you know. Maybe I wanted to believe that

Enre had arrived for me." The next words refused to come because voicing them would make them real. When they did flow, they were barely a whisper. "But my dreams were a warning about him, weren't they?"

I thumped my forehead onto the table. The wolf whined inside me, rolling and nudging. Images of what Enre and I did in the woods sent shivers up my thighs ... and elsewhere. Couldn't my body see I had been used? I'd behaved like some desperate wulfkin in heat while Enre played me to get insider information.

"How could I not see through his charm?"

Sonia patted my arm. "Honey, don't blame yourself. He's a fine specimen of a wulfkin, and most of the girls in the pack have been hoping for a chance with him."

"You're not helping. He's our enemy, remember?" I lifted my head, and a tarot card stuck to my brow.

Sonia was quick to snatch it. She hummed as she studied it, her lips tightened. "Interesting."

"What?"

She set the card face up on the table.

It showed a massive medieval tower pitched on a mountain with lightning bolts striking it from blackened skies. The structure was burning and crumbling, people leaping out of windows. It was the same card from an earlier reading. Tower—the destruction card.

My stomach clenched. I hated that card.

Sonia fiddled with the twigs around the table, turning them over repeatedly. The sound was hypnotic.

"The tower card's been coming up for the past few weeks." She tapped it with a crimson fingernail. "Change is imminent. And this is a chaotic type of change, where everything we know will be twisted on its head."

"Not a fan of it."

Sonia collected the tarot pack in one swipe and set them at the corner of the table. "Sometimes change is necessary. We should have left this place months ago. Destiny is forcing us because we've been dragging our feet."

"What can we do?" I inched closer to the edge of my seat.

"Very little. The wheels are in motion, so be prepared for a hard landing."

A sinking sensation plummeted through my insides. "How can you be so calm when you pronounce doom and gloom?"

Sonia shrugged. "Panic isn't going to help."

"It helps me." Up on my feet, I tugged down on my jacket

and slipped the hood on with shaky hands. So, life was going to get worse. Great. "Thanks for listening to my ramblings. I better go feed Ash, it's almost noon." The reason I'd been avoiding the chore was a hesitation to confront Enre.

I pushed open the door to a light flutter of snowflakes coating the line of trailers. "I'm always here for you, Alena."

"I know you are," I said over my shoulder and hurried outside.

A jittery sensation weaved through me. What was I supposed to do now? Wait for doom to hit? Father had said Enre had nothing to do with me and that I better not leave the circus grounds today. What was happening? Why wouldn't he tell me about his plans to rescue Nicolai? Was he rescuing my brother today?

Shameful guilt blazed in my cheeks. The ache in my chest threatened to split me in half.

I stomped through a thick layer of snow and slush on a path between the line of trailers and the big top. My hands were tucked in my armpits. The sun didn't warm the arctic chill settling in my bones. Voices from the tent filtered out; the pack was practicing for the show. Life appeared normal.

After making a quick detour to the mess tent for meat and a bucket of water, I reached Ash's trailer. Her whimpers echoed from within, more than likely starving for food. She could eat nonstop. I'd love her metabolism.

Once inside, I shoved the curtains aside and found Ash pacing back and forth in the dimly lit space. Her breaths raced, her tongue hung out of the side of her mouth, and a permanent grumble trickled from her chest. I'd never seen her this upset.

My gaze drifted over to the cage Nicolai usually inhabited during full moons when he transformed into his wolf form. A limp body lay crumpled in the center of his prison.

Enre. My heart jumped into my throat. I dashed to unlock

his door, struggling with the key, realizing I had to use the new one on my keychain. Why did Father keep changing the locks on these stupid cages? It clicked open, and I burst inside.

"Enre." He lay on his side, curled in a fetal position, his chin tucked into his chest. I felt for a pulse at his throat—faint. His skin was ice-cold, his breaths shallow. "Can you hear me?"

Hollowness lanced through me. This was Father's work, had to be. Ash's low grumbles continued, grating on my nerves.

"He's okay," I said.

Though I had no idea if that was the case. A massive purple bruise smudged the side of his face, and a trail of blood dripped down from his mouth and over his chin.

I sat back on bent legs and rubbed a hand down my face.

What was I doing? Nerves bounced through my veins with uncertainty as I stared at him. *Why couldn't we have met under different circumstances?*

Okay, I would heal him for no other reason than that he'd shown me sympathy and helped me try to rescue Nicolai. Somewhere inside him lay a decent wulfkin.

Climbing to my feet, I hurried out of his cage and retrieved the bucket of fresh water. I took my coat off, dipped a corner into the water, and cleaned his wounds.

Knowing my father's bodyguards, surely there were more injuries. When I lifted his shirt, I gasped at the yellow and green welts on his ribs.

Enre's hoarse voice snapped me from my thoughts. "Checking me out?" I jerked back, hitting the bars behind me.

Ash yelped, drawing his attention.

"I'm okay." His voice was scratchy and dry. He attempted to drag himself up onto his elbows but collapsed onto his back and moaned.

"Stay down. I'll try to ease the pain."

"Don't," he said. "Your f-father'll be p-pissed."

I didn't care. I rubbed my hands together, visualizing healing energy building around them.

When I met his stare, movement whirred behind his bright, blue eyes.

Father should have tried talking to Daciana after she took over their pack. She might have been open to negotiations. Women weren't as quick to jump into battles … Maybe the packs needed more female alphas.

Regardless, two of our scouts had been butchered by Sandulf. Father demanded payback. I suspected that once he drilled Enre for further insider information, he'd attack the Romanian pack.

Leaving my gloves on to avoid depleting myself of energy, I inhaled and placed my open palms inches above his ribs. Too many questions buzzed in my mind. Did Enre plan on killing my father? Had he meant what he said in the woods about us running away?

And did he know about my mother's death? But a different question spilled from my lips. "Why'd you help me with Nic?"

His attempt at shrugging made him wince in pain, and his lips warped into a silent whimper. "Nic being in prison is a danger to us all." His eyes clasped shut while he obviously rode a wave of agony.

During those few seconds, I yearned to lean in and kiss his worries away. The thought was crazy.

My eyelids closed as I imagined a white light streaming from my palms and into his injuries. I delved deeper into my mind, forgetting myself, and drove every last particle of positive energy into Enre's wounds.

A soft touch on my arm roused me out of my focus. My

eyelids flipped open, and a wave of nausea swept over me. The world tilted. I fell against the bars behind me.

"Are you all right?" Enre was sitting by my side, hands clasping my arms, his face so close his warm breath danced across my face.

"I'm okay." The exhaustion gripping my limbs after a healing wasn't new. At least it hadn't knocked me out.

"Thanks for helping, but don't ever endanger yourself for my sake." He sat back on his bent legs.

I shrugged, uncertain how to respond. Why was he being a martyr?

He lifted his long-sleeved shirt to reveal his exquisite torso. *Nope, don't go there. It's an ordinary chest.* My wolf rolled around in protest, demanding we climb under his shirt with him.

"Some of the bruises are gone," he said. "You have a magical touch."

I leaned in closer, puzzled, and ran a hand down his firm stomach where the yellow and green marks had reduced in size. I'd never healed anyone this quick, ever. It was new. And I hadn't passed out, either.

"I have no idea how you did that, but thanks. Even my thigh's better." He slapped a palm on his leg without so much as a twinge of pain on his face. "You've got some strong mojo. Your hands were on fire."

I'd never expected my healing to be that strong through my gloves. Had my ability changed? I recalled Mother once telling me about my grandmother, who'd also had the touch of healing but then had gained the ability to control the wind with a single thought.

"Enre, why didn't you tell me who you really were?"

He ran a hand through his hair. "I wasn't sure how you or your father would react. But I can make him see reason if given the chance. I wanted to protect my family, like you trying to rescue your brother. Is that a crime? I never injured any of your pack. And I'd avoid that at any cost." He cocked an eyebrow. "Maybe I laid a few punches into Blackie … I mean Damir … but he deserved it."

"I don't think Father will listen," I said. "It's your Varlac family and … " The rest refused to come, and the rock in my throat hardened.

"What are you talking about?" His eyes narrowed.

I struggled with each breath, and my vision blurred behind tears. He had a right to know. "Levin Ulf murdered my mother."

Wiping my eyes, I refused to cry in front of Enre. I'd finished with grief years ago, yet the wound seemed as raw as the day it happened.

He reached for my arm. I jerked back and climbed to my feet, holding onto the bars to steady my balance. I hurried across the cell toward Ash's cage.

"I had no idea my father did that. I'm sorry," he said.

So, it *was* his damn father. Part of me had hoped it was an uncle or distant cousin. At least that would make it less personal. "I don't need your sympathy."

He shuffled behind me, but I didn't turn.

"I left my Varlac family at the age of fourteen after I'd had enough of my father's beatings." His voice grew firmer, never quivering. "Father insisted I would be stronger for it. But how does a child fight against an untouchable lord?"

"That's horrible." I turned around.

Enre was barely a pace from me, arms by his sides. A crease marred the bridge of his nose. "I'm not my father."

We stood there in a daze, paralyzed in each other's gazes. Ash shoved her snout into the back of my thigh, nudging me into Enre's arms. Strong, secure, and familiar. His heat pressed in around me. His lips were inches from mine. My breathing sped up.

My life was one messed-up pile of confusion. That moment was wrong on every plane of existence, and yet all I yearned for was to drown in his stare and never resurface.

"I came here to find a way to protect my pack." His hands pressed into my back, drawing me closer, our bodies joining. "But I never expected to fall for you."

His words brought more trembling, but I couldn't lose myself in him. Too much was at stake. Pieces of my dream returned. Was Father at risk? I pried myself from Enre's hold and ran to the door, desperate for fresh air before I did something stupid like declaring my love.

"I can't do this. I'm sorry." Slamming his cage shut, I locked it, in case Father returned. After I placed fresh meat in Ash's cage, I rushed outside. The air squeezed out of my lungs, and my heart splintered.

An icy snap curled around me, my jacket rustling as I hurried around the trailers draped in white. The slush and mud had disappeared, and new snow compacted beneath my shoes.

Regardless of every doubt trickling through my veins, Enre's admission that he'd fallen for me resurrected the tingles in my stomach. They were the same ones that had persisted ever since we met.

A cacophony of voices broke out around me, eclipsing my thoughts. I halted, ankle- deep in snow. Wulfkin spilled out of the big top and throughout the caravan of trailers, bottle-necking the mess tent's entrance on their way inside.

What had I missed?

Spotting Sonia amid the horde, I grasped her wrist. She twirled to face me with worry worming its way behind her distant gaze.

"It's started," she said. "The chaos."

"What's going on?" My mind twisted into a tangled knot.

"Alena." Father's voice sliced through the murmurs and

shuffling. He stood beside the tent's entrance with his hands by his sides in a stiff posture. "Join us."

Sonia eased an arm beneath mine, and together we joined the other wulfkin. Seated halfway toward the back, I studied Father for a clue about this meeting. Every nerve jumped beneath my skin.

His shoulders curled forward with arms folded across his chest. Speckles of snow dotted his black hair, aging him instantly.

Tightness worked its way up my throat, reminding me of the last time he'd worn such a mournful mask and defeated posture—Mother's death.

Once everyone was seated, Father stepped in front of the pack and stood with parted legs, hands laced behind his back. "I have received some alarming news about Nicolai."

My body froze.

"He's being transferred tomorrow morning across the country to Sofia, in the south of Bulgaria."

Tears pooled in my eyes. No one said a word.

A furnace of lava streamed through me, and I scooted to the edge of my seat. How could this be happening? Nicolai would transform tomorrow night. Sofia was a four-hour drive from Ruse, and the prison had maximum security. It made his current jail seem like a day camp. How would Father rescue Nicolai now?

Sonia touched my arm and whispered, "You've turned white."

I shook my head, unable to process anything except Nicolai's situation.

"Tomorrow's the full moon," Eevi called out. "Nicolai's going to turn. And we have a Varlac with us. We're all going to get punished for this."

The soft murmurs increased into loud chatter.

"Quiet," Father said. "I'm not telling you this to create

panic. I have solicited someone inside Sofia prison who will get him out before he turns. I'm going down there today." He rubbed his chin. "I will take Nicolai straight to Transylvania from there. I want all of you to prepare for our move into Romania tomorrow night, and we'll meet you in Transylvania soon after. Our time in Ruse has run out."

"What if Nicolai doesn't get out before the full moon?" someone else asked, voicing my concerns.

After a long pause, Father studied the back wall of the tent and replied, "Whatever happens, you will still leave for Transylvania tomorrow night."

A wulfkin stood up. "What about the Varlac?"

Then another. "They'll shoot Nicolai if he changes."

"You—"

"Keep calm." Father's rushed words were anything but calm, yet it had the effect of silencing everyone. "You've all known this was coming, and together as a pack, we are stronger. Follow me, and I'll keep you safe. I give you my word."

My pulse sprinted too fast, and my head spun. Was this really happening?

"Now I urge you to move with swiftness and not breathe a word of this to anyone outside the pack." He stepped back. At first, no one shifted from their seats. "You are dismissed."

It was as if the air had been sucked out of the tent and the pack had forgotten how to use their legs. Then, one by one, they exited. A few gathered around Father.

I couldn't move. Tears trailed down my cheeks.

Sonia leaned in close, wiping one of my tears with her thumb. "It'll be all right, honey."

My head shook of its own accord.

"Come, I'll get you some water."

"What if Father can't get Nic out in time? What if it goes wrong?" This might be our last day alive.

"I'm certain your father has given this a lot of thought. He'd never allow anything to happen to either of you."

Considering our predicament and Father's promise to get Nicolai out, I wasn't convinced. What if my dreams were a premonition? Maybe this was my mission—to rescue my brother. Keeping my voice low, I leaned closer to Sonia. "Maybe I can get Nic out before he leaves Ruse, but I need a decoy. Will you help?"

Sonia shook her head, her hand squeezing mine. "No way. I'm not disobeying Maxim. You're going to get burnt if you do this. Leave it to your father."

My knees bounced with desperation.

"Sit back and trust someone else," Sonia said.

My heart raced, and I refused to accept that. Not when so much was at stake. I could do it. Somehow.

"But Father won't know it's you," I said.

"Alena." Father's voice made me jump out of my seat and Sonia alongside me.

He eyed Sonia, who lowered her head and scurried away. Wonderful.

He approached me. "Can I trust you to pull the pack together for tomorrow's departure in my absence? I'm putting you in charge while I'm gone."

My hands curled in my pockets. "Of course, but are you sure about rescuing Nic?

And what will you do with Enre?"

"Leave your brother to me. I'll deal with our intruder once we reach Romania." Father rubbed his lips. "It's in my jurisdiction to deal with him as I see fit, but I must tread carefully since he's a Varlac."

"So you're not going to kill him?" My voice quivered. He sighed, took a seat, and patted the chair next to him. I joined him.

After a quick scan of the entrance, he spoke in a voice

barely audible. "I've never killed a single intruder."

I stiffened, uncertain if I'd heard right. "You've told us you have."

"I've threatened trespassers, Damir provided the heavy hand, and we sent them on their way. Every wulfkin and pack is trying to find a place in this world, so who am I to take their life? When your mother passed, I made myself a promise to never kill again."

"Then how were you planning the takeover of Transylvania?"

"Keep your voice down." He glanced around again, then turned back to me, his brow furrowed. "With the sheer number of wulfkin in our pack we'll push the Romanians out. No blood will be shed on either side. I simply said I would kill to keep the rumors alive." His words were monotone, as if he'd said it to himself many times before and now they were a line he recited with ease.

"Why didn't you tell me?" An ache settled across my brow.

The tent fluttered around us in the wind, and its raspy crinkle annoyed me.

"No one can know. It'll make us targets to every single pack out there, especially the

Varlac."

"Then what will you do with Enre?"

He reclined in his seat, and the crease forming slowly across his brow told me he'd been giving this heavy thought. My father ran a hand through his thick hair, lowered his gaze, and inhaled deeply. "Ever since Enre arrived, I've been waking up thinking your mother is still around, only to find myself alone."

When his gaze met mine, a pitiful expression captured his face. It belonged to someone who'd lost all hope, not my father. He'd risk everything for those he loved.

"I can't touch his father directly, but I can show that butcher the pain of losing a loved one when his son dies at my word."

I flinched, and my hands curled against my stomach. "But Enre's innocent. He told me he left home at a young age and has nothing to do with this. And I doubt his father will care if his son dies."

"Every parent feels the agony of losing a child, no matter what they pretend. Varlac are brought up to show no emotions, but his parents do love him. I'm certain of that." He stood and turned away. A heavy silence folded around us.

I touched his arm and stood up beside him. "You're my father and the strongest, most caring wulfkin I know. Don't allow revenge to blur your judgment."

He wrapped an arm around my shoulder and kissed the top of my head, holding me for a long moment.

"Don't worry about Nicolai and Enre. You focus on packing up. Do you remember the location in Transylvania where we decided to meet if we were ever split up during the move?"

"Yes." I trembled, and it wasn't from the chill.

"Let's get going. You have a lot to prepare," he said.

I nodded, unable to form a response. Our world was crumbling in on itself.

He returned to his trailer in preparation for his trip to Sofia, and I hastened to mine.

I trusted Father with my life, but I also believed in having a security blanket.

What if his contact in Sofia wasn't able to get Nicolai out in time? Plans went to crap all the time. Look at my life. Nicolai and I could both die tomorrow night. The idea left me gasping for air. The situation couldn't possibly get worse.

Already, a plan was forming in my mind. I'd risk facing Father's wrath to get Nicolai out.

CHAPTER 18

ENRE

I gripped the metal bars of my prison and shook them. Aside from the raspy groan of the hinges, it remained locked. Alena had left me to clear her head. Or at least I hoped.

"Whoever built these cages knew what they were doing."

Ash sat in the opposite cell, a wall of bars separating us. She studied me. If she could speak, she'd probably tell me to forget trying to escape, otherwise she would have left this place ages ago.

Approaching her, I threaded an arm through the bars and scratched her head. "Don't worry. When I get out, I won't leave you behind. I'll take you to Transylvania, where you can live with my pack and be free in the woods."

She pressed her head against my palm as I ruffled the fur behind an ear.

A nagging thought pestered me—why hadn't Maxim finished me off? If it were Sandulf or any Varlac, I'd be long dead. Don't get me wrong, I'd fight to my last dying breath to stay alive, but I couldn't work out Maxim's reasoning. Maybe everything we'd been told by Sandulf about this pack was wrong. And thinking back to all the fucked-up shit Sandulf had done, why had I believed him anyway? I kicked the straw at my feet and gritted my teeth.

Ash scurried away from me, to the back wall of her cell.

"Sorry to scare you."

And why had I believed replacing Maxim would gain me a pack, or that afterward the

sun would shine out of my ass? I should have gone to Maxim from the beginning and proposed an agreement between our packs. It seemed that even from beyond death, Sandulf managed to mangle our lives.

One day, I planned on becoming the kind of alpha whose pack stayed together out of loyalty, not fear. Where life was anything we wulfkin yearned it to be—freedom in the forest, or mingling with humans. If Daciana's human boyfriend accepted our existence, others might, too. A few months ago, I'd have slammed down anyone who told me I'd even consider merging our kind with humans.

Clasping the bars, I throttled them again.

First things first—find a way out of this prison. Then I'd make Maxim listen to me so we could sort out this shit. Lastly, somehow, I'd convince Alena I was her wulfkin mate. Staring at the locks, I noticed they were pretty new ... Did that mean they might be harder to pick?

The door to the trailer burst open, and the tiny grilled window facing both cages rattled.

Ash jumped to her feet, the fur on the back of her neck bristling until she spotted Alena.

"Wasn't expecting you back so soon," I said, surveying how delicious her backside looked in those tight, black pants as she closed the trailer door.

"Well"—she careened toward my cell with a strange half smile planted on her lips— "this is your lucky day."

"Somehow, I suspect our interpretations of that aren't the same."

Her eyes rolled. She huffed and kept glancing to the entrance and back. "No, they're not."

"You going to let me out then? I'm assuming you're not a fan of your father killing me."

The edge of her mouth twitched, and she did a double take in my direction.

"I know I have sexy eyes," I said, "but I doubt that's the reason you're visiting me."

Alena shook her head as if she'd vanished into a thought of her own. When she refocused, her gaze could have pierced a hole through my chest.

"I want to make a deal with you."

Moseying closer, I gripped one of the bars. What was it with girls and deals today? "Go on."

She retreated, her back hitting the wall, even though the metal barrier separated us.

Her voice lowered. "Help me break Nic out of prison, *tonight*."

My mind raced. "Because of the full moon tomorrow?"

"Yes. And he's being transferred to another prison in the morning. It gives us a window of opportunity to rescue him."

The wind outside howled as if it were a distant wolf pack warning of encroaching danger.

"Why me? Ask one of your pack friends. Your father will kill you if he finds out. And me twice over for helping."

"This doesn't concern my father." She dropped her arms to her sides and chewed on her lower lip, her gaze bolted to the entrance of the trailer.

"He'd beg to differ," I said.

She approached the bars and brushed a loose strand of hair from her cheek. The pleading softness of her voice lured me away from my worries. "Father hasn't killed anyone since my mother died."

If she spoke the truth, maybe there was hope for Maxim, after all. "I could see that."

Her brow pinched. I might have pushed my luck. "Well, because of your father, mine wants to kill you in revenge. Do you see that too?" Her eyes widened, and her cheeks were ablaze. "I'm sorry, I ... I shouldn't have said that."

The sinking sensation deepened through my gut.

"No one else will go against the alpha's word to help me," she said. "Father says he'll rescue Nic tomorrow in Sofia, but I'm scared it'll go wrong before the full moon. I want to believe those words you said to me in the woods were real and not part of your plan to take over our pack."

"I meant everything I said, but I'm not going with you until I speak with your father."

"You can't," she said, her attention anywhere but on me. "H-he's not here.

"You're lying."

"If you see him, you won't stay alive for long. Help me, and then you can return to your pack and be free."

"Free?" I scoffed and ran a hand down my face. "There'll be no freedom when your father turns up to destroy my family. I'm not leaving until I speak with him."

Fidgeting with the fur collar on her black bomber jacket, Alena hesitated. "He told me he won't slaughter your pack, but that doesn't apply to you."

Was she telling me the truth? I didn't take her for someone who lied. But this was her father telling her these things ... Maybe he intended to protect her from the truth of his real intentions.

She unlocked the door to my prison and opened it, freeing me. "Please, Enre. If you stay, you'll get killed. And if you don't help me, Nic and I might die."

I flinched back. "What?"

Our eyes met, and a quiver captured Alena's words. "The moment Nic or I die, the other does too. Every other generation in our family has linked souls. My grandmother did, and her grandmother, and so on." She rubbed her palms down her jeans.

My thoughts whirred, convinced I'd once heard Sandulf tell me about a wulfkin family cursed by a witch. All twins in their family were destined to have joint souls. At the time, I'd figured it was a stupid fairy tale, especially since it was set in ancient times ... But what if it referred to Alena's lineage? And if that was the case, did that mean the other witch-related stories Sandulf had told me were true, too? I hoped not.

"Are you sure of this?" I asked.

"Why would I make this up? Yes, it's real. My mother suspected it, but after Nic got hit by a car and we both fell into a coma, she knew it had to be true. Afterward, she kept us both so overprotected, we were one step away from being wrapped in cotton and locked in our trailer." With a raised eyebrow, she said, "And we don't tell anyone, for obvious reasons. Makes us easy targets."

An invisible fist collided with my chest, emptying my lungs of air. "Why didn't your father rescue Nic earlier?" A prickling sensation ran down the back of my scalp.

"Exactly," was all she said, as if it felt reassuring to share the demon she'd been harboring.

If Nicolai turned in prison, they would shoot and maybe dissect him. Alena would also die. The media would be in a frenzy over the discovery of a real-life werewolf. The Varlac would blame the Bulgarian pack and kill every last one of them, not to mention what the trigger-happy humans scouring the forests would do to all of us. We'd never be free again.

I stepped cautiously closer, out of the cage. "Are you certain your father won't harm my pack?"

She offered me a quick nod, which meant when her father did approach Transylvania, it would be a face-off between him and me. That, I could handle. I was a big wulfkin and could take care of myself. But if Daciana didn't agree to share her land with Maxim, he'd challenge her as well.

Alena extended a shaky palm for me to take. "Please, will you help me?"

I studied her gloved hand and open fingers. The simple gesture of offering the exposed veins on one's wrist was used to show defeat when cornered, or to present oneself to a mate. Did she like me that much, or had she been beaten down by the situation? Dreading for her life, I had no other option but to join her crazy rescue attempt. Again. At least this way, I'd be able to watch over her.

I wrapped my hand around her wrist and drew her into an embrace. My lips captured hers, and for those few seconds, the ache in my heart threatened to split me in a thousand pieces. I wasn't sure I'd be able to leave her behind if the time came. We'd bonded, and everything about holding her in my arms felt right. With her by my side, anything was possible.

When her lips broke away from mine, her smile caressed my insides. "So, I'm taking that as a yes."

"It was yes from the first moment I laid eyes on you."

CHAPTER 19

ALENA

*D*arkness had spread across the skies with haste tonight, and the adrenaline pumping through my veins readied me for a battle.

Father and Damir drove out of the parking lot. They edged the family's beaten-up Beemer onto the main road and headed out of town toward the capital of Bulgaria— Sofia. Once I'd lost sight of them, I turned and bolted across the snowy grounds toward my trailer. Chairs were stacked outside the great tent, and wulfkin busied themselves packing the circus. I should have experienced some guilty feelings for not helping, but with the greater scheme of events, the only emotion stirring inside me was dread.

After changing into black clothes, for camouflage, I grabbed my backpack and hurried back to Ash's container.

My dream replayed for the hundredth time in my mind, and no matter how I twisted the events to make sense of them, only one plausible explanation remained: it was up to me to rescue Nicolai.

One way or another, by the end of the night, Nicolai

would be free. I didn't care what punishment Father dished out as long as Nicolai was safe.

Ash, Nicolai, and I would cross the Danube River from Bulgaria into Romania this very night. And Enre ... My mind stopped flat. He'd come with us, of course, but what would happen when Father and the whole pack arrived in Romania? My head ached as I contemplated how much worse the situation could become. After realizing Enre was actually a good guy, I couldn't bear to have him butchered. But I wasn't sure how to change Father's mind.

Pushing the concern to the back of my mind with every other problem, I dashed into Ash's trailer, causing her to jump. Her wolf senses should have been keen, but every time I entered the small trailer, she flinched. Enre froze, as if he'd been pacing in his unlocked cage. Illumination from the fairy lights outside revealed the worry written across his furrowed brow.

"What's the plan?" he asked, pulling on his coat.

"We wait by the police station. When they start moving prisoners for the transfer, we strike."

Enre stepped out of his cage, shadows dancing in his eyes. "We strike? Be more specific."

"They'll probably be loading the prisoners into a bus behind the jail. Once we spot Nicolai, you pretend to attack them in your wolf form, and I will—"

"Whoa ... Back up a bit. Me in my wolf form? Was sacrificing me your plan all along?" His eyes widened.

I hadn't meant to wound him. "You're not being sacrificed. You're simply deflecting attention, causing a distraction. While you do that, I'll dash for Nic and cut him loose." I retrieved the pliers from my backpack and showed them to him. "I can't think of a better way to do this."

"They'll have lots of guards with guns when the prisoners

board the bus. And they'll just shoot me." He rubbed a hand across his lips. "Not liking this plan."

I sighed. "I don't either, but I want Nic free."

Enre walked past me, his elbow grazing my arm, and a new kind of tingle replaced the nervous ones. The wolf's desire to have Enre folded around me. *Not now.*

"Your brother boards the bus. Then we follow. Once we're away from civilization, we pull out in front of the bus, forcing them to stop. Then we strike. This way, there'll be fewer police and guns aimed at me.

Rage built in my throat as I stuffed the bolt cutters into my back pocket. "Not going to work. What if the officers don't get out of the bus when we stop them on the road, but they call for backup?" Pacing in a circle, I kept shaking my head. "No, we need to do this my way. We'll get Nic out, return to the circus for Ash, then cross the border to Romania tonight, before the rest of the pack."

Enre's mouth opened, but no words gushed out at first. "I'm guessing you're not going to change your mind on that, huh?"

"Nope."

"Then let's at least take Ash with us. We can park away from the prison, and we don't have to return to the circus. That delay might give them enough time to capture us here. It's the first place they'll look. We can make a quick getaway before every policeman in Bulgaria is put on alert to track us down."

The idea had merit. Why not?

Every nerve in my body tingled, and I recognized the wariness in Enre's gaze too well. This was a massive risk based on my fickle dreams and Sonia's readings. Geez, just thinking about the fortune-telling made this plan sound ludicrous. If tonight turned sour, it would be a catastrophe.

"Look, I know I'm asking a lot. If we get caught, there's a

high chance we'll get killed one way or another. Though, I don't know who will get to us first: the humans, my father, or the Varlac. So I understand if you want to back out."

He stepped closer, his warm breath on my face. "And how will you manage on your own?"

I shrugged. "I'll find a way. If you join me, it needs to be because you want to, not because I'm forcing you. You can leave now, walk out of the trailer, and head home. I won't tell a soul."

Enre didn't move. He touched my cheek, sending a shiver down my spine. "If we're heading to Romania tonight, we'd better get going."

"Okay," I said.

The next inhale jammed in my throat, and my feet weren't doing any better, as they remained glued to the wooden flooring. We were really doing this. *Pull it together. Remember Nicolai, the dreams, the stakes.* When Father found out about my plans, which included Enre, he would murder me.

Enre's fingers pressed into my arm, his touch easing my knotted muscles. A hard expression slid across his face— tight jawline, body rigid, and distant eyes. I'd seen that expression on wulfkin many times, usually before they jumped into a fight.

"Are you certain you're up for this?" he asked.

"Yes. I'm ready to go." Wishing my voice sounded less shaky, I grabbed the cage keys from my pocket and handed them to Enre. "Take Ash and meet me on the other side of the empty lot, behind the circus. Give me a few minutes to retrieve the van."

Ash was already close to the cage door at the sound of her name. She whined to be released.

"See you soon." I hurried outside and shut the door behind me.

The scattering of snowflakes was beautiful, falling through the glow of fairy lights in the distance. Wulfkin voices floated on the breeze, and my chest tightened, but I couldn't allow one ounce of guilt to affect me, not now.

Running around the outside of the trailers to avoid bumping into anyone, I soon reached Father's RV and scampered inside. No one ever kept their doors locked, not in a pack family where everyone trusted each other. Once inside, I found all the spare keys for the vehicles located at the back of the third drawer of his bedside table, alongside several books. *Voila.* The extra-long one. With it in my hand, I hurried outside and shut the RV door behind me. Between two trailers in the distance, several figures moved, but it was too dark to see who it was. Hopefully, they couldn't spot me in the shadows.

"What are you doing?" The voice came from behind me.

I flinched and spun to face Lutia, who was wearing a furry white coat that reached to her ankles. The shadows concealed most of her face, but I sensed her scowl. I'd never liked her. She was the kind of wulfkin who flavored her words with so much sugar, you choked on it. That was why Father always sent her on missions—to stop the constant arguments and drama she created amongst the pack members.

"Why aren't you helping the others?" I asked. Father *had* put me in charge in his absence.

She shrugged. "Figured since I was going to get kicked out, it wasn't my business to help."

"You know, a bit of sincerity is all it takes to make you a better wulfkin."

She scoffed and focused her stare at my fisted hand—the one holding the key.

"What were you doing in there?"

That simple question made my pulse speed up. Had she seen me leave Ash's trailer?

Did she see Enre and Ash leave their cells? I didn't have time for her meddling.

"What do you want, Lutia?"

Then I spotted it. Several feet behind her, in the shadows, the dark shape of a large bag.

Following my gaze over her shoulder, she said, "I'm leaving."

"It's against pack law to go without the alpha's consent," I said, my fist tightening around the key. "You bailing on us confirms you're guilty of Enre's accusations." Every feature on her face twisted into an unrecognizable expression.

"Be warned about Enre. He already gave his heart to Daciana. He doesn't give up on what he desires." Lutia retreated and lifted her bag onto her shoulder.

"He's using you to save his pack and his precious Daciana."

"What would you know?" My chest flared up in a blaze at Lutia's accusation. Was I his stepping-stone? I kept reminding myself that Lutia was a spiteful wulfkin prepared to do or say whatever it took to deflect attention away from herself. Except, what if Enre *had* said all the right words to me just to get his way? Then why did our wolves react this way ... No denying it, he felt the lure. My head swam with confusion. Considering what lay ahead of me tonight, this kind of doubt was the last issue I needed. *Damn you, Lutia.*

A smirk split her thin lips. "I know you and Enre are up to no good, but that's none of my business. And what I do is none of yours."

My shoulders stiffened, a drowning sensation worming itself through my stomach. "If you leave, the whole pack will be instructed to kill you the moment they see you again, and

Father will report you to the Varlac. You won't be safe anywhere."

Shrugging, she turned away and strutted into the darkness, heading toward the main road at the front of the circus. Her voice wavered in the breeze. "If I stay, I'm as good as dead. I like my chances on my own."

It was my job to stop her. I could call the other wulfkin to take her before she got too far. But that meant delaying the rescue attempt for Nicolai and drawing unwanted attention to me. *Crap.* Enre and Ash were probably already waiting in the field behind my trailer.

Lutia had completely vanished from sight.

My belly churned with unease. I didn't have time for her distractions. She'd be a problem for us to deal with later, when and if everything went to plan. I spun on my heels and sprinted to the edge of the circus where several of our vehicles were parked.

Surprisingly, no wulfkin crossed my path on the way to our Dokker panel van. The engine roared to life. Maybe luck was on my side. Father loved this little van with its two seats in front and the empty space in back, so I'd need to keep it scratch free. While reversing, I spotted Sonia in the side mirror standing alongside the vehicle. *Shit.*

Rolling down the window, I stuck out my head. "Just going on an errand."

Sonia cocked her head and walked over to my window, one of her eyebrows arched and her gaze filled with curiosity. Oh yeah, she knew me too well.

"You going to stand there, staring at me?" My words, fast and fueled by adrenaline, came out more aggressive than I'd intended. "Sorry, I'm in a rush."

"For your errand?" Sonia rubbed her earlobe.

"That chaos stuff you were talking about," I said. "It's hit all right, and it's massive." How could Sonia always appear so relaxed? Droplets of sweat tickled as they rolled down my back. "Don't look at me as if I've done something wrong."

"Have you?"

"Of course not." Not yet, anyway. Running a hand down my face, I struggled to control my bouncing knee. What if someone spotted Ash outside? What if Enre couldn't control her? I kept checking the side mirror, expecting someone to block me in.

"Are you sure you want to *leave*?" The way she said the word *leave* made me think she questioned my plans or had seen something else in her tarot cards. But I couldn't let doubt in or I'd never go through with my plan.

"Well, I better go." Guilt gnawed at my gut for not telling Sonia where I was headed, but I'd share it with her once this was over. Until then, I refused to draw her into my problems.

"Okay then. Off you go." Her hand flicked for me to leave, and she strolled away. Geez, talk about making me feel worse. *Focus. Worry about Sonia later.*

I reversed the van until I emerged clear of the other parked circus vehicles. The

snowfall had increased again as I put the gear into drive and merged onto the main road. My foot pressed the accelerator, and the engine grunted as it protested being woken up on such a cold night. It rattled and blew smoke out the tailpipe. Soon enough, I was on the backstreets, driving toward the lane facing the empty lot behind the circus. Darkness and the blowing snow made it difficult to see, but the closer I got, the more certain I was that Enre and Ash weren't anywhere around.

Attempting to strangle the wheel, I scanned the area, the empty land coated in snow. Anyone out here tonight would be easily spotted with the background of white. Farther behind the lot, the circus fairy lights cast dancing shapes on the line of trailers.

"Hell. Where are you, Enre?" Had they been spotted or, worse yet, stopped by other wulfkin? What would I do then?

Parking alongside the curb, I spotted movement near a dumpster on my far right. Two figures slipped out ... Enre and Ash. They rushed over. I reached into the back and slid open the side door. Enre leapt inside, followed by Ash. I slammed the door shut and drove us along the wintery road away from the circus, my pulse in a frenzy.

Enre had already scaled the center console to get into the passenger seat. "What took you so long?"

"Don't even ask. You?"

"Aside from Ash trying to chase a cat, and me running after her like a lunatic, we're dandy."

With the winds picking up and the snow sloping at an angle, the steering wheel became difficult to control. At least the snow tires kept us from skidding if we moved slower than thirty-five miles per hour. My nerves were eating away any last remnants of calm as I contemplated returning to the circus. I struggled to inhale. *Calm down, you can do this. Think of Nicolai.*

Darkness had claimed the city, and outside the glow of the streetlights lining the road, the houses and buildings vanished into a blurry background on either side of us.

"I've never done anything this dangerous before," Enre said while staring out his window, his gaze studying a hatchback vehicle overtaking us. It fishtailed farther ahead, struggling to remain on the road. The idiot turned onto a side street, still speeding.

"Throw me at any animal," he said, "and I'll jump at the chance of battling it, but this is different. We're meddling with humans, and it goes against everything we've been told."

"I know." From the moment we joined a pack, the dangers of dealing with humans were drilled into us, along with the punishment—death by the Varlac. In fact, the Varlac threatened wulfkin with death any chance they got, and if I hadn't seen their vile ways firsthand, I might have suspected they were empty threats.

Varlac. One sat next to me in the van, and instead of planning my revenge, as I'd always anticipated, I yearned to crawl into his embrace and forget the world around us. Stopped at a red light, I said, "If you're not comfortable with this, you're free to go.

No hard feelings." Oh, the pain would surface if he abandoned me, but I had no right to force him into breaking the law.

"I'm not walking away." He glanced over.

My heart beat a bit too quick. This whole attraction thing was going to land me in so much shit.

Ash's head popped out from in between our seats, nudging me as she attempted to get closer to Enre.

He folded an arm across the back of her neck, drawing her closer to him. When she licked his cheek, he pushed her away.

Ash released a protesting whine and sat back, her chin resting on the console between us, her hot breaths accompanied by constant mewls. The moment Enre scratched her head, she calmed down. Yep, he sure had a way with the girls.

A honk blared behind us, startling me, and I realized the traffic lights were glowing green. When we were driving again, only the occasional car passed us. The deeper we drove into the center of the city, the brighter the lights, the loftier the neo-baroque buildings, and the fewer the trees. Ruse was often called the Little Vienna, though with the buildings covered in snow, I couldn't see the resemblance.

We neared the police station, and my knees were bouncing again.

Slowing our pace, I took a side street a block away from the well-lit station.

When we reached the end, I swung left onto a back road overshadowed by tall buildings on both sides, and we were instantly facing floodlights in the far distance. I hit the brakes and killed the van lights. One policeman glanced our way and waved his hand for us to leave.

"We're too late. They're loading the prisoners." My pulse pumped. This was bad. Enre leaned forward in his seat, staring out the window.

Police officers were marching the prisoners from inside the station into a small transit vehicle parked outside. It resembled an old bus, except this one had bars over the boarded-up windows. The accused were linked by a chain around their waists, ankles, and wrists. They shuffled as their heads bopped up and down with each step.

My chest constricted as I imagined Nicolai treated this way.

When it appeared no more prisoners were coming out, the police officers dispersed. Most headed back inside the yard.

"They're moving them earlier than Father said." Panic gripped my voice.

A police officer whistled and walked quickly toward us, his flashlight pointed in our direction.

"Crap." He would see Ash.

Enre pushed open his door, and a gust of icy wind rushed into the van. He jumped out and smacked the door shut before circling around the front of our vehicle, hurrying to my side.

Opening my door, he said, "Move over, I'm driving."

My gaze remained locked on the officer who was halfway down the street and closing in fast. Not that we were doing anything wrong. But in case tonight went wrong, I didn't want a cop able to recognize us spying on the prisoner transfer.

"Move." Enre pushed my arm, and I climbed over to the passenger seat.

Once inside, he revved the van to life and reversed back past the street we'd come down. Enre threw the gear stick into drive, but the vehicle choked and died.

"Son of a bitch." He turned the key, the engine only squealing. He tried again and again.

"Don't flood the motor." Every part of me tensed, and my gaze refused to move from the officer several paces away, his flashlight blinding me. His mouth moved, but no words reached me. "Oh, shit."

"Come on, come on." Enre turned the key for the fifth time, and the engine came to life.

I released a long breath. He threw the gear stick into drive and swung the van left down the lane we had come up originally, the policeman still following.

My heart pounded against my rib cage, resonating in my ears.

"Change of plan," Enre said, his voice a bit too cocky for my liking. "We're doing this my way."

Every part of me tensed. This wasn't how tonight was meant to go down.

CHAPTER 20

ENRE

"Slow down." Alena's voice barely broke through Ash's howls from the back of the van. If the slippery road didn't kill me, the girl's fussing, coupled with the wolf's howling, would do the job.

"Ash." My voice climbed.

The growls silenced.

Alena clutched the door handle with a death grip, and her other hand pointed right, as if I didn't know which way to go once we exited the narrow lane.

A quick glance in the side mirror showed no sign of the police behind us. Good.

Emerging from the alley, I swerved the van onto the road. The back tires slid sideways. A thump in the back suggested Ash had lost her footing. Alena scrunched her eyes shut, holding onto the door.

If Alena and Ash got injured, I'd never forgive myself. Spinning the steering wheel in the direction of the swerve to stop the skidding, we came to a dead stop in the center of the road but facing the wrong way. A truck was heading in our direction, and every hair on my body stood on end.

"*That was stupid!*" Alena's words were close to a scream.

Taking a deep inhale, I accelerated, did a U-turn, and caught my breath. The transit prison bus was down the road ahead of us, almost concealed by the heavy snowfall.

"Have you ever driven before?" she continued.

"I've driven in worse weather than ... " I spotted a police car ahead of the bus as they turned left at an intersection. "Shit."

"They have an escort?" Alena asked.

Refusing to lose sight of the prisoners, I trailed behind them, keeping a safe distance away. "We have two options. Return to the circus and forget the rescue mission, or—"

Alena made a low, gravelly noise, and her brow creased. Was it from my suggestion or my driving?

"Or we keep to my original plan," I said. When we took a left onto Borisova Boulevard, the bus came into view once again, along with several others cars. "I suggest the latter."

"I don't think we have a choice." Alena kept her sights fixed on the road ahead.

We passed trees peeled bare of leaves. The contrast of dilapidated apartments next to gothic architecture reminded me of Brașov.

How are we going to deal with the damn police car? I should have seen that coming. But the rescue had to be on the highway. No cars, no streetlights. Just us and them. *Think, Enre, think.*

"Are there any deserted roads on the way to Sofia?" I asked.

Alena didn't respond right away. "Yeah. Not far out of Ruse, we'll pass through the national park. There's nothing but trees either side of the highway."

"That's where we'll cut them off."

The whole scene reeked of danger. Then again, we were dealing with humans, not manipulative alphas who'd feed you to demons the second they got a chance. I tossed away the doubts and glanced at Alena. Her hands were tucked under her thighs, and her knees bounced.

I promised myself that after this I'd do what it took to take Alena as my mate, keep her close, and protect her. Except ... were such dreams foolish?

Then there was Daciana, who had no idea what was coming, and I had no way of telling her, either. Perhaps I should have given in to her nagging to memorize the new pack house phone number. *Dammit.*

Ash stuck her head in between Alena and me.

Patting her, I said, "Better hold on, little one."

She retreated, her claws click-clacking against the metal flooring of the van before quieting down.

Ahead, the bus swerved onto a ramp behind the police car escorting them. They passed a sign listing upcoming cities, including Sofia. We took the ramp, too—no other car did. The curvy road had fewer lights, fewer cars, and fewer homes, and the farther we traveled, the more my muscles tensed.

Alena shifted in her seat. "We're at the park." Her words sounded strangled.

We'd left the buildings behind, and a small metal railing on either side of the road held back the plush explosion of trees. Aside from the car lights, everything else fell into the night's grasp.

"How long do we stay on this road?" I asked.

"About twenty-five miles. I think once we cut them off, you transform and distract the policeman in the car while I sneak up and knock him out. Then we do the same with the bus drivers. But you'll have to be fast to avoid getting shot. Cops will be called, so we'll need to be ultra-quick to get Nic out."

I glanced over and noticed how pale her cheeks were and her strict focus on the road ahead.

"We can do this." Her words quivered, as if she was attempting to convince herself rather than me.

"We will. We're doing this for your brother." *And you*, I almost said, but I figured that already played on her mind.

Ten miles deeper into the park, I stared at the taillights in front of me. The windows were boarded up, and there was no rear door. Considering the light spattering of snow and the sludgy, slippery road, the bus was traveling faster than it should have.

No cars had passed us for a while. It was time. "Hold on. We're doing this now."

Alena's loud exhale made my own breath hitch in my throat. I sped up, the distance between us closing rapidly, and pulled up alongside them.

Their wheels were sliding slightly.

"Get ready."

Alena laid her hand on my forearm, her warmth sizzling.

"Enre, no matter how tonight goes, I'll do everything to stop Father from challenging you. And ... And I do like you more than I should." Her soft touch vanished, and she gripped her seatbelt tight across her chest. "I'm ready."

Too many thoughts bubbled at the front of my mind. Emotions tugged at my heart. This wasn't what I needed mid-assault. I shoved it aside because I couldn't do the mushy stuff. Fuck, not now.

Words slipped out before I could stop myself. "Alena, I want you as my mate."

Before she could respond, my foot struck the accelerator. We were thrust back into our seats, and the engine grunted as the van's rear end fishtailed. The police car's taillights were dots in the distance as we sped up, starting to overtake the speeding bus.

I swerved into the bus's path, and it veered off the road.

Sparks flew from the opposite side of the prisoner bus as it scraped against the metal railings.

Reacting quickly, I pulled the steering wheel back to avoid our own van skidding out of control.

I held our speed alongside them, watching, waiting for them to slow, but they didn't. Now the police car far ahead had its brake lights on.

The bus shook and wobbled as the driver obviously struggled to keep it steady. They twisted at an awkward angle as the rear of the vehicle grated the railing, groaning. Then a loud bang resonated, and smoke billowed out from the grill on its rear. The bus slid into an uncontrollable sway, then its nose glided across the road, right into our path.

Alena screamed.

I slammed on the brakes. Our van trembled, skidding sideways on the snowy road. My arm shot out across Alena's stomach as we came to a halt. Ash crashed against the back of my seat and snarled.

Suddenly, the tires of the prisoner bus lifted off the ground, and the first flicks of golden flames sparked from its engine in the rear.

Ahead of us, the bus flipped onto its side with a thunderous clap, taking up the width of the road, its undercarriage facing us. White and black smoke swirled upward on the wind along with fire. The pungent stench of gas filled the air.

"No." Alena shoved the door open, leapt out, and sprinted toward the overturned vehicle. Before I could get my head on straight, Ash had shoved herself in between our seats to the front, squishing me against my door. Her hind leg kicked me in the ribs. She jumped outside.

My side pinched. "Ash, get back."

In the rear-view mirror, tiny yellow headlights were

encroaching upon the scene. "Fuck." Rushing out of the van, I bolted after the girls. I contemplated transforming.

My wolf was grousing inside me, insisting it come out now. Ahead, the flames were gaining momentum, crackling and licking the breeze. The faint drizzle of snow did little to put it out.

In one giant leap, Ash bounded atop the front of the bus, her bronze fur burning golden from the fire's reflection. Halfway along the vehicle, she scratched at the metal as if digging a hole. She must have located Nicolai. Alena rounded the front of the vehicle and tugged at the corner of the front windshield, which had come loose from the warped frame of the bus.

Sprinting closer, I yelled, "Ash, get back to the van!"

When I reached Alena, her alarmed voice elicited my own toxic fear in the form of shudders. "The bus is lying on its side door. We have to get Nicolai out before the fire engulfs everything."

The night had turned into one great pile of crap, and until I got the prisoners out, I couldn't release my wolf. I needed my hands to get everyone out of the bus. The plan was to rescue Nicolai, not murder them all.

The accident must have twisted the side of the bus since part of the window lay pulled away from the shell. Alongside Alena, I grasped the window and yanked with all my strength. It gave slightly, peeling away further. We'd get this open in no time.

Beyond the bullet-resistant glass, the driver and policeman were bleeding and unconscious. Farther behind the plastic barrier separating the inmates from the driver, a roar of panicked screams resonated. It was too dark to see faces or bodies, let alone identify Nicolai.

Then movement at my side drew my attention. I stepped back for a better view.

The escorting police car was parked about twenty yards away, and someone was climbing out. Over the person's arm was a crossbow. I squinted, panic lurking at the back of my mind. Then I saw her face—Kalina, the Interpol agent from the circus. What was she doing here?

Dressed in black leather pants and jacket, her hair pulled off her face, and her eyes locked onto me, she approached. Retrieving a bolt from the satchel dangling from her hip, Kalina set the crossbow up. Had she spotted Ash? When I looked up, Ash was nowhere to be seen, and yet Kalina wasn't taking her sights off me.

She aimed and fired.

I threw myself sideways, out of her reach, but not before the crossbow bolt grazed my arm, tearing through my jacket. When I touched the wound, blood stained my fingers. *Bitch.*

Sliding in front of Alena, I shoved her around the front of the bus, toward the undercarriage and out of range of Kalina.

"Enre, stop it," Alena said. "Get out of my way."

Turning to face her, I said, "Leave now. Something's wrong here."

Her head shook, and the growing flames behind me danced in her eyes. "I'm not going

anywhere without Nic."

My heart bounced against my chest, the beat thumping in my ears, and a faint moment

of dizziness took hold. I shook it off. Something about this situation seemed set up—all of it, actually. Down the road, the flash of lights drew closer. Ash had run off somewhere. The fire was growing in size, and soon it'd engulf the bus with Nicolai inside.

Kalina reappeared, from around the front of the vehicle, wearing the widest open- mouthed grin I'd ever seen. The kind that gave shivers the creeps. Her crossbow was again aimed in our direction.

Alena gasped. I blocked her with my body and faced a blurry Kalina. Rubbing my eyes, I shook my head again. What was happening to me? Was there poison on the tip of the arrow that grazed me?

"You better lower that. I'm only warning you once." Were my words slurring? "Goddamn werewolves," Kalina said. "I should kill the lot of you."

CHAPTER 21

ALENA

I plunged after Enre, who reeled backward. I seized his arm to keep him upright. It was Kalina's arrow. Since it had scratched Enre, he'd been stumbling all over the place. She must have poisoned or drugged him.

Enre's gaze remained fixed on Kalina. "Psst ... Put it down." His words slurred, his arms flailing outward for balance.

Kalina's armed crossbow remained aimed at Enre's chest from several paces away.

Ripping my gloves off, I funneled healing energy through my body, down my arms, and into Enre. I had no idea if it would work, but I wasn't going to sit around and do nothing. I had to try. On the bright side, Kalina had no idea what I was doing.

I glanced at her, meeting her stoic stare. "What did you do to him?" My voice rose above the distant crackle of the fire. The ferocious winds blew snow sideways, pelting against me, my body leaning with it.

"I knew he was a werewolf the first time I met him. It was in his eyes, and his name Ulf confirmed it. I killed one of your kind a few years ago, and he'd gone on about some Ulf family targeting me for revenge." Beneath the words, her tone was dead.

The idea that she knew what we were thrashed in my head. I only wanted to get Nicolai and drive us the hell away from this freaky woman. But if Kalina knew of our existence and maybe even hunted us, that spelled disaster for wulfkin everywhere.

"What are you doing here?" I asked, thankful my voice didn't quiver. "Are you even an Interpol agent? And why aren't you helping the prisoners?"

"I don't give a shit about the prisoners, and yes, I am an agent." Her chin lifted high. The screams from inside the bus clawed at my guilt. Nicolai. I wouldn't let us die.

"Then what do you want?" I shouted the words over the fire.

"Revenge for my father's death." Her lips warped in an awkward downward turn.

And reality struck. A werewolf killed her father? Was that how she knew werewolves existed?

"Weeks ago, a woman was attacked. At the last full moon." Her voice dipped. "I found her torn and dead body several blocks from your circus. And I saw the demon werewolf flee the scene. If I'd had my knife, I'd have skinned the beast."

Her expression turned grim, packed with hatred. She spat on the ground. "He had a silver streak that ran from the tip of his tail to his muzzle. The rest of the fur was black."

My insides iced over, and my knees wobbled. I'd only ever seen one wulfkin with that pelt pattern—Nicolai.

One of her eyebrows arched, and she offered me a knowing nod.

"No, y-you're wrong," I stammered.

"The same butcher has been killing humans at full moons for years and slaughtered my father two years ago in

Serbia. I recognize his coloring. I know it's him. I saw him transform back into a human behind the circus at the last full moon. But when I went to search for him, he'd vanished."

"You're lying." The words shot from my mouth, but I couldn't deny parts of her story. We *had* been in Serbia two years ago, and the police *had* hounded us about a dead human there, too. Could she be telling the truth?

Too many questions and doubts spun in my head. I recalled the metallic odor reeking from Nicolai the morning after the last full moon. I'd put it down to him gorging on too much meat. And the new locks on the cages. It wasn't the first time, either. Father changed them regularly. He always insisted on being the one who released Nicolai from the cage each morning after a full moon, saying it was a male bonding ritual. *Hell!*

My next breath hitched. Father. It couldn't be. He wouldn't hide such a crime. And I still refused to believe Nicolai had been responsible for so many deaths all these years. That wasn't the brother I knew.

Enre shook himself, bumping into me, as if trying to clear his head. "Sss ... Stop spinning shit."

"Shut up, foul beast. Did you have to watch your father being ripped to shreds? See these?" Kalina pulled the collar of her leather jacket down to reveal scars scoring her collarbone and lower neck. "That's her brother's handiwork, from when I tried to save my father. It reminds me every day of what was taken from me." For a smidgen of a second, something flickered behind her eyes. The raw pain of losing a loved one. Then she shook her head. "Dead bodies have been left behind in most cities you've visited. It all points to him." She nodded toward the bus. "His last kill confirmed it for me. I also witnessed one of your crew transforming into a werewolf at the back of the circus in Serbia. It wasn't the one who killed my dad, but that's when I knew I was dealing with a pack of demons."

"If it was Nic, he's caught now. You've got your justice, what more do you want?" My body quivered. This couldn't be happening.

The idea of releasing my wolf tapped at the back of my head, but while I changed, she could easily shoot Enre or me.

Kalina's lips opened in a silent snarl, and she broke into laughter that made the hairs on my arms stand on end. "I haven't even started with my justice. He'll suffer as much as my father did when Nicolai ripped him to shreds. And all of you will die tonight. Maybe I'll keep one of you alive and have you arrested for this escape attempt. The police are on their way."

My voice faltered, and despite all the defenses, excuses, and negotiations spinning around in my head, it was Enre who responded.

"Why travel with crossbows? Makes you look c-crazy." He wavered on his feet. "Have you considered getting help?"

Raising her crossbow to target his face, she said, "Time for your farewell."

"No!" I shoved him behind me. "Leave him alone."

"Fine by me if you both want to die." Her gaze flickered to the bus and back.

"I planned to kill your brother in Sofia after he transformed in front of everyone at the full moon tomorrow night and revealed your kind, but if I have to do it now ... "

She shrugged. "So be it."

My mouth fell open at the same moment a flash of high beams and the tooting of a horn came from behind me. I spun to see a car approaching fast, but the whir of a crossbow bolt whizzed past my ear and pierced the front windshield of the oncoming vehicle.

The vehicle fishtailed out of control, sliding wildly across the snowy road. That's when I recognized Father's BMW. Every inch of my body snapped to attention.

The car came to an abrupt halt about fifteen feet from the bus, and before I could make sense of why Father was here, I ran toward him. *Please don't let him be hit, please no.*

"Stop, or he dies." Kalina's voice boomed across the night.

The terror coursing through my veins tripled in speed. Halting a few paces away from the Beemer, its blinding headlights preventing me from seeing beyond the windshield, I turned around. My entire body shuddered.

Enre was on his knees, blood pouring from his mouth, and his body swaying. Behind him, Kalina stood, the crossbow pointed at the back of his head. "Come back, nice and slow, or your boyfriend dies."

Enre kept rubbing his face, shaking his head. Dread crawled through me.

"There's enough poison on the tip of the bolt to kill him instantly," Kalina continued. "Lucky for you, I only grazed him earlier." Tilting her head to the side, she stared down at Enre, who'd collapsed on all fours, his arms trembling, his back arching. Was he going to shift?

"He's really struggling, isn't he? Poor little doggy." His head snapped up, his brow and mouth pinched as he fought through the pain.

"Don't do it." My words were for Enre not to transform, but Kalina took them as hers. Her boot collided with Enre's butt, sending him sprawling to his stomach on the snow-covered road.

"Move." She gestured to me with the crossbow. "Free the prisoners. I want your brother to see you die."

Standing there, my limbs numb, I stared at Kalina. Rage burned through my veins. I yearned to tear her to bits and smash her into the ground. I might have been the pacifist of our pack, but in this situation, I'd gladly break her neck.

"Now." She stepped away from the bus. The forest was at her back, and Enre remained between us.

Without another thought, I hurried to the bus, grabbed the corner of the windshield, and pulled, but it wasn't budging. I scanned the inside of the bus for the officers' weapons.

The creak of a car door opening farther down the road drew my attention. Over my shoulder, I spotted two figures climbing out of the BMW—Father and Damir. This was officially the first time I'd been thrilled to see the quick-tempered, aggressive wulfkin.

"I had this under control, Alena," my father said, his tone gritty and filled with venom. "Why is he here?" He pointed to Enre, who crawled away from Kalina. Father shook his head. "This is the exact reason I didn't tell you Nicolai's transfer was tonight, or that I would be breaking him out on the road rather than in Sofia. Because I knew you'd do something stupid like this."

A sinking sensation swirled through my belly. "But I could have helped you."

"You never listen," he said.

"Fascinating," Kalina butted in. "Family squabbles. Well, if it helps, neither of you were going to succeed." She broke into a cackle. The sound grated along my spine.

My next words flew out, fast and dead-on, targeting Father. "You knew Nic was killing those humans, and you covered for him? Why didn't you tell me?"

"Ha, this is getting good," Kalina said. "Told you, Maxim, I'd pin you down soon enough." Her voice lowered, growing heavier and louder. "Did you also cover for your son when he killed my father in Serbia, you monster?"

Even from my distance, the glow of the dancing flames revealed Father's frown.

"You know nothing, Kalina," Father said, turning toward me. "Alena—"

"Save me your pity story," Kalina replied.

"So it's okay for the innocent lives to be taken because I don't understand your bullshit. Well, fuck you, and welcome to my life."

Father stepped closer. Damir followed with his hands clenched at his sides. Enre was already climbing to his feet. The crackling tension in the air wasn't from the lofty fire or the muffled voices from within the back of the bus. It was from the fight about to break out.

Convinced all the blood had drained from my face, I clutched my fists to my chest, quivering from the truth. I faced Father, but my response was barely a whisper and I doubted anyone else heard it. "How could you?"

"Stay right where I can see you," Kalina said toward the other three wulfkin. "Or she gets it. You know what I want. Retribution."

Shivers slithered up the back of my legs as the crossbow pointed poison in my direction from a few paces away. I was an easy target. Father and Damir stood near the Beemer. Enre was farther in front. Three sets of eyes locked onto Kalina.

"Get inside the bus now." She spat the words in my direction, her gaze narrow and crammed with the promise of death.

I yanked on the corner of the window again, using my wulfkin strength, but made no progress. The crunch of snow made both our heads jerk toward Father and Enre. I spotted a flash of Damir vanishing around the back of the bus where the fire roared.

"If your pet mutt doesn't return by the count of three, she dies."

Father and Enre said nothing but stared at Kalina as if they were hunting a deer.

"One."

My body quivered, and a crackle at the back of the bus told me the fire was spreading. "Two."

No footfalls. Where was Damir? Hell.

"Three."

A sudden explosive pain struck my back above my shoulder blade. Thrown forward onto the bus's windshield, I slid down the glass and crumpled to the side. My world slanted. A momentary blindness took hold, and my throat seized up.

CHAPTER 22

ALENA

*W*as this death?

Father. I was leaving him behind. Nicolai would also die. I'd lose my pack family and Enre. I could no longer deny it. I loved him and had made too many excuses to avoid him. Too late. I was dying. All the missed opportunities speared my heart.

My eyelids flipped open. My next inhale was sharp and agonizing as I gasped for air. A throbbing ache lanced across my shoulder. I shoved the confusion away, convinced the poison was making its way through my body. How long did I have?

Whimpers fell from my lips as I tried to push myself upright.

Screams from inside the bus echoed around me, and the stink of gas filled my nostrils. My whole body trembled. Sonia's words cascaded into my head, the ones about me influencing huge change. Except what difference would my death make?

Each breath hitched in my chest, and every slight movement was excruciating. Nicolai. I had to tell him how sorry I was for getting us killed.

Behind me, a cacophony of voices, snarling, and a distant howl blurred into the background as I pushed myself to my hands and knees. Each move had me crying. I refused to die. Not like this. I collapsed again; my body curled in on itself. Clenching my jaw tight, I rode the torture flaring down my spine. *Take small breaths. You can do this.* I kept repeating the mantra in my mind. Dragging myself up onto my arms, I reached out for the window.

My hand slipped. I tried again, except someone snatched my ankle and dragged me backwards on my stomach away from the bus. My gaze stayed locked on the vehicle, my insides turning to cement as my fingernails dug into the snow to claw my way back. And then I saw Father's feet near the front of the bus. He ripped away the rest of the glass in one grunting move and leaned in, smoke billowing out past him.

Prisoners, one by one, staggered out. Father was there, taking the police officers outside and placing them on the side of the road. Where was Nicolai?

I came to a stop, and within seconds, a wet nose pressed against my cheek. Ash? On my next inhale, I corrected that. Enre, in his wolf form. He was alive, thank the moon.

Slowly, I lifted my head, wanting to thank him. But the side of the bus, engulfed by flames, caught my attention. Prisoners were emerging, coughing, stumbling away from the accident. Most sprinted down the road, back toward the city.

The roar of the wind gushed past, snowflakes hitting the side of my face, landing in my open mouth. The vision ahead became a blurry haze of oranges and grays. My head swam, my body numb from the cold. A pair of bare feet stepped into my vision.

"Alena, I'm going to remove the crossbow bolt. It's going to hurt, but I'll make it quick." Enre's voice wavered. "Use your healing, focus on that."

Wasn't he a wolf a second ago? He remained out of my line of vision as I lay there, convinced death was coming for me. I still hadn't seen my brother.

A sudden and excruciating gnawing twisted through my shoulder and down my arm. The torturous explosion of pain deepened around the wound. My screams escalated.

Enre said something, but his words were lost in my agony and my cries for him to stop. A bolt landed in front of me, the tip covered in blood. My blood.

He applied pressure to the lesion and wrapped his jacket over my shoulder and under my armpit, all while I lay on my side, whimpering. The blinding torture spearing through me eased slightly, but not enough to stop my shaking. The care Enre showered on me was equal to that of a family member, not an enemy. I owed him my life.

I visualized a funnel of energy pouring into my shoulder, stronger and wilder by the second. Drawing healing from the world around me, I shut my eyes and pushed beyond the suffering, past the arctic chill settling in my bones. I imagined myself warm, free of horrific torment, and anywhere but in the middle of the road with my head in the snow.

Silence fell around me. It was too quiet, in fact; not even the wind blew. Opening my eyes, it took me several moments to take in the scene. I lay between the bus and Father's car. The fire crackled, but I no longer felt the heat. The wind and snow had stopped.

Ahead, Father dragged a coughing Nicolai from the bus. Blood dripped down my brother's face.

I scrambled to my feet; the inflamed soreness had dissipated from my shoulder, but haziness still circled in my head.

Kalina came into view from around the front of the bus, her crossbow aimed at Nicolai. Behind her, Lutia appeared with an arm wrapped around Damir's throat and a bolt aimed at his temple. Where had she come from?

"Stop." I took a step forward, but my knee buckled and I fell over. Quickly, I scrambled to my feet again, fighting the fog in my head threatening to knock me out.

"Lutia?" Father asked.

"You were going to report me to the Varlac," she said.

"We can still work it out. Stop now, or you'll be an outcast. No pack will take you in."

"Not if you all die tonight."

My insides scorched. With each passing second, my strength returned tenfold. My wound barely stung now. How was my body healing so fast? I moved forward, step by step, holding myself upright.

Then a blur flashed past my side—Enre in wolf form—toward Kalina.

She released a crossbow bolt, dead straight for Nicolai.

I screamed.

Father threw Nicolai aside, and the bolt slammed into his chest, sending him crumpling to the ground next to my brother.

"No!" Shivers captured my limbs. My throat was raw from yelling.

Enre crashed into Kalina, bringing her down, the crossbow tossed out of her reach. In that same moment, another wolf appeared from behind the bus—Ash—who leapt onto Lutia's back, ripping into her neck. Lutia's shrieks pierced the night.

Every nerve in my body exploded with fire, another yell howled from my throat. Then I stumbled forward, not a single twinge across my body. My muscles tightened.

I bolted, snow crunching and sliding beneath my boots.

My sights were set on Father. Nicolai leaned over him, pleading for help.

Throwing myself to my knees beside them, I reached for the bolt sticking out of Father's chest above his heart.

Father caught my hands in his icy, weak grip. "Don't. It's too late." His breaths grew raspy, slower.

"I can heal you, hold on."

Nicolai was on his feet, pacing toward the BMW and back, murmurs coming from his mouth, his head shaking.

"Alena." Father's voice was barely a whisper. "Nicolai doesn't know what he's doing in his wolf form." He sucked in a short breath, his face twisted in agony. "He doesn't remember what he's done. Don't break his spirit."

"Don't worry about that now." My voice wheezed as I placed my palms on the entry point and called for the energy that had buzzed around me seconds earlier.

"Pull out the bolt, Nic," I called out. My gaze never left Father or his struggle to keep his sleepy eyelids open. "Stay with us. Don't go." My throat stung. I poured everything I had into Father, healing him, wiping away the poison. It had to work.

"I love you both. Take care of e-each ... oth ... " His voice faded, and he froze, eyes open, no life behind them.

Tears blurred my vision as I sobbed. I clasped my eyes shut and hauled the energies from around me, not caring if I offered every ounce of my own strength.

The sensation of fire trembled through my limbs and streamed into him. I continued drawing more energy ... more than ever before. It wasn't enough. Tears ran down my cheeks and off my chin.

A faint voice said my name. Was it Father?

I snapped open my eyes and found him still lying there, not moving. My hands pressed to his bloody chest but felt no pulse.

"Alena," Nicolai said as he ran a hand over Father's eyes, closing his eyelids. "It's too late, let him go."

"No!" My body went numb.

My brother's face resembled how I felt inside: sadness pulling his features down, his eyes glistening, and his skin snow-white. When I glanced around, the trees on either side of the road were bent over, curved inward, as if reaching for us, for me, for Father.

"You did that," Nicolai said. "During your healing." He leaned across Father and placed a kiss on my brow, his warmth spreading through me.

Little made sense, and I didn't care to understand it right then. But I did know one thing. My dreams had, in fact, been a warning. A premonition. And I'd done nothing to stop them from coming true. To save my father.

CHAPTER 23

ENRE

*K*alina quivered beneath me. My paw pressed to her throat above the Interpol badge, claws drawing blood. My jaws were inches from her blurry face. *Shit, I'm losing my grip.*

With lips peeled back, teeth exposed, I was ready to tear into her flesh. Every hair on my back stood on end as my wolf demanded we finish her. My muscles tensed, and I salivated at the idea. After all, she knew our kind existed and deserved to die after killing Maxim.

Nausea refused to leave my gut, sending uncontrollable shivers through me. Alena's healing mojo helped a bit. I needed more. The icy poison still coursed through my veins.

"Do it already, you disgusting monster." Kalina's eyes narrowed, and her mouth twisted. "I welcome death if it means seeing my parents again."

Oh, she'd get her wish soon enough.

Ripping Kalina's life away would give me the ultimate pleasure, but it wasn't mine to take. Alena deserved that right because of Maxim.

Squirming under me, Kalina shifted her hips slightly.

Movement to my left caused me to jerk my head around. Her hand gripped a blade aimed at my face.

I jumped back and snapped onto her wrist, teeth biting down hard. The blade fell on the ground as she screamed. Her cries did nothing to loosen my grasp, and neither did the weak punches she threw into my ribs.

Near the front of the bus, I glimpsed Blackie hauling Ash by her tail away from Lutia's limp body. Ash released Lutia and snarled, fighting against Blackie's pull. A part of me pitied Lutia. If she hadn't spent so much time backstabbing wulfkin, she wouldn't have ended up as wolf chow.

Free from Blackie, Ash pounced toward me.

A deep growl rolled through my chest. *This isn't for you.*

Ash slipped a few paces away, then sprinted toward Nicolai, who knelt next to

Maxim. Leaping up, her front paws landed on his shoulders. Nicolai embraced her in a hug, his face buried in her fur.

Towing a protesting Kalina, I dropped her arm and released a throaty grumble to Alena.

She was on her feet, pacing in a small circle near her father and brother, her arms tight across her stomach and her mouth moving but no words coming out.

She stopped her frantic pacing and turned. I retreated a few steps to indicate that Kalina was all hers.

The shriek of sirens closed in from behind me.

Kalina, cradling her injured arm against her chest, pulled herself upright to a sitting position. "You're all murderers. Even your own kind loathes you. Lutia betrayed you. She told me of Maxim's plan to break Nicolai out after overhearing him talking about it." Kalina's voice shook. "And killing me won't hide what you are. The truth always comes out. You kidnapped the missing girl, Ash Antov, too. Your brother probably ate her." Trembling, Kalina's gaze scanned the road behind us.

"We were trying to save Ash from humans like you." Alena pointed to Ash by Nicolai's side. "She's stuck in her wolf form, and we've been trying to help her because I doubt her human mother would accept her this way."

I kept glancing over my shoulder, expecting police cars to appear any second.

Kalina's eyes narrowed at Ash, who pushed her muzzle into Nicolai's side. Alena faced me, dread clear behind those pale, gray eyes. We had to get out.

I morphed into human form. The moment my fur vanished, a chill closed in around me. "Finish her, Alena. We should have left five minutes ago." I scanned the road for my clothes and retrieved them in haste.

Quick to get dressed, I returned to Alena. Kalina continued dragging herself away from the group on her butt.

"Alena," I said.

She marched after the human, Ash by her side.

"Nic, get Maxim in the van, now," I said. "Blackie. I-I mean Damir, you take Maxim's car. Take Lutia's body and put her in your trunk. We can't leave it behind." All the prisoners had fled the scene, rushing toward the city. Hopefully, they'd be caught by the police, slowing their approach.

Damir climbed to his feet first and offered me a confirming nod, the kind that a pack member gives another. Despite past encounters with the wulfkin, I saw him now for what he really was—caring and loving when it came to his alpha, his family, his pack. That, I respected.

The sirens and the snowfall intensified as I approached the girls, eager for us to leave. I couldn't work out how Alena had managed to warp the trees on either side of us. Had the recent Lunar Eutine changed Alena as much as it had

Daciana, when it had given her the new ability of being able to tell if someone was lying with one touch?

A sudden crack resonated from the bus. The fire had spread across its belly. Another spark. Hell, it might blow.

"Alena, we have to go. Right now." The jitters captured my limbs.

"Kalina," Alena said, standing over the human, her voice soft and slow, yet strong enough to be heard over the breeze. "My brother might have taken your father's life, but I'm giving yours back."

Kalina stopped her fidgeting and stared at Alena.

I gasped. "You're letting her go?"

Alena's focus remained on Kalina, seemingly calm and in control of her emotions, until I noticed the whiteness of her knuckles fisted at her sides and the shakes snaking up her arms. Snow was falling horizontally now, slamming against her back, and yet she stood there immobile, frozen in the moment.

I reached across to Alena, cupping her hand in mine, pulling her away. No words were exchanged—anything I said would have been empty of meaning. At times like these, knowing you weren't alone was what mattered, or at least that's how it had been for me when Sandulf passed.

Alena withdrew her hand from mine and wiped her eyes. She patted down her torn and tattered jacket and hurried toward the van, her boots kicking snow, Ash on her heels.

Kalina watched her, gripping her bleeding arm against her chest. Her expression froze somewhere between shock and confusion.

The sirens were close. Nerves crawled up my spine. Leaning in to Kalina, I said, "If I get a whiff of you near Alena, the circus, or me, you won't even see me coming. I won't be as generous as Alena. Count yourself lucky." My hands curled into fists. "And that applies to telling the police anything about who we are or our involvement in any of this."

Kalina curled her knees into her chest and bowed her head. I took her submissive response as confirmation that she believed my threat.

Red and blue lights flickered through the mass of trees behind us. I sprinted toward our van, climbed inside, and turned around to see Ash and Nicolai in the back with Maxim's body. Alena belted herself into the passenger seat, her face pale and tears trailing down her cheeks. The BMW inched closer, with Damir at the wheel.

"Let's go." I sped past Kalina and the overturned bus. Damir was behind.

The first full glow blue and red lights emerged on the road in the distance.

I left our headlights off a while longer. Once we were farther down the road and clearly concealed by the forest, I flicked the beams on and drove my foot into the accelerator, further increasing our speed. Damir kept up.

An explosion erupted behind us.

"Shit." Alena covered her mouth.

"Must have reached the fuel line," I said, not voicing the fact of how close we'd been to the vehicle minutes earlier.

Alena placed a hand on my thigh but kept her gaze on the road ahead. Judging by the inferno burning in her touch, I figured she was continuing to heal me. How could I ever repay her?

"I'm so sorry about your father."

She nodded silently, and her next breath hiccupped. I saw her brother bow his head in the rear-view mirror.

Snow pelted our windshield, the wipers doing little for my vision. With no other cars on the road, I guessed we were safe to go a bit faster. We needed to put distance between us and the scene. The police would spend time trying to track the escaped prisoners first. By the time they realized Nicolai was missing, the rest of the pack should have left Bulgaria.

My mind whirred with options. The complication of having Ash and two corpses with us meant we couldn't return to the circus. Revealing a dead alpha would surely cause panic. But they'd hear the news soon.

"Are you all right, Nic?" Alena asked.

"In shock." His words were smothered in sniffles. "I'll survive."

Once we arrived in Transylvania, I'd have to convince Daciana that the army of refugee wulfkin I'd brought to her doorstep was in no way a threat. I hadn't convinced myself of that yet, but I'd try. Even bringing Alena and Nicolai, the alpha's offspring, promised little. When an alpha was killed, kin could step up to be the next in line, but if challenged by anyone in the pack, they had to fight for the position. One option was the pack merging with Daciana's, which made more sense. I almost laughed to myself thinking about how Daciana hated being an alpha, yet I'd be offering her close to forty more members to join her family. How would she react? She wouldn't be thrilled—I was sure. Of course, there was another option. With the predicament of my father and my twenty-fifth birthday being tomorrow, there was the possibility of me stepping up for the alpha position. But I wasn't sure Alena and Nicolai would accept my takeover.

Maxim was the kind of father I wished I'd had growing up. I'd overheard him tell Alena how Nicolai had no idea what he was doing. Maxim had protected his son from the truth. So, who was I to tell Nicolai what he'd done? We'd all made mistakes in our past, let our wolves take too much control. Now that Alena knew, she could find a way to ensure he never hurt another person again. And I'd gladly help her if she'd let me.

"I'm thinking we should head straight to Transylvania as

per your father's original plan," I said, "as long as the police don't call the border to alert them of the prison break and ask them to search cars."

The soft sobbing from the back of the van could only be Nicolai. I glanced over to Alena, but her gaze remained fixed outside the passenger window on the dark forest passing by.

"I know someone at the bridge checkpoint who might be able to help us," Alena said, breaking her silence. "A friend of Father's." When she looked at me, her features were concealed by shadows. "Thank you. You owe our pack nothing, but you're still helping us." Her hand lingered on my leg, fire coursing through me.

At first, I couldn't find my voice. For too long I'd believed the Bulgarian pack was savage, ready to fight and kill us, but those were ideas put into my head by Sandulf. I should have known better than to believe anything he said after what he did to our own pack. These wulfkin were like us—trying to survive in a harsh world where running and hiding were our only options. Maxim had done what any alpha would—he fought to save his family—and I was fully convinced he'd been a reasonable wulfkin.

I lifted Alena's hand to my lips and sniffed her faint scent of lavender. "I do what it takes to help a wulfkin in need." I glanced across to her. "Especially you."

She returned to staring out the window and drew her hand away.

Somehow, I would make our situation with Daciana work. Now that we knew what Nicolai was capable of during the full moons, I'd personally build him a cage he'd never escape. My future with Alena was still uncertain, but first we had to deal with the small problem of getting out of Bulgaria in one piece.

CHAPTER 24

ALENA

"We're going to come to a T-intersection at the end of this road," I said, my body still numb. I couldn't believe that Father lay in the back of the van ... dead. Still, my words poured out as if on autopilot. "Turn right. The road will take us to an old freeway that heads back into Ruse. Unfortunately, we'll need to go through part of the city once we leave the park. There's no other way to reach the bridge."

Enre nodded, his hands practically strangling the steering wheel as the vehicle swayed across the road from the wind and snow. "Hope this contact of yours at the bridge is the real deal."

"He works nights, and anyone from our pack can cross the bridge into Romania without a passport." Father used to send wulfkin across the Danube River to spy on the Transylvanian pack. I remember how excited he was about finally finding us a permanent home. And now he wouldn't even get to experience it with us. Tears flooded my cheeks again. I couldn't stop them or the splintering in my chest. Every part of me shook as I hiccupped my next breath. *Hold yourself together. A bit longer.* But Father was dead, and it felt as if someone had stolen everything I'd owned while I wasn't looking.

Enre glanced my way, sorrow and concern burrowing behind his eyes.

I willed away the rush of grief clawing up my throat. We had saved Nicolai. That was something. No, it was everything. Maybe I should have listened to Father about tonight and stayed back at the circus. If I hadn't tried to rescue Nicolai, would Father still be alive? *Moon goddess, give me strength.* Lifting my feet up onto the seat, I hugged my knees to my chest and laid a cheek on them, staring out at the blur of forest. Each time I closed my eyes, I pictured Father lying on the road, struggling to keep his eyes open. He stared at me without a hint of blame in his expression. I bit my lower lip, failing at keeping the tears at bay.

Enre touched my shoulder, and his warmth spread through me.

Once we reached the intersection and Enre turned right, the sound of sirens found us. I gripped the door handle as my heart slammed into my sternum. With my feet back down, I stared into the side mirror. No sign of flashing lights.

Shit. I had to warn the rest of the pack. Even though Enre said the police would be busy rounding up the escaped prisoners, I couldn't count on that. Grabbing the cell from my pocket, I dialed Sonia's number. *Please pick up.*

"Hey, girl."

"Sonia." My voice wavered. "You need to get everyone to leave for Romania as soon as possible. Don't wait until the morning. Do it now if the circus is packed."

"Why? What's going on?"

"Cops will swarm the area looking for Nicolai. Leave now before they try and stop you."

"You're scaring me, Alena. Are you all right?"

"I'm fine." My next inhale hitched as tears threaded down my cheeks. "Please, Sonia. I'll tell you everything when you and the pack arrive in Transylvania. Call me, and I'll give you directions once you're in Braşov."

Her shallow breaths sped up. "Of course. We're almost packed. We can leave very soon."

"Love you." I hung up before I blubbered more and completely lost it. With the phone back in my pocket, I wrapped my arms around my stomach.

Enre accelerated, and we fishtailed; he steadied the van, and we raced ahead. Damir maintained his distance behind us in the Beemer.

I glanced into the back of the van at Nicolai and Ash. "We'll be fine." I had no idea if we would be, but it seemed like the right reassurance to give. Father had always spoken such kind words whenever we battled other problems.

"How far to the bridge?" Enre asked, his voice tense.

"About twenty minutes." Fear swept through me once more. "If Kalina tells the police it was us, the pack will be arrested."

Enre's gaze remained fixed on the curvy road we sped along. "She'll keep her mouth shut, I made sure. Plus, by the time the police track down all the runaway prisoners and finally realize Nicolai is missing, we'll be long gone. And if the rest of the pack leaves soon, they should also make it out before they are suspects."

"You sound awfully confident in that," Nicolai said from the back. "Who are you, anyway?"

"I'm Enre, a pack member from Transylvania helping you out. When you're neck- deep in shit, you take help from wherever you can find it, no matter who's offering."

"How would you know? Were you stuck in a bus, battling for each breath, convinced you'd never see your family again?" Nicolai's tone was sharp and sarcastic.

"Nic," I butted in. "He's with me."

"It's okay," Enre said. "My whole pack almost got killed because of our ex-alpha. He raised a dracwulf. But I never stopped fighting to survive, so I do understand."

I gasped, knowing too well what a suicide decision that was for the whole pack. It was well documented in wulfkin history that one of those berserk animals had once slaughtered an entire village of humans. They were illegal, and any wulfkin caught rearing one had their whole pack sentenced to death. Courtesy of the Varlac, of course. Our leaders were fearful of them, and for good reason.

"How could he have risked your lives like that?" I asked.

"It was Sandulf's way of dealing with your encroaching pack. Except he lost control of the animal. The dracwulf claimed me, dragging me into its lair, and Sandulf happily obliged. He left me for dead in the dracwulf's cave." His voice deepened. "I had a severe bite from the dracwulf." He glanced over at me. "That's why it took me so long to heal from the bullet wound."

A tightness crawled through my chest.

"I wasn't ready to die," Enre said. "Each day, I attempted to escape. And I always believed I'd get out alive. In the end, Daciana rescued me."

Silence filled the van. Only the distant sirens wailed.

"I'm sorry you went through that," I said.

"If I didn't perish while at the mercy of a monster, I sure as hell am not going down in this situation."

Shivers crawled up my legs. We kept driving along the darkened forest road, and the closer we got to Ruse again, the louder the sirens became. Emerging from the national park, we entered the main road. The flashing lights of a police car brightened the sky from a cross street ahead.

My breath froze in my lungs.

Enre lowered his head but didn't change lanes. Smart move not to draw attention.

"Shit, we'll be caught." Nicolai's words were strangled.

"Keep it together." A growl rolled from Enre's throat.

"I'm fine, you look after yourself." Nicolai's voice deepened. His wolf instincts were kicking in. Tomorrow's full moon was already affecting him.

The police vehicle zoomed past us, then a second one. They were headed to the scene of the accident.

"Take the next right," I said, tucking my jittery hands beneath my thighs. "And follow the back roads."

No one spoke for the next mile or so as we drove between apartment buildings on one side and the frozen Danube River on the other. Stripped of leaves, the gnarly trees along the bank wore an icy skin, resembling an arctic forest sculpture. Up ahead, the enormous metal bridge came into view. Lights dotted its length across the frozen river that divided Romania and Bulgaria. I prayed Father's contact still manned the bridge on the night shift. Usually, we gave him a heads-up when we were coming. Too late now.

Enre glanced at me. "It's your turn to shine and get us home."

CHAPTER 25

Shuffling sounded from the back of the van.

A rush of panic, guilt, and sickness swirled in my belly. My pulse drummed beneath

my skin, and I took a peek over my shoulder to see Nicolai covering up Father and Ash, probably just in case we were searched.

We curved toward the border crossing where only one of three checkpoints was open. A massive semitruck sat at the operational booth. The barrier lifted, and the truck moved forward.

Enre inched our van toward the booth and locked us into park. Looking across to me, he asked, "You good to do this?"

I nodded, though the rest of my body had different intentions—mostly not moving from the seat. When I spotted a young, pale-haired guy emerge from the booth, my stomach lurched. That wasn't Father's friend.

Grabbing my wallet from my jacket's pocket, I took out the wad of euros I had with shaky fingers, not paying attention to how much it was, and climbed out. Frost closed around me, the light splattering of snow an icy kiss each time it touched my skin.

I plastered a fake smile on my face.

"Hi, is Ivan working tonight?" Probably not a smart question, but my head wasn't functioning.

"Passport for everyone in the van." He stuck out a hand and tucked the other into his pocket, shivering on the spot.

I stood there, immobile, with no response coming to mind. We had no passports, only a wolf and two dead bodies. *Oh, hell.*

The man's eyes narrowed, his fingers wriggling toward me. "Hurry up, it's cold."

"Ghiţă," a man's voice said from near the booth. "I've got this. Go inside."

I glanced toward the checkpoint and spotted an older, stockier man with black hair emerging from the booth in a huge duffle jacket and hugging himself. My muscles eased. It was Ivan—Father's connection. *Thank the goddess.*

Ghiţă grumbled under his breath and slowly walked back inside.

Ivan offered me a knowing smile. Father had made connections with humans everywhere he traveled to benefit the pack, but none of them knew wulfkin existed.

"Did I miss a call from your father?" Over my shoulder, he studied our van and the Beemer.

My throat seized up, the words wedged inside me along with tears, and shivers claimed my legs at the notion of talking about Father as if he still breathed. I shook my head. "This is a last-minute crossing. Two cars for now."

Momentarily glancing over his shoulder at the camera above the booth pointed in our direction, he shifted his back to it and stuck his hand out. I stuffed the euros into his palm. A sleight of hand with money guaranteed you anything you wanted in this part of the world.

A quick count of the money, and his head jerked up. "This is half the usual."

I rubbed the chill in my arms, doing nothing but spreading the cold through me. "That's all I have."

Some had been stashed in the car, but we might need that later on. And I didn't want to use Father's bank account. It would leave a trail. Though, with the camera at the booth, the police would know we crossed anyway.

"Please." I refused to glance back, despite the howl of sirens in the city behind us. "The circus is crossing over to Romania in a few hours, and I'll make sure they pay you double." My limbs shivered uncontrollably, and my teeth chattered.

"I just received an alert to shut the border." He stared at me. With the mess clouding my thoughts, for the life of me, I couldn't pinpoint his expression, especially with his hooded eyes. It sent all kinds of mixed signals.

If the border closed, we'd be stuck in Bulgaria and hunted down by the police.

"Triple, and you have a deal," he said.

My breaths refused to leave my lungs. "Done."

His fingers curled around the money. He stuffed his fist into his jacket, spun on his heels, and hurried back into his booth. I presumed that was a good-to-go sign, so I rushed back into the van, slamming the door shut to stop warmth from escaping. I blew hot air into my cupped hands.

"So? What's going on?" Enre asked.

"We wait and pray he lifts the barrier. Then we're free to go."

After five minutes, I was still shifting in my seat.

"What's taking so long?" Nicolai asked from the back.

I shrugged and peeked behind me. Nicolai remained in the back, shrouded in shadows.

When I turned back around, the barrier was lifting, and the heaviness in my chest eased. We were driving again.

Damir stayed close to our bumper as if worried we'd leave him behind. I kept glancing in the side mirror, holding my breath, and that's when I saw the flash of blue and red lights appear in the distance.

"Oh, crap."

Enre checked his rearview and side mirrors. No one made a sound during our crossing.

"They're shutting down the border," I said.

The beating of my heart refused to slow. With us clear and moving forward, I scooped out my cell. I sent Sonia a text telling her the border was closed and to delay crossing for a day. I felt horrible changing plans on Sonia again, but better they sit tight for another day than wait in limbo near the border and draw unwanted suspicion.

A pair of stone towers flanked the road as we entered the actual Danube steel bridge that connected Bulgaria to Romania. The metal railings of the bridge swooshed past us, lights guiding our path along the two-lane motorway. On either side of us, night claimed the river. A large sign with the word *Romania* printed on it appeared in the distance alongside the blue-, yellow-, and red-striped flag.

As we approached the exit booth, the barrier rose.

Once we entered Romania, a sense of calm crept over me. I slouched in my seat, and Enre's arms relaxed on the steering wheel. We had made it across. I couldn't believe it. Still, no one breathed a word.

An hour into the drive, Enre pulled into a gas station. He made sure to park at the side of the building, not far from the toilets.

Out of the car, I stretched my body, unable to take my eyes off Enre, who strolled into the store. He'd risked so much for us. How could I ever repay him? Damir parked nearby and climbed out, also heading for the store.

The moment Nicolai slipped outside, I dragged him into a hug, no matter how horrible he stunk of perspiration, dirt, and smoke. "It's great to have you back."

He still wore his clothes from the day he was caught by the police, bloodstains concealed by filthy patches. Small-time detention centers didn't waste money on prison clothes. Soot marred his face and hands and was smeared across his nose. It was obvious he'd been in a fire.

"I still can't believe what happened, you know," he said. "I thought I'd die in that bus." The pain was raw in his eyes. "And Father ... " His words ended abruptly, his gaze falling to his bare feet. "What happens now?"

"We find a new home. The rest of the pack will join us shortly. It will work out for us in Transylvania. This was Father's plan, what he wanted."

His head jerked up as if startled. "I don't want to lead the pack, Alena."

I nodded. This was uncharted territory for us, and so much relied on Enre now. We were in his hands, but for once, I had no doubts about him. I trusted he had our best interests at heart. However, he wasn't the alpha of his pack—Daciana might not want us.

"I'm not too sure what happens now, but we'll get through it. I'll take charge of the pack temporarily." In all honesty, I didn't want to run the pack, either, but what other options remained? And I refused to let everything Father had worked so hard for go to waste.

Nicolai took me into his arms, rubbing a palm down my back just like Father used to do. I wiped away my tears. Breaking from our hug, I nudged him back into the van. "Wait in there, and I'll get the keys to the toilets so you can clean up a bit."

I hurried into the store and bought several bottles of water, a towel, beef jerky, a belt, socks, and a *Welcome to Bucharest* sweatshirt for Nicolai. I grabbed several cupcakes too.

After Nicolai had washed up, we got back on the road. Silence filled the van again. In the early-morning hours, we reached the capital of Romania, Bucharest, before the sun put in an appearance. We passed huge glass buildings. There were offices, villas, and other modern structures. The traffic was heavy, and the side of the road was littered with cars, probably from drivers intent on overtaking other vehicles.

Enre swerved the van, barely missing a dog, and cursed under his breath. "I feel sorry for all the strays in this city."

I gripped the door handle, my pulse on a rampage, convinced we'd hit something before we made it out of the jungle of chaos. Behind us, Damir stayed closer.

"Let's take the dogs with us." Nicolai piped up. Why didn't his suggestion surprise me?

Enre half snorted, probably thinking Nicolai was joking around. I didn't have the heart to break it to Enre that Nicolai meant every word, even piling our car with stray dogs.

Driving through the city, we passed rows of cement apartments, balconies adorned with satellites. I could never live cooped up in such blocks. I pitied the people who did.

We passed one historical building, complete with sculptured goddesses flanking the front gate. I made a mental note to return to Bucharest and discover what else this city offered.

When Enre glanced at me, his mouth morphed into a grin, the edges of his eyes creasing. "You all right?"

I studied his hard jawline, the exhaustion beneath his eyes, and his curled shoulders. "What is Daciana like?"

"She's unlike any other wulfkin you'll ever meet. Strong,

independent, and she'd sacrifice her life for another wulfkin without a second thought. And she would have preferred to be born a human." He shrugged. "But we all live with our demons." He nodded to himself as if recalling memories between the pair. And I recalled Lutia's words about Enre having a crush on Daciana. Had that only been in Lutia's warped imagination?

"What's the likelihood Daciana will be open to sharing her land with us?"

"Very high. She'd never turn away a wulfkin in danger." Not a hint of doubt or hesitation accompanied his response.

"Sounds positive."

"You two have a lot in common. At the last Lunar Eutine, Daciana also transformed from moonwulf into wulfkin, and the moon goddess also blessed her. She has this heightened sense. With a single touch, she can tell you a wulfkin's true intent. Whether they're lying or being honest."

I glanced down at my hands. I wasn't wearing my gloves, and I didn't feel the slightest exhaustion after healing both Enre and Father with my ability. And the healing seemed different, almost as if I drew energy from around me, not within me. Did that explain the bent trees? It both terrified and intrigued me, though any gift from the moon goddess must be a blessing.

"Handy ability," Nicolai said from the back.

"Yeah, we better keep her away from you," I said, "or she'll reveal each time you lied about letting Ash out of her cage or when you snuck out of the circus to attend discos."

Nicolai released a loud huff, followed by Ash's whining sound.

Then I gifted Nicolai with two cupcakes and Enre with one. He reached over to take it from my palm, but Ash's snout shoved forward from the back of the van and snatched it out of my hand in one bite, paper holder and all.

"Ash. That wasn't yours."

She licked the icing off her nose.

Enre laughed. "It sure did look good."

"No food is safe around that food-muncher extraordinaire." Funny how the smallest actions easily squashed the pain riding inside me, even if only for a moment.

"You can have mine," Nicolai said.

"Nah, you enjoy it," Enre said. "I'm fine."

A cop whizzed past us in the opposite direction. My breath hitched. They chased a speeder, not us. Taking a shaky inhale, I glanced over at Enre and offered a nervous smile. His pale face reflected my mood.

Even though Enre promised us Daciana was reasonable, what if he was wrong? What if she only wanted her existing pack? We outnumbered them, so she might see us as a threat. Emotions knotted my insides into an untameable mess.

Well, I guess if she said no, then we'd continue onward from city to city as we had with Father, until we located another place to call home. And the thought had me wondering how I'd feel about leaving Enre behind. It was ridiculous, of course …

Except, he'd endangered himself to help us when he didn't have to. Would Enre roam the countryside with us while we hunted for a place to live?

CHAPTER 26

ENRE

$\mathcal{E}$xhausted, I drove through the Carpathian woods. The sight and fresh scent of the tall pine trees reminded me how much I missed home. Snow coated the curvy path as we made the slow, slippery climb up the mountain. The bumpy ride had everyone in the van jostling around. Damir kept close behind us.

Soon enough, we emerged into an open area, clear of trees, where the Transylvanian pack house lay. My gut tightened. For the past few days, I hadn't been sure I'd see home again.

The sun peeked out from behind the clouds, lighting up the snowy yard and roof. Smoke billowed out of the chimney of the cottage-style building. Sandulf's old Land Cruiser sat in the driveway. Daciana had swapped her old car for Sandulf's.

Nicolai stuck his head out between our seats. "Wow, this place looks like it belongs in a fairy tale."

Unbuckling my seatbelt, I said, "Stay here a moment. Let me see who's home."

Outside, I inhaled fresh kindling on the breeze and

236

hurried along a pebbly path shoveled clear of snow. Cheerful curtains hung at the windows. Someone had been keeping house, though I suspected it wasn't Daciana. Probably Boltof, the oldest in the pack. The last time I was home, we'd finished repairing the laundry room after our battle with the dracwulf. Now, no one would suspect such a fight took place here. Any human stumbling into this area might have mistaken it for a getaway home or some hippie hangout.

The crunch of snow drew my attention to the back of the house, out of sight of the van. I turned the corner and found Daciana approaching, her arms filled with wood for the fireplace. Dressed in jeans, knee-high snow boots, and a furry coat the color of night, she seemed a world away. The breeze blew through her brown hair. She stopped on the spot, her head jerked up, and her gaze landed on me.

"Enre." Tossing the timber to the ground, she ran toward me.

She hugged me with the warmth and comfort of a sibling welcoming me home. Strange how the last couple of weeks had changed me. Despite Daciana's choice to love a human, I was happier for her now than I ever had been. I guess it came with my own happiness.

Breaking our hug, she said, "Thank the moon you're home." She smacked my arm. "I hate it when you pull this shit and go off on your own. Why didn't you talk to me first?"

"Because you would've stopped me, and don't say you wouldn't have. I can see it in your eyes even now."

She shook her head. "You'll have to tell me everything over dinner."

"Well ... " I started, and her furrowed brow stole my words. "You're not going to like this ... "

The narrowing of her eyes reminded me of the multitude of times she'd pushed me away, making it clear we weren't meant to be together. She'd always have a place in my heart, but not in the way Alena made my pulse skip, or the way my wolf instantly responded to hers, or how my every thought was consumed by her.

"Most of the Bulgarian pack will be arriving in the next couple of days," I said. Daciana's cheeks paled. "They're attacking?"

"No." I took her hand and drew her toward a wooden bench Botolf had crafted from a

dead log. Brushing the snow off, I guided her to sit and joined her. "It's much more complicated." And then everything from the last couple of weeks poured out, from Nicolai's capture by the police, him murdering humans without knowing, to Maxim's struggles to find a safe home for his pack, Ash, Kalina's revenge, and the whole bus incident. I even told her about Alena, and how she made me feel, which was completely unlike me. But it seemed nothing would stop the words from steamrolling out.

"Their pack has nowhere to go," I said. "I thought they might share our land. I can build Nic a cage to make sure he never gets out again during the full moon. Either Nic or Alena will lead their pack, or maybe I could ... " When Daciana didn't say a word, my voice stopped flat. "Or we could propose to them that we merge the packs and you become the overall alpha. You can then run the biggest pack in Europe." I stood and paced in a small circle, nerves licking the length of my spine. "They're vulnerable, but a great group of wulfkin who've had a string of bad luck in finding a home."

I glanced over at Daciana, who sat there, her eyes on the house and hands gripping the bench.

"Say something," I said.

When she looked my way, a new expression met mine; one filled with desperation, pain, and guilt. "I didn't even want to be alpha of our pack, why would you think I want to lead the biggest?"

"Easy. You don't have to merge with their pack as long as you are okay sharing the land with them."

She lifted herself from the seat with the grace I was used to witnessing in Sandulf and even Maxim ... a true alpha, controlling one's emotions, which I always failed at miserably.

"Definitely, they're welcome to share the land." Her words were strangled. I couldn't pinpoint the sentiment behind her voice.

"What's wrong?"

"Your father." She fell silent, staring at me. Then she went on, "He's here, in the house. I've had to entertain the prick since yesterday."

Dread seeped into my veins. *Fuck!*

Daciana hugged herself, her eyes darting around in a nervous way. "I told your father I wanted to hand the pack over to you and asked him if he'd officiate at the ceremony."

A bulldozer of emotions slammed into me. It was difficult, but I doubted Father would have been thrilled with Daciana's request. He believed wulfkin deserving of alpha status had to claw their way to the top.

"Why would you want to give up being an alpha?" The idea was foreign to me. I'd dreamt of the position for too long. Perhaps because of the overshadowing pressure to have my own pack by the age of twenty-five or I'd die.

"I plan to live with Connell in the city, continue my research on saving wild animals, and scout for our pack. I know this puts me at the bottom of the pack rank, but I don't care." She smiled briefly and shrugged. "Sandulf had hoped to give you the pack all along anyway. If you'll still have me, this is what I choose."

"Of course I'll have you. You're not going anywhere." I

opened my arms and took her into an embrace, rubbing her back, realizing how difficult this decision must have been for her. Thinking back to the trials she went through to save her relationship with her human, standing up to Sandulf and killing him, it wasn't a surprise. Though it still struck hard. I didn't share my concern that my father might not agree with her. First, I'd pay him a visit.

Daciana broke away. "This also means you no longer have to worry about not meeting your end of the Varlac pact. There's no reason for your father to challenge you and demand your death since you have your own pack now."

My spine stiffened. "You're doing this for me?"

Her voice was stern. "No. I'm doing this for *me*, but we're both benefiting from it." This was the Daciana I remembered so well.

"I don't give a shit about my father. He can rot in hell."

An icy wind blew, threatening snow again at any moment.

A smile spread across Daciana's lips, but it vanished in a second flat. She lifted her head and sniffed the air. "Someone's here. Wulfkin."

The wind fanned across my back. I found myself smiling and turned around. "A few of the pack came with me."

Alena walked around the corner of the house, her arms over her stomach, followed by Nicolai and Damir. Ash already pounced toward me, kicking snow behind her. My eagerness to tell Alena she was welcome, along with the whole pack, tickled the back of my throat.

Ash lunged at me, her huge paws crashing into my shoulders, and she pushed me down in the snow. Her wet tongue licked my cheek. I couldn't stop the laughter. "Down, Ash."

She shook herself, snow flying in every direction, and immediately coiled around Daciana's legs.

Scratching Ash's ears, Daciana's gaze locked onto the three wulfkin closing in.

I climbed to my feet. "Let me introduce you to Alena Novac; her brother, Nicolai Novac; and Damir. Daciana has no problems with you and your pack sharing her land."

Alena stepped forward first, and Daciana accepted her in a hug. Seeing the two wulfkin who held a special place in my heart hugging and inhaling each other's scent aroused all kinds of thoughts. My wolf was ready to come out and party.

Damir's and Nicolai's gazes were set on Daciana, and not in the enemy kind of way, either. She'd kick their butts across the yard if they tried anything, but hey, I'd allow them to discover that the hard way.

"We appreciate you accepting us on your land," Alena said.

Daciana slipped her hands into her pockets and shrugged. "You're most welcome. No one should ever turn away wulfkin in need."

Alena's gaze landed on me, and I rewarded her with a smile.

Daciana refused to take her eyes off Alena. I swore a sliver of jealousy crossed her expression. Oh, yeah, now we were even. I'd had the same reaction, but much worse, when Daciana first shacked up with that human.

Color hit Alena's cheeks. "Do you have a problem with us burying Father on the land then? Somewhere deeper in the woods, if possible, to say our farewell?"

"Not at all," Daciana said. "I'll take you to a perfect spot while Enre speaks with his father." The bridge of her nose creased at the mention of my father.

"And Lutia," Damir piped up.

"She should be buried very deep in the woods," Daciana offered. "Maybe close to Sandulf."

"Your father's here?" Alena's gaze bore into me, her voice high-pitched.

Kissing the back of her hand, I said, "Don't worry. I'll join you shortly."

"Come, I'll help you with the bodies." Daciana started toward the front of the house with Damir and Nicolai behind her. Ash romped ahead.

Alena stared at me, so many emotions whirring behind her pale-gray eyes.

"Go, I need to see my father."

After a simple nod, she leaned into me, her lips grazing mine. My arms swept across her back, drawing her closer. I inhaled her lavender sweetness and returned the kiss, permitting myself to forget the horror of my father being here for those few seconds.

Once she'd left my side, I headed toward the back door of the pack house. My gut twisted into a knot with each step. I opened the door and stepped into the kitchen.

Father's scent—a sour, tree-sap odor—collided into me. Too many fights and punishments from my younger days flooded back, the ones I'd worked so hard to forget. Except now they were as raw and fresh as if they'd happened yesterday.

The first wave of shivers clawed up my spine. He wasn't the kind of wulfkin who took any pleasure in of social niceties. *"Get the task done and go,"* he'd say. *"Lingering is a female's job."* Everything with Father came with a mission, a purpose that somehow benefited him. And considering today I turned twenty-five, I knew exactly why he was here.

From the time I'd left my Varlac clan in Hungary eleven years ago, this day had been niggling in the darkest recesses of my head. The moment when I'd declare either that I had a pack of my own or that Father had the right to take my life in any way he desired.

Taking a deep breath and squaring my shoulders, I pushed past the swinging kitchen door and stepped into the main living room. The air was thick with the smell of fur, perspiration, and kindling from the roaring fireplace.

A quick scan revealed five wulfkin. Botolf sat on an over-stuffed chair, dressed in a pink Hawaiian shirt, while Radu huddled on the wooden floor next to him, hugging his knees. Both their smiles were a welcome sight.

"Good to be home," I said in their direction, not expecting a response. It was for show, nothing more.

My sights landed on Father, who lounged in the center of the large sofa, his arms folded across his lap, still bear-like in stature. The only hint of him aging was the presence of a few silver strands streaking his short black hair above his temples. Behind him waited his muscle—two large wulfkin. I didn't recognize either of them, but it had been a while since I'd left home.

"Father." I stopped several paces away. "A pleasure to see you."

With his hands on his knees, he pushed himself up. "Don't kid yourself." Growing up, he'd beaten into me the notion of never talking to wulfkin while sitting, or I might as well join the females in the kitchen. "Here I was thinking my visit would be like our good old days, until Daciana spoiled the fun."

Yep, straight to business. Who needed niceties when dealing with the devil? One side of his mouth curled upward, and the look in his eyes held the same evil I'd seen each time he prepared for another punishment.

The bastard enjoyed every punch he threw my way, and a quick glimpse of his large hands as he wiped them down his black shirt brought back the memories: the thunderous pain his strikes left, and my struggles for breath each time his fist collided with my chest.

"Sorry to disappoint." I made no attempt to keep the sarcasm out of my response.

He motioned his disinterest with a curt wave of his hand, as if I were no more than a pesky fly. "I'm used to your disappointments." He strolled across the room toward the window, his boots thumping the wooden floorboards with each step. He turned his back to the window, a halo of light cast around his large frame.

Another wulfkin emerged from the hallway into the room with us.

I did a double take. "Matias? When did you get back?" Matias had been part of the Transylvania pack, but once Daciana had killed Sandulf, he'd vanished and none of us had known where he'd gone.

"He's with me," Father said, dragging my attention back to him. "The only wulfkin from this pack brave enough to tell me the truth about what's been going on."

A snarl lodged in my throat. Matias sold us out to my father.

"I thought you were killed by the dracwulf," Matias added. "So I did the right thing and sought help."

"Well, you can continue considering me dead," I said, "seeing as how you sought immunity from Varlac punishment and not caring for the rest of the pack."

Matias straightened his posture, his gaze fallen. Pack members stood up for each other. They didn't run away the second life got hard.

"Enough of your squabbles." Father stomped toward me. "So, Sandulf created a dracwulf, and yet I had to hear about it *weeks* later from someone other than my son?" His voice grew sharp. "We had an understanding. You report *everything* back to me."

"There was no such agreement." My response flew back fast, and I tucked my fisted hands into my pockets. "Maybe if you had treated me as a son rather than target practice, I might have understood your intentions better."

"Pfft," he hissed through clenched teeth. "I gave you a Varlac upbringing, something any wulfkin would have cherished. If you have no backbone, then that rests on your shoulders, *son*." He spat the final word.

He circled me, and I stood there, refusing to let him intimidate me. Never again.

"So, now I'm left with the difficult decision," he said. "Sandulf is dead. The rules clearly state that if a pack member creates a dracwulf, the entire pack pays for it. Death is the punishment."

I swallowed the boulder in my throat. Playing the *son* card wouldn't work. There was nothing else between us. No love, no connection.

"I can instruct the council not to kill you as a favor to me, but the others ... " He tsked. "The council can't bend the rules for everyone, not without something in return."

Rage pumped through my veins. He hadn't changed one bit. "You're the Varlac leader of Europe, the council will do whatever you ask them to. This is bullshit."

"Well, I have been trying to delegate recently. Anyway, considering Daciana only has a small pack of four, this is too much territory." Rounding me, he stopped and faced me at eye level. "But I want to show you I can be an understanding father."

The poison in his eyes was anything but understanding. "As such, the Transylvanian land will be given to your brother, Marcin, and his pack of twenty or so. The four of you will join his pack, taking Marcin's orders. For that, I will present your case to the council to see if the punishment can be spared on this pack."

Radu made a gasping sound, his shoulders hunched, his eyes wide.

From what I remembered of Marcin, he was as ruthless as Father, and Daciana's pack would be treated like outsiders, or worse. My insides were boiling, every nerve twitching.

I fought to rein it in, but not before my response flew free. "That's going to be a bit difficult considering I've just taken over the Bulgarian pack. This officially makes me the alpha with the largest pack in Europe. And if I'm not mistaken, under your rule, the alpha with the largest pack decides who may join his pack." My lips peeled back over sharp teeth, and a growl droned in my chest. I hated lying or presuming Alena would agree to me being alpha, but since we were in the same boat of shit, I couldn't imagine her disagreeing too quickly.

"The pack is on its way here," I continued. "They'll arrive in a couple of days, and we'll reside in Transylvania. Now, if my brother is having difficulty with his pack, I'd gladly take his members under my leadership, but I won't accept Marcin into my pack. He can live with you in Hungary."

Father's gaze dropped momentarily.

I couldn't believe his arrogance to take our land, as if we meant nothing. To hell with it. I'd fight him and every last Varlac to their graves before I gave in to him.

"Well then," he said, "it seems I've been wrong about you."

For a long while, only quickened breaths filled the room. The fire crackled and spat out embers.

Father's gazed stabbed into me. A low grumble resonated from his chest. "So, you killed Maxim, you say?"

I swallowed the knot in my throat. "Maxim is dead, and his offspring are here to confirm this. In fact, I have Maxim's body, too. They are burying him now in the woods."

Father stared at me. I refused to allow the jitters to take hold.

"This changes everything." He strolled to the window and back. His lips thinned as they started to curl upward into a horrid smirk. "You and Daciana will present your case and request approval for her to hand over the Transylvanian pack in front of the Varlac council. If agreed, I'll no longer hold this pack responsible for Sandulf's actions."

"Fine." I wouldn't back down, though I knew too well what would happen if we failed.

"You and Daciana will accompany me back to Hungary. You will do this properly. I don't want anyone challenging my son about how he gained the Transylvanian land."

A truck might as well have smashed into me. I'd lost my thoughts, and my legs weakened beneath me. Everything Father did came with ulterior motives. He didn't need to say it, but I saw it in his narrow gaze. He wanted us in Hungary for another reason. "But—"

"Life has changed back home." Movement whirred behind his eyes. "Without the council agreeing to the changeover, Daciana remains the alpha. And that gives me the right to punish the pack for Sandulf's mistake. Lucky you got yourself a new pack then. You've just saved your ass in case the council doesn't approve the changeover."

"Fuck you. You're not touching this pack."

One of his eyebrows arched, and the back of his hand flew forward, striking the side of my face.

I didn't move or make a sound.

He turned away and stood next to the couch. "Delightful. You mouth's as foul as your brother's."

The wolf was halfway up my throat, and every muscle rippled. I would rip his fucking head off and tear his spine out. I stepped closer. My breathing raced. My vision locked on my father, who was using his fingernail to clean the ring on his index finger.

"Enre." Botolf's voice rang in my ears. "Don't."

Clenching my jaw, I stood there and wiped my cheek. Blood coated my fingers. "You can leave my home now.

Daciana and I will arrive in a few days." I spat the words, eager for him to go. "I need to be here when the pack arrives."

Except he stood there, folding his arms over his chest. "I'll give you a few days to get your affairs in order, and then we're going to Hungary together."

My arms trembled, but the response about how I was going to force him to leave stung my throat. No matter how much I yearned to beat the man and make him feel the years of agony I'd faced as a child, it wouldn't be worth the payback he'd inflict on my pack members.

Alena popped into my mind. I imagined her panic when I told her the news, but while Daciana and I were gone, she could settle in with the rest of the pack. This would work. It had to.

I bit my tongue. Here I thought my life was set. In Hungary, I was sure I'd not only have to fight alongside Daciana for her pack's lives, but knowing my father, he'd somehow endanger mine.

CHAPTER 27

ALENA

The freshly turned soil marked Father's grave, contrasting against the white snow around it. No wooden crosses or marble headstones were needed. Father was returned to the earth, where all life had begun.

Enormous pine trees surrounded us, their branches heavy with the burden of snow, watching over Father's remains. Several feet behind Nicolai, the woods opened up to a cliff's edge ... a valley for Father's spirit to overlook. It was a post-card image of endless sloping woodlands coated in white.

Tears blurred my vision, and I wiped them away, battling the blackness threading through me. The same blackness I'd kept as a friend for too long when Mother was killed. My shoulders shook. I couldn't hold back the emotions. I let them flow, wild and free, just how Father would have wanted.

Nothing was fair. I dropped my face into my hands, unable to stop the tears or the sensation of my chest breaking in half.

Around me, the wind howled, and Nicolai's soft whimpers reminded me I wasn't the only one who'd lost a father.

Maxim was the alpha, mentor, and Father to everyone in the pack.

When someone placed a hand on my back, rubbing it like Father used to, my head jerked around expectantly.

It was only Daciana, her eyes glistening. "I am truly sorry for your loss." Her warmth awakened a sliver of my spirit. "But you're home now."

She didn't know me, and yet she offered us her land, accepted our pack, and shed a tear for a wulfkin she'd thought had wanted her dead. I was wrong to have accepted Father's decision to kill this pack. Death wasn't the solution to anything.

"Thank you." My words sounded brittle.

"I'll go brew some coffee for your return."

I replied with a smile that seemed awkward and wrong on my mouth. Daciana turned and trudged through the thick snow.

Across from me, Nicolai remained kneeling, his gaze lowered. Damir stood at the foot of the grave, sniffling.

Ash trotted past and brushed against me. I ran my hand down her back, her fur soft against my skin as slight static raced up my arm. Her ears perked up as she glanced back at me.

She stood in a section of deep snow overlooking the valley below and released a howl. The lonely sound roused my own wolf, and a piercing urge rose to the back of my throat. Before I could stop it, my head tilted back, and a howl broke free. Nicolai and Damir joined in our song of grief that drifted on the wind. In the distance, our cries were joined by other wolves. This was now our home, where wolves roamed free, where the woods were our backyard. The first blossom of happiness swirled inside me.

Ash paced past me, and I patted her again. "It's okay, my

friend. We're safe." She released a strange guttural sound, as if something was lodged in her throat.

Nicolai stared in her direction and rose to his feet. "Ash?"

Ash's body vibrated and shimmied in the sunlight, then she started to morph. Her legs lengthened, fur vanishing.

Giddiness tickled my chest. After all this time! It was a miracle. The moon goddess had finally answered our prayers.

Nicolai was by my side. Before us, Ash stood in her human form, crouched in the snow. She looked up with wild, green eyes framed by blonde hair in need of a major wash. Her mouth opened.

"Nic." Her voice was rough and grave. She broke into a coughing fit.

"Don't try to speak," I said. "It'll take time since you were in your wolf form for so long."

Nicolai peeled off his coat and draped it over her back, helping her up. But she stumbled forward. He caught her and swept her off her feet into his arms. Ash held the coat around her, teeth chattering, but her beaming smile said it all.

Had my magical touch incited something in her? Why now, and not the other times I'd patted her? I thought back to the bent trees when I'd tried to heal Father. Maybe my ability had changed, or possibly it was Ash knowing she was finally safe with Nicolai. The latter explanation made more sense.

Nicolai dashed past, giving me an open-mouthed smirk. His eyes lit up as he hurried toward our new home. The idea of *our home* sounded foreign in my head. Damir followed the pair.

Tonight was a full moon. We'd have to lock up Nicolai with extra security.

When I turned back to the burial ground, the soft crunch

of footfalls resonated behind me. Over my shoulder, I found Enre approaching, his chin dipped to his chest. If Father had had the chance to know Enre as a wulfkin rather than a Varlac, he'd have seen him as I did and given us his blessing. Enre was a wulfkin with a pure heart who wanted peace and harmony. This whole time I'd been wrong to doubt him because of his heritage. It was a mistake I wouldn't make again.

Enre knelt next to Father's grave and scooped a hole in the snow. It wasn't long before he reached dirt. He took a fistful of soil and sprinkled it across Father's burial to show his respect. Head low, he remained that way for a few long minutes.

Up on his feet, he brushed down his jeans, revealing wet marks on his knees. He took my hand and raised it to his warm lips. "How are you doing?"

"I'm all right."

"Do you want me to leave you alone?"

"No." I wasn't ready to leave Father, but I didn't want Enre to go anywhere either. "We need to talk."

"I don't like the way you said that."

He paced to a tree and back, his footprints creating a path through the snow. "I need to go to Hungary."

Thoughts banged inside my head as a sinking sensation hit my belly. "Why?"

"Father had planned to give this land to Marcin, my brother, who would then become alpha over Daciana's pack. Marcin is a tyrant like my father. So I said the only thing that would stop him—that I was now the alpha of the largest pack in Europe and that I killed Maxim. But I am in no way trying to take your pack, this is for show only."

I wasn't sure how to respond, and while I kept telling myself I should act shocked, I couldn't stop the tingle of excitement swirling in my gut. I'd never wanted to rule the pack, and neither had Nic, so was this the answer? Enre had the caring nature, strength, and leadership attributes of a great alpha. "You'd make a great leader of our pack." I offered him a wide smile. "But why are you going to Hungary?"

"Daciana told my father she wants to hand over her pack to me, but apparently the Varlac council needs to give approval for that to happen." He stared at me for a long minute, concern swirling behind his gaze. "If we don't go, Father will kill Daciana's pack as punishment for Sandulf creating a dracwulf." He released a long breath. "I have no choice."

My knees turned to mush. "I *hate* your father. I will never forget or forgive what he did to my mother, and I can't guarantee I won't stick a blade in his throat if I find him alone. But I trust you."

Enre smirked. He wrapped an arm around my waist, placing a kiss on my nose. "I share your loathing for him, and if the opportunity came, you'd be lucky to get to my father before I finished him off." His voice trailed off as his eyes slid upward momentarily. "Daciana and I will leave for Hungary in a few days."

"I don't like what your father's doing. It feels like a trap."

"I give you my word. I'll be back."

"If not, I'm coming for you, and the first person on my hit list will be your father."

"That's my girl." He brushed a strand of hair off my cheek. "It's going to work out, you'll see. Once your pack arrives, you settle in and make yourselves at home until I return."

Enre's eyes widened. "Crap, it's a full moon tonight. I have to go get Nic's layered cage prepared. He's not breaking out again."

I slipped my hand into his, our fingers intertwined, as we hurried through the woods toward our new pack house.

CHAPTER 28

"The hunt begins." Enre's voice streamed across the semicircle of forty or so wulfkin in the yard behind our pack house. "Remember, only kill what you'll eat, and don't start until you've crossed the valley. Now, be free."

Silver moonlight danced across the bare shoulders and backs of my family as they undressed and transformed out in the open. The sound of skin splitting echoed in the air, a cocktail of fur, musk, and other wolf scents drifting on the breeze. I couldn't picture a more perfect family image.

Our pack had arrived the day after we did. The Bulgarian border reopened, and the police had no reason to stop the circus from crossing over to Romania. I figured the authorities would still snoop around, but living out in the woods, there was no reason for us to draw unwanted attention as wolves.

We'd spent the last day convincing the pack to play along with our story while Enre's father remained in Transylvania. So far, so good. Except, tomorrow, Enre and Daciana were leaving for Hungary. My belly twisted. That's why Daciana spent the night in the city. Love comes in all kinds of packages: a human for Daciana, and a Varlac for me. Who would have guessed?

Enre moved closer. His hand slipped beneath my blouse, finding my stomach. His touch ignited the fire within me, the one that had been burning ever since we'd first met.

The first wulfkin sprinted away from the group and into the forest, followed by another. More vanished into the darkness until only Enre and I remained on a lawn covered in discarded clothes. In the distance, the glint of our caravan revealed the line of trailers snaking their way up the driveway.

Enre's arm slid across my lower back.

"You think Nic is all right?" I asked.

"He's locked up in a new cell with thicker bars, several layers of bars, in fact, and extra bolts, like he was last night. Better he spends a couple of nights in a cell to be sure his wolf is abated. Plus, he's got Ash down there. She said she wants to spend the night watching over him."

I imagined it was more than that for Ash. If I'd been trapped in my wolf form, as she had been, I'd have no desire to shift back for a while. And being a wulfkin, she was no longer controlled by the moon. Plus, I suspected she liked Nicolai a lot.

"So, you getting naked?" Enre's eyebrows waggled.

I winked at him. Soon, we were nude, my skin tingling from his embrace. He turned and lunged into the woods while transforming. So, it was a race he wanted. I'd show him. But he'd vanished.

I transformed in no time and chased after him. The ground flew beneath my paws, my heart galloped faster, and I inhaled the familiar musky scent—Enre. I followed him away from the valley and deeper into the woods.

Then he crashed into my side, bringing us both down. In an instant he was back on his feet, nudging me up. He trotted farther into the forest, and I followed him until we reached a mountain. In front of us lay a tiny, wooden hut with no windows. To my surprise, a fire waited inside, along with a fur blanket large enough to fill the space of one room. Enre had arrived prepared. His actions made me choke up.

We transformed into our human forms. In his presence, the trickles of happiness reminded me that Father wouldn't want us to mourn him, but remember him as a great wulfkin. The rawness of losing my father would never leave me. But he'd want me to live life to the fullest.

Enre scooped me into his embrace, showering me with kisses and cradling me in his arms. I melted whenever he flashed his sexy smile my way. "As far as I'm concerned, I've claimed you as my mate forever."

This time it was me who grinned. "Me too." And when his lips pressed against mine, his arms tightened around me. For the first time in too long, a tiny glimmer of hope swirled through my chest.

He guided me onto the furs, and we lay in each other's arms, my head resting against his chest. The warming flames crackled while the winds outside howled. The tornado of events over the last couple of weeks still seemed surreal, but the way I adored Enre was honest, natural.

"Sometimes, I wish we had run away, like you suggested when we were in Bulgaria," I said. "I should have taken you up on the offer then."

"Sure would have been easier, except for Daciana and the others." He pressed in close, placing a kiss on my cheek. "I'd fight every single wulfkin if it made you happy."

"Well, I don't need you to fight anyone." I lifted my chin to better reach his mouth. "But I wish you weren't leaving so soon."

"I don't want to think about that now." He captured my lips with his, our tongues tangling.

As I shivered beneath him, other thoughts were abolished from my mind. Only Enre and I existed at that moment. Our bodies clung to each other, his warmth spreading through me. His earthy, musky scent was intoxicating. His left arm squeezed around my shoulders, and the other caressed one of my breasts, kneading it.

I moaned against his mouth. He kissed me harder as his touch trailed down my stomach. Shivers followed everywhere his fingers grazed my skin. He broke our kiss and studied me with his breathtaking blue eyes, framed by dark lashes. His wandering hand skipped to my inner thighs, spreading them, and I eagerly obliged. The moment Enre's fingers stroked the length of my silkiness, a raging excitement overtook me.

A purr vibrated in my throat. His action quickened, and he dipped his head, taking my beaded nipple into his mouth, sucking, flicking the tight bud. I mewled, my pulse thumping as every nerve ending buzzed. Eyes clasped shut, my concerns and problems vanished, and only one thought remained: how much I desired to have Enre inside me. I had to get my fill to last until he returned from Hungary. For now, the world consisted of just the two of us. Tomorrow would come soon enough.

Opening my eyes, I found him sliding down alongside me and positioning himself between my legs. When he spread them wider, electricity charged throughout my body.

"Staggering how you can do that." A wicked grin appeared on his mouth as he pulled away to stare at all of me. "I love watching you get so wet because of me. I love the way you taste, your fragrance ... Fuck." He shook his head. "I want you to come in my mouth. Now."

His words made my heart trip.

He bent forward, burying his face between my thighs, and licked my sex with purpose. My body was scorching, and every muscle softened as I moaned with intoxication. He raised his head, his gaze meeting mine. When he winked, a quiver enraptured me, taking me to the brink of an orgasm. Thrusting his tongue into me, over and over, his fingers dug into the flesh of my hips. My libido responded, the desire drumming forward. My howl echoed in the hut as he ravished me, refusing to let go until every last bit of my passion escaped.

Pulling himself back onto his knees, he licked his lips. I propped myself up on shaky elbows and reveled in his arousal. I adored the idea of him sitting there with me, my legs spread wide open in front of him. Already the anticipation of his touch prickled across my skin.

"Your cock going to keep teasing me from a distance?"

He grabbed my hips and pulled me across the blanket toward him. I arched my pelvis, and he positioned his tip at my opening. "I've been waiting to fuck you again since our first time in the woods. And now I have no plans to stop until you beg me for mercy."

My nipples and sex tingled with his promise. He slid deep into me, pushing, stretching every part. I cried out, gripping handfuls of blanket as Enre thrust forward, rocking into me, his hands on either side of my shoulders. His hips jackhammered, and his hard mouth claimed mine, his tongue surging inside. My body arched against his sweet friction.

Our panting was synchronized and charged, and our moans escalated. Enre making love to me exceeded any wet dream. I hope no one expected us at the pack house tonight. He wouldn't stop until I begged for mercy, and that was the furthest thing from my mind.

Thanks for reading Shadow Shifters.

Reviews are super important to authors as it helps other reader make better decisions on books they will read. So if you have a moment, please do leave a review.

Find more Mila Young books.

Gods and Monsters
Apollo Is Mine
Poseidon Is Mine
Ares Is Mine
Hades Is Mine

Wicked Heat Series
Wicked Heat #1
Wicked Heat #2
Wicked Heat #3

Elemental Series
Taking Breath #1
Taking Breath #2

Fallen World Series Co-write with C.R. Jane
Bound
Broken
Betrayed

Broken Souls Series Co-write with C.R. Jane

<u>School of Broken Souls</u>
<u>School of Broken Hearts</u>
<u>School of Broken Dreams</u>

Haven Realm Series
Hunted (Little Red Riding Hood Retelling)
Cursed (Beauty and the Beast Retelling)
Entangled (Rapunzel Retelling)
Princess of Frost (Snow Queen Retelling)

Beautiful Beasts Co-write with Kim Faulks

Manicures and Mayhem
Diamonds and Demons
Hexes and Hounds
Secrets and Shadows
Passions and Protectors
Ancients and Anarchy

SPIRIT SERIES
Spirit of Christmas

ABOUT MILA YOUNG

Best-selling author, Mila Young tackles everything with the zeal and bravado of the fairytale heroes she grew up reading about. She slays monsters, real and imaginary, like there's no tomorrow. By day she rocks a keyboard as a marketing extraordinaire. At night she battles with her might pen-sword, creating fairytale retellings, and sexy ever after tales. In her spare time, she loves pretending she's a mighty warrior, walks on the beach with her dogs, cuddling up with her cats, and devouring every fantasy tale she can get her pinkies on.

Find me on: facebook.com/milayoungauthor

For more information...
milayoungarc@gmail.com

www.ingramcontent.com/pod-product-compliance
Lightning Source LLC
Chambersburg PA
CBHW030804200726
48285CB00014B/625